BUNGLE IN THE JUNGLE

Science Traveler Series

Book 11

BUNGLE IN THE JUNGLE

Science Traveler Series

Book 11

J. L. Greger

Bug Press

Bernalillo, New Mexico

Bungle in the Jungle

Bug Press
An imprint of IngramSpark
Bernalillo, New Mexico 87004
http://www.jlgreger.com

ISBN (paperback): 9781735421445
ISBN (EPUB): 9781735421452
Library of Congress Catalogue Number: 2023900051

DEDICATION

In remembrance of Dr. Nancy Johnson who delighted in telling
of her adventures during her USAID assignment to Manaus,
Brazil, in the 1980s.

ACKNOWLEDGMENTS

I want to thank John Byram for editing this manuscript. I also want to thank Barbara Hodges for her patience and creativity when designing all the covers for my books.

Over the years my fellow writers from the now defunct Oak Tree Press, the Public Safety Writers Association (PSWA), and the local chapter of Sisters in Crime have provided intellectual and emotional support for my writing. I appreciate them as authors, advisers, and friends.

MAP OF BRAZIL

CHAPTER 1: Sara Almquist at the U.S. Embassy in Brasília

"Your plan won't work."

"Yes, it will."

"No, it won't."

Sanders's upper lip quivered "It will, *if* you are your usual talkative, do-gooder self."

Sara Almquist ignored Eric Sanders's uppity tone. He'd become more edgy since he'd been assigned to head the U.S. diplomatic mission to Brazil. It wasn't surprising. He was the temporary replacement for a U.S. ambassador who had become too enmeshed in Brazilian politics. Sanders had been warned not to make the same mistake. The State Department hadn't even conferred the title of ambassador on him but had given Sanders the title of chargé d'affaires.

Sanders had confided to Sara that his direct boss, an undersecretary in the State Department, had promised him a promotion, which would take him back to Washington, D.C., if he solved two clandestine problems faced by the U.S. embassy in Brazil.

Sara knew a bit about his secret assignments but assumed she would learn more when she had accepted his invitation to spend two weeks in Brazil as a scientific consultant. Ostensibly, she was the U.S. State Department's representative to a conference on "Vector Control of Tropical Diseases" being held in Manaus, Brazil. She was also expected to advise the embassy staff on possible initiatives to mitigate the spread of these diseases from Latin America to Florida and California.

Sara couldn't believe it. She and Sanders were arguing already, and this was the first time they'd been alone together in a month. She reviewed how they'd come to this junction.

***

Sara had been annoyed by the sparseness of the briefing document sent before her trip. However, she had hidden her feelings and engaged in light banter as Sanders and a small entourage escorted her on a tour of the embassy when she arrived in Brasília. Once Sanders had closed the door to this tiny conference room, both she and Sanders lost their formal smiles.

Sara had noted during the tour Sanders didn't look as crisp as usual. He evidently had nicked his chin while shaving and a drop of blood was on his starched white collar. There were bags under his dark eyes. She figured the less said, the better. "Are you okay?"

He had shrugged. "You look rested. I'm glad you spent a day in Rio after your overnight flight from Miami got in at five yesterday morning."

She had paced around the barren room. It had no windows or mirrors. Only a whiteboard that could be used as projection screen, a credenza, a small table, and four chairs were in the gray room. Sara traced her finger along the edge of the board.

"It's not wired. At least it wasn't when I checked yesterday." Sanders had fumbled with a refrigerator under the credenza. He had handed her a bottle of diet cola and took a bottle of water for himself. "The consulate in Rio reported you picked up all the documents I left for you about the conference."

She had nodded before she uncapped the bottle and took a slug of the cola. The room had been hot and stuffy, and the cold fizz had felt wonderful on her throat.

He had poured water from his bottle into a glass on top of the credenza. "Well, what do you think?"

"Your plan won't work."

***

Sara didn't want to review in her mind their verbal exchange, but she wanted to vent her frustrations about Sanders's hair-brained scheme. "Let me get my assignment straight. You think someone at this conference will know the location of a scientist named Al Caputo who disappeared in the Amazon region about a year ago?" She snorted. "And you think I can induce this unknown someone to divulge secrets which confirm your theory that Caputo was working for Brazilian drug traffickers?" She snorted again.

J. L. Greger

She thought her deadpan delivery of her summary of his plan and her laughs indicated her disdain. They must not have. Sanders began tinkering with his computer as soon as she began her second sentence.

A map of Brazil popped up. He pointed to a wiggly blue line. "Al Caputo disappeared from a ferry sailing from Manaus up the Rio Negro."

Sara could see the Rio Negro flowed from Colombia and joined the Amazon River at Manaus. "Okay. I can see Manaus is probably a thousand miles closer to the site of his disappearance than Brasília where we are now. But pirates almost killed my friends while on an Amazon cruise and...."

"Not that story again," sighed Sanders. "You've taken much more dangerous assignments for the State Department through the U.S. Agency for International Development. Besides, the U.S. needs to send a representative to the conference in Manaus. As an experienced medical epidemiologist, you are a logical choice."

"Okay, but I don't see why attendees at a conference on mosquito eradication would know an expert on frogs, like Caputo."

Sanders's lip quivered.

"Don't be cute and say, 'Frogs eat mosquitos.' I'm sure frogs are not one of the vectors being discussed. I need more concrete background materials than the almost worthless briefing document your staff sent me before I left my home in New Mexico."

"Take a look at these." He handed her several pages that had been folded in a pocket inside his jacket—a special feature which Sanders had a tailor add to all his jackets. "We know Caputo spent two days at the National Institute of Amazonian Research in Manaus before he embarked on a five-hour ferry ride to Barcelos on the Rio Negro."

"It's not surprising Caputo visited the institute. Its freshwater biology program is famous."

"No. Ray Curtis, my new information officer, checked."

Sara smiled because "information specialist" was Sanders's euphemistic way of referring to a spy. "What's his official title? Does he have much experience?"

"Science attaché. He worked two years in Cuba before I brought him here two months ago."

Sara looked at the ceiling and groaned. This was going to be a long, hot two weeks with what appeared to be inadequate facilities and support staff.

"Don't underestimate him. He's not as experienced as I might like but he seems to have been thorough and discreet as he investigated Caputo's disappearance."

"What's Ray's supposed expertise in science?"

"Climate change." Sanders swiped a handkerchief across his forehead and loosened his tie. "The engineers can't get the air conditioning in this embassy to work well. It's one of a hundred reasons why my predecessor's predecessor had a new building designed but Congress never appropriated the needed funds."

Sara stared at Sanders hoping it would force him to spit out the relevant details. Then they might even have time for *pleasantries*.

"You're right. I didn't tell Ray that I trust you implicitly." He rose and draped his arms over her shoulders and gave her a peck on the cheek. "This miserable room is more effective than a cold shower for reducing libido." He gave her a long deep kiss. "I also didn't tell him that I love you." He sighed and returned to the chair across the table from her.

Sara finished the cola in the bottle in one slug. "I suspect many on your staff know more about us than you think. Our relationship is no secret in Washington."

Sanders sipped his water. "Ray knows I've worked with you before in Bolivia and Cuba. He also has been told of your continuing appointments as a scientific consultant for the FBI and the State Department."

"That would be hard to hide. Are you sure he doesn't know about our personal relationship? He might think a secret relationship would be a way to bribe you."

"I should tell him that my bosses in the State Department are aware of our relationship. It's just...."

"You want to test him? So, I need to second guess the meager data in my briefing document..." Sara paused. "...and the info you just handed me?"

"Perhaps. We wouldn't be meeting in this windowless sweat box if I was sure about anything in Brazil. Ray's the smartest and most energetic staff member in the embassy, but he's too inexperienced to know his limits."

Sara stood and pulled another diet cola from the refrigerator. "Sounds like your prestigious appointment here really sucks. It's worse than you've admitted on the phone during our daily calls. And your trip with scientists up the Amazon was… just an exercise in grandstanding."

"Not really. Locating Caputo is part of one of the puzzles I must solve to get back to Washington. The trip with the scientists was a way to see where Caputo disappeared and talk to several who had been on the ferry with him." He paused. "And to see the Amazon. You have no idea how vast the river is. It discharges ten-fold more water than the Mississippi. There are places you can't see from the banks on one side of the Amazon River to the other side."

Sara noticed Sanders had closed his eyes as he began to speak of the Amazon River. It must be really something to impress Sanders. But it was stuffy in the tiny room, and she wanted to get this briefing over with quickly. "Cut the ad for the Amazon. Give me the facts I need. Then maybe we'll have time for pleasantries in a cooler location."

Sanders stood and began to pace. "Everyone Ray spoke to at the National Institute for Amazonian Research made similar comments. Caputo only talked to those in the institute's administrative offices and in its entomology facilities. Look at the pages I just gave you."

She scanned the first page. "It's not surprising. Zoo officials have told me that they have two main nightmares when importing exotic animals. One, officials confiscate the animals they've collected because of minor mistakes in paperwork. Two, the animals die in transit or at their new location because they reject the food offered. I assume the National Institute for Amazonian Research often facilitates the preparation of paperwork necessary for sharing animals with collaborating foreign research institutes, like the St. Louis Zoo."

"Note the date on the first page." He pointed to date by the signature at the bottom of the page. "Officials at the St. Louis Zoo had cleared all those details before Caputo arrived in Brazil."

Sara shrugged. "Perhaps Caputo was just nervous."

Sanders shook his head. "Ray learned Caputo asked a lot of questions about importation of animals and biological tissues by private—*not* public—collectors and researchers."

"Strange. It suggests he was ready to engage in free enterprise."

"You mean—illegal smuggling."

"Okay. I agree Caputo may not have been honest about his plans. However, frogs eat insects. It was logical that he spent time with the faculty in the entomology department."

"Several faculty members noted he asked about the diet of the golden poison dart frog." Sanders stared at Sara. "Admit it."

"Okay, you win. Golden poison dart frogs are *not* found in Amazon jungle but in the jungles on the Pacific coast of Colombia. Which suggests Caputo's stated plan to study amphibia of the Amazon and bring back examples to the St. Louis Zoo was *not* consistent with his questions."

"It gets better. Caputo asked every faculty member if any of their staff had indigenous origins or were from Colombia? And then spent much of his time at the institute with three of the individuals identified."

Sara rummaged through the new pages. "I see Gabriela González Gómez is a postdoctoral trainee at the institute." She paused to study a transcript and a photo. "She did her undergraduate and graduate training at Florida State University and presumably speaks fluent English." She scanned several more pages. "She was born in Colombia and is registered for the conference. I should have no problem getting to know her. It might be more difficult to question the graduate student and technician with indigenous backgrounds."

"Agreed. However, their father, Will Anderson, spent five years at the institute working on his graduate degree in the late nineties. He returned to the institute most summers during the next twenty-five years to do research. I bet they speak passable English."

Sara thumbed through more pages. "Seems the son Juan Silva Anderson got a research assistantship at the institute after he graduated from the Federal University of Amazonas with a degree in biology. Reasonable, but how did the daughter—with no training—get a job in a lab?" She studied a page. "What happened to the father? It says he died."

                                                    J. L. Greger

"Ray didn't think to ask the first question. The father died in a river accident about a year ago. You'll note Will filed several requests for the U.S. to allow his family to emigrate. There always seemed to be a mistake in the paperwork."

"Okay. I have an excuse for visiting with…" Sara thumbed through the pages. "…Juan and Maria at the institute. Maybe Ray Curtis is a better information specialist than the briefing report he sent to me suggested."

Sanders shook his head. "It was the consulate's public affairs officer who showed me the file of letters from Will Anderson last week. She thought it would be a great PR opportunity to help these two indigenous Brazilians immigrate to the U.S."

Sara stood and sidled over to Sanders. "I wish I didn't have to rush off to the conference in Manaus."

Sanders stood and wrapped his arms around her as he gave a slow, deep kiss. She could easily forget the heat in the room, but the lack of time prevented anything more from happening.

CHAPTER 2: Sara at a Reception in Manaus

Sara's travel schedule allowed no room for delays or relaxation. She whizzed from the embassy to the airport in a cab, barely had time to catch a three-hour flight from Brasília to Manaus, hailed a cab to the starkly modern Ramada Hotel, and walked rapidly from the hotel to the nearby campus of the Federal University of Amazonas. Even so, she arrived thirty minutes after the conference's opening reception began.

Before she entered the conference headquarters, she noticed a woman in a blue shirtwaist dress. Sara thought she'd seen her before, maybe on the flight from Brasília. One thing was sure—Sara wished she was as thin. Sara sighed and slowly donned an ecru linen suit jacket to hide her thickening waist, plastered a smile on her face, and tried to walk briskly into the building.

The lobby was empty except for two women at a table piled high with half-empty boxes of folders and tote bags. A yellow poster on an easel was labeled in large blue letters: "Vector Control of Tropical Diseases." Noisy conversations almost overpowered the bossa nova music streaming from the room beyond the table.

"*Olá*. My name is Sara Almquist."

One young, dark-haired woman swallowed hard and sped into the large room behind the table. The other stood. "Dr. Almquist, we were worried you would not arrive in time for the opening ceremonies."

Sara looked at her watch. It was six-thirty. "I thought the opening ceremonies were at seven."

"Yes, but our biological sciences dean wanted to talk to you before he introduced you." The young woman quickly filled a blue and yellow tote bag with a conference brochure and a badge lavalier.

A middle-aged man with thick gray hair emerged from the reception room behind the table. He extended his hand. "Welcome to Brazil. I'm Manuel Castro Braga."

Sara was relieved Manuel had skipped the welcoming kiss on each cheek. "*Muito prazer*. Chargé d'affaires Sanders told me this morning about how disappointed he was not to attend this event. I am honored to be here." She wondered how many diplomatic rules and Brazilian customs she'd violated, but the pleased expression on Manuel's face suggested it didn't matter.

"I heard Mr. Sanders accompanied several scientists on a trip to the northern area of Amazonia to study the effects of global warming on amphibian populations." He paused and looked as if he was trying to phrase his next sentence carefully. "He must have a keen interest in science or...?"

Sara had no intention of filling in the blank but recognized Manuel might have guessed the real reason for Sanders's trip. She shrugged. "He likes to get info firsthand."

"The area he was visiting is believed to be near the headquarters of a drug cartel. Mr. Sanders is known in South America as an experienced diplomat. He must have known the dangers."

Manuel Castro Braga had just politely informed Sara that he suspected Sanders was continuing to track the movement of illicit drugs as Sanders had during his other assignments as a senior information specialist in Latin America. It was time to change the topic. "I'm more interested in your background, Dean Braga."

Manuel frowned.

"I've never been good at remembering names. The double last names used in Brazil are more than I can handle." She bit her lip. "Do you mind if I use only your second last name?" Sara had told him the truth at least part of it. She had a good memory for faces and had studied pictures of the fifty scientists registered for the conference, but she hadn't tried to remember any of their double last names. "I guess it's obvious I'm a scientist, not as diplomat trained in etiquette."

"You underestimate yourself. The first question the head of the Cuban delegation asked was if the charming Dr. Almquist had arrived yet. He was most eager to speak to you."

Sara racked her brain. She hadn't recognized the names of the three Cuban scientists registered at the conference. "I don't remember seeing the name of any Cuban I knew on the conference registration list." She had been pleased because scientists from Havana might know besides organizing scientific exchanges between Cuba and the U.S., she had helped Sanders identify members of a Miami-based drug cartel who had infiltrated Cuba a couple of years ago.

"He didn't preregister for the conference. His name is Carlos Moreno, and he is a physician associated with a tropical medicine institute in Havana."

Sara forced the muscles in her face not to move. Carlos Moreno was a Cuban intelligence officer. He knew about her continuing relationship with Sanders and her dual roles. "I thought Dr. Moreno specialized in research on tuberculosis, not tropical diseases transmitted by mosquitos."

"Ah, yes." Manuel shrugged. "Countries sometimes send scientists with multiple roles to conferences such as this. It is unfortunate."

Sara decided to turn the focus on him again. "You too are here in a double role. You're a dean and a scientist. What is your background?"

"I'm a pharmacist by training and my research is about extracting and identifying useful compounds, such as curare, from jungle plants." He shrugged. "My expertise, like Dr. Moreno's, has little to do with mosquitos or tropical diseases."

Sara was stunned when she heard Manuel's area of research. Curare was a dart poison used by indigenous people of Brazil. She wondered how much he knew about another dart poison—the toxin produced by the golden poison dart frog. The compounds were different chemically and were found in different jungles. One was plant-based; the other was believed to be derived from beetles and concentrated in the skin of frogs. However, she'd bet Manuel knew quite a bit about all the poisons used by South American indigenous people to poison their darts. And his insistence on meeting her immediately on her arrival seemed unnecessary. "Do natives in the Amazon still use curare as an arrow poison?"

"Yes." He deflected further conversation by saying, "Moreno said you were a thorough investigator besides being a well-known epidemiologist."

***

The reception was like an overstocked fish tank at feeding time. People were packed around the refreshment tables. The crowd was too large for the room because all faculty, research associates, and graduate students in the biological and agricultural sciences at the Federal University of Amazonas and the National Institute of Amazonian Research had been invited, not just the fifty registered participants in the conference.

Sara's goal at the reception was to locate and talk to Gabriela González Gómez, the Colombian postdoctoral trainee whom Al Caputo had contacted, but she didn't want to signal her interest by asking for Gabriela by name. The daunting task became impossible when Manuel Braga called four people, including Sara, to assemble on the speaker's platform.

Sara first thought Manuel was isolating her so he could observe her actions. She decided she was being paranoid. The U.S. embassy had contributed a significant amount of funds to facilitate the conference. She assumed the others assembled on the platform also represented entities which had made large contributions.

Manuel Braga's effusive introductions and the flowery responses of a representative of the World Health Organization, the Mayor of Manaus, and the leader of a non-profit organization called the World Mosquito Program were long and boring. As the crowd dwindled, Sara saw the woman in the blue shirtwaist dress enter a back door to the reception.

Sara had a brainstorm. After Manuel finished his embarrassingly long introduction of her, Sara stood and said, "*Olá*. The Acting U.S. Ambassador to Brazil wants to offer scholarships for further scientific training in the U.S. to several of you. It's his way of thanking Brazil for conducting this important conference. I hope all graduate students and research associates who are interested will contact me at the end of this reception." She sat down amid applause, probably because the crowd appreciated her brevity.

She hoped Gabriela Gómez and Will Anderson's two children would respond. Sanders would complain about her splendiferous offer but then would admit it was a good business investment. He would also chide her for incorrectly giving his title as the "acting ambassador" but would accept her argument his real title of chargé d'affaires sounded too stuffy.

The woman in the blue shirtwaist dress was one of those who approached the platform after Manuel Braga officially announced the start of the conference. Sara remembered now where she'd seen the woman in the blue shirtwaist dress—the woman's photo was in the papers Sanders had given Sara this morning.

Sara asked those gathering about her to each write his or her name, area of study, and email address on sheets of paper as she shook hands and read name tags. Finally, she was close enough to read the name of the woman in the blue dress—Gabriela González. A man pulled her away from the group before Sara could read Gabriela's second last name.

Sara fixed the woman's image in her mind. She was willowy and about Sara's height of five-eight with brown eyes. Her black hair was pulled into a knot at the nape of her neck. Her manicured appearance made it difficult to guess her age, probably in her thirties. It didn't matter; Sara was sure she could recognize her again. The man would be harder to identify. He was dark, probably about forty, and looked more muscular and had shorter hair than most of the academics at the conference.

The last person to sign the sheet was a short, chubby-cheeked young woman with straight black hair. She looked like a girl of sixteen but probably was at least eighteen. The girl hesitated and looked in all directions before she said, "I want to walk with you to your hotel." Sara noticed the young woman wore no name tag. She had signed the list as "Maria Silva Anderson."

CHAPTER 3: A New Point of View

Maria smiled. "I know a shortcut back to your hotel."

Sara ignored Maria and sped up her pace to join the last few guests leaving the reception at the front entrance of the building. She found two men who said they were returning to the Ramada Hotel immediately, but Maria was nowhere in sight.

Sara knew she should talk to Maria but being lost in Manaus at night was too great a risk. Sara pulled a pen from her purse and held it in her closed fist like a knife. It wasn't much but it might be enough to ward off an attack. She rushed to catch up with the men who had already left the building.

Maria was suddenly at Sara's side. "I *stoppe* to *telle* my brother I'll be late. Why do you not *truste* me?"

"That's not the point. I prefer to be in a group when wandering about a city at night. We can talk as we walk if we stay close to the two men." Sara decided to test Maria with a question for which she knew the answer. "You look too young to work at the National Institute for Amazonian Research—you must be a student. What are you studying?"

"I study biology but *worke parte* time in the entomology *departmente* of the institute."

Sara had to think hard to understand Maria. Like many Brazilians, Maria added an "e" sound at the end of many words. Sara also had trouble believing Maria's statement. The embassy background check had indicated Maria was not enrolled in any classes at the Federal University of Amazonas and worked full time at the institute in the entomology department.

The two male scientists were only a couple of steps in front of them. Sara decided to continue the conversation with Maria although she doubted Maria's honesty. "What do you do in the entomology department?"

"I take care of the insect colonies. We joke and call them the bug farm. It has some rare insects which need special care."

"Can you give me an example of a rare insect? I'd never thought of any insects as being rare or close to extinction."

Maria's mouth twisted. "Not what I mean. Some of our insects are not in other collections."

"Like what?"

"Bullet ants."

Sara had scanned the Web for information on dangerous animals of the Amazon in preparation for her trip. She thought she'd seen comments on the pain caused by the bites of certain ants. "Are those the ants with the poisonous sting?"

"Yes. They're nasty. I wear gloves and am careful not to let them sting me."

"Do you tend colonies of poisonous beetles, too?"

"Why do you ask?"

Sara was surprised by the sharpness of Maria's voice. "I thought if you tended poisonous ants, you might tend other dangerous insects." Sara decided she might as well be gutsy because they were now in the brightly lit parking garage at the rear of the Ramada Hotel. The two men from the conference were only twenty feet ahead. "I know golden poison dart frogs accumulate poison in their skin when they eat certain beetles. But I've never heard the name of the beetles or anything about them. Do you know anything about those beetles?"

"You ask strange questions." Maria suddenly flinched and stepped backward.

Someone grasped Sara's left arm and brought his right arm around her neck.

Sara knew she'd better act quickly. She stabbed with the pen clenched in her hand at the man's shoulder.

He cursed and dropped his hold around her neck, but his grip on her left arm remained firm.

Sara lowered her head and shoulders, reached between her legs, and grabbed the back of the man's bare knees. She pulled hard.

The man loosened his grip but not enough for Sara to escape.

She brought her right knee up and kicked backward hard. She'd connected with his groin or thigh.

The man cursed and released her.

She swung her free hand to punch him, but her fist connected only with air, and she lost her balance. She thought she heard Maria screaming and the sound of running feet.

The next thing she knew, she was crouched on the ground on her hands and knees. She was surrounded by legs. Two sets of men's legs in gray trousers. The legs of a man in navy slacks. The legs of a man in jeans. The bare legs of a middle-aged woman. Maria was kneeling by her.

The man in navy slacks announced, "You were lucky. We heard screams and these two gentlemen rushed into the hotel lobby yelling."

Sara didn't feel lucky. She could see the sleeve of her linen jacket was torn. As she placed her foot on the ground to stand, she saw a blood-stained hole at the knee of her linen slacks. "Will someone give me a hand to help me stand?"

Both men in gray trousers extended their hands and pulled Sara to a standing position.

Sara felt stiff. Both knees hurt. She took a tentative step and then another. She hadn't done any real damage to her knees or ankles.

The hotel attendant muttered under his breath, "It's been six months since a guest was attacked in the parking garage." He led her to bench at the back entrance to the hotel. It appeared he didn't want her to sit in the hotel lobby where others could see she had been mugged. It would be bad publicity for the hotel.

Unfortunately, none of those around her could provide a good description of her attacker. The two men in gray trousers and the hotel employee disappeared into the hotel.

Maria whispered, "I was afraid this might happen. That's why my mother and brother were following us. My brother tried to grab the bad man, but he ran too fast."

Sara for the first time studied the older woman. She looked like many Native American women back home in New Mexico with black eyes, a broad nose, and her long gray hair pulled back in a braid.

The features of the man in jeans confused her. He was probably almost six feet tall and had blond hair and brown eyes. He did not look like he could be Maria's brother. Then she realized his straight nose and thin lips were like those of Will Anderson in the photo Sanders had given her.

"Are you Will Anderson's son, Juan?"

"Yes." He gave a tentative smile. "Have you seen the embassy file on my father?"

"I know your father was trying to obtain green cards for the three of you."

"Is that all?"

"I know he died in an accident about a year ago."

"It wasn't an accident. He was killed thirteen months ago."

"Are you sure?"

"Pai was too good a swimmer to drown."

Sanders had not indicated any doubt about the cause of Will Anderson's death. *Odd.* Sanders often speculated deaths during accidents were successful murders. Sara usually assumed Sanders's had worked too long in the intelligence field. "Did your father do anything unusual in the month before his death? Or did anyone threaten him?"

Maria murmured, "She asks strange questions."

Juan shook his head. "Not strange. She knows more than she's admitted. Why else would she ask about the beetles that the golden poison dart frog ate."

Sara tried not to stiffen. He and his mother must have been closer than she realized before the attack to have heard her questions. She should have noticed their presence a*nd* they should have been able to trip the attacker. She was missing key data about this family. The bench by the brightly lit back entrance should be safe, but she was uncomfortable. "Let talk more over coffee in the hotel's café."

Maria darted a glance at her brother. "We should go home."

Her brother shook his head. "We have time."

***

After they were seated round a small table, Juan pointed at Sara and held up two fingers. "Two men have asked about those beetles. One asked Pai shortly before Pai's accident." He nudged his sister. "Remember how upset Pai was."

Maria nodded. "He called the man 'evil.'"

"Then the U.S. scientist who disappeared on the Rio Negro stopped by the lab and asked to see our beetle collections a couple of months later."

"He was so jumpy."

Juan covered Maria's hand with his. "She means nervous."

"So, Juan, do you work with the insect collections, too?"

Juan straightened on his stool. "Pai was an anthropologist, but he was friends with an entomology faculty member. We both work for Pai's friend now. I am his graduate research assistant, not a technician in the bug farm."

"Sara was bit confused. She wished she understood Portuguese but had accepted years ago that she had little ability to learn languages. "Is 'Pai' your dad's nickname?"

He frowned. "Pai is how we say 'Dad."

"How did Maria come to work in the same lab as you?"

"When Pai died, Maria quit school and went to work full time." He winked at Maria. "At the bug farm. We needed the money."

Sara relaxed slightly. Juan's answers were consistent with the data in the embassy file. His English was perfect to Sara's ears. But Juan was older and more experienced—perhaps at lying—than Maria. Sara had no choice but to accept his answers on face value and have a long talk with Sanders later. "You said two men have asked about the beetles. Do you know the names of the men?"

"The second was Al Caputo. He supposedly drowned the day after we spoke to him." Juan shrugged. "But I don't think it's true. My boss thought he saw him in Manaus two months ago."

"What?"

"There is a rumor that Caputo went to work for the drug gangs."

"Do you know anything about the first man?"

"Not much. I never met him. Pai said he wasn't a Brazilian and called him 'Spider.'"

"Why?"

"I don't know. Pai didn't like spiders."

The mother placed her hand on her son's hand. "Ask."

"Too soon."

"Ask."

"Mãe wants to know if you can help us get the papers to immigrate to the U.S. You spoke of the embassy offering help to those who wanted to study in the U.S." He leaned forward. "At least, Maria claimed you made that offer at the reception."

"I did. Are both you and Maria interested in studying in the U.S.?"

"Mãe needs to leave Brazil, too. It is not safe here."

"I realize crime is a problem in Brazil, but it is in the U.S., too."

"You do not understand. It's personal. You were attacked because you were with Maria. They thought she'd given you Pai's diary." He lowered his voice. "They broke into our house twice."

"Who's they?"

"We don't know."

"Who are you guessing?"

"Those interested in the beetles. When our house was broken into before Pai died, Pai told me they were looking for his diary. He said they wouldn't like what had written in it about Spider."

"And?"

"Pai told me to take the diary to the U.S. consular office in Manaus. I did. A woman called Camille told me no one wanted a diary written in Tupi."

"What did you do then? And what is Tupi?"

"I returned the diary to where Pai hid it. Tupi is a language once used by some of the indigenous people of Brazil."

"I'm surprised Tupi has a written form."

"The early Jesuits here created the written form of the Tupi language, but it's not used much now. Pai had to learn Tupi to study old Jesuit documents for his research."

"Can you read Tupi?"

"Pai tried to teach me, but it was boring."

Sara was in a quandary. If the attacker was looking for the diary, he should have taken her purse, but he'd made no attempt to grab her purse. This could be a trap, but Sara believed the Andersons sincerely wanted to leave Brazil. *Why.*

Sara pulled from her purse one of the pages that students had signed at the reception and handed it to Juan. "Give me your email address and phone number. I'll try to get back to you tomorrow afternoon. Meanwhile, I think the diary is probably safe where it is hidden.” She lowered her voice. “Can you give me a hint on its location?”

CHAPTER 4: Questions

"Honey, I'm in trouble."

There was a sigh. Sanders said, "What phone are you using?"

"The secure satellite phone you gave me. I'm in my hotel room."

"What happened?"

"I was mugged in the hotel parking...."

"Are you okay?"

"Yes." Sara heard Sanders talking to someone else in the background. It was annoying. He hadn't even waited to listen to her full reply. "I don't think this was a random event because the lone mugger didn't try to get my purse or attack the smaller woman with me."

"I'm sure you looked more affluent."

Sometimes Sara wished Sanders was more romantic, but he was right—this wasn't the time. "Here are some things you should know. Carlos Moreno from Cuba is here. He informed at least one conference organizer Manuel Castro Braga I was more than an epidemiologist."

"Damn."

"I saw Gabriela Gómez in the distance. I couldn't decide if she wanted to talk to me in private or was hiding from me. But I might be paranoid."

"Interesting."

Again, Sara could hear Sanders engaging in a second conversation.

"Maria Silva Anderson sought me out. She lied a bit, but she's no mastermind. Her brother and mother appeared around the time I was attacked. I didn't catch Juan in any lies, but he's clever."

"Could they be involved in the attack?"

"The thought occurred to me. They have an agenda and are frantic to get to the U.S. They think they can trade their father's diary for green cards. Strange. Anyway, it seems this diary might identify a man who would know the location of Al Caputo. This man and Caputo both asked the kids about the beetles. The kids...."

"Hardly children, but I understand."

"They are the caretakers of the beetle collection at the institute. I don't know why Caputo and not one of them was kidnapped."

"Anything else?"

"The kids expect an answer tomorrow."

"They may have to wait."

"Oh, before I forget, Camille is a poor employee. And I need a new pair of slacks. You know my size."

"You should be getting a visitor in a couple of minutes. Only open the door if the woman says she's Camille Draco. She's the public affairs officer at the Manaus office. As you spoke, I contacted her. I'll stay on the phone until she arrives. By the way, she's the one who flagged this conference to me and identified the three people to watch. The Manaus consular office has a guest house of sorts. She'll take you there."

"Thanks."

"She knows I've worked security at several embassies and you're a frequent science consultant for government agencies, but she doesn't know anything about us. Keep it that way."

Sara again heard Sanders engaging in another—or perhaps two—conversations. Finally, he said, "I knew you'd uncover clues needed to find Caputo but not this fast. Unfortunately, your cover has been blown. I should have realized your success in Bolivia and Cuba would be known. It's my fault."

"Oh, I forgot, this diary is written in Tupi and is hidden. All Juan would tell me was it was 'well hidden.'"

There was knock on the door.

"Who is it?" Sara looked through the peephole.

"Camille Draco. I'm alone." The woman shoved a badge toward the peephole.

Sara could see a seal with *U.S. Embassy* stamped on it. *So, what?* She couldn't identify a fake. She described the woman to

Sanders as having short, black hair with green and purple highlights.

Sanders said, "Let her in," before Sara completed her description.

***

While she listened on the phone to Sanders, Camille pulled at the drapes, unscrewed the receiver on the hotel phone, and ran her free hand behind the headboard of the bed and around other pieces of furniture. She said, "Nothing" and "Yes" twice.

Sara had plenty of time to study Camille as she repacked her suitcase because Sara had only removed two items from the case before she'd rushed to the conference. Camille was a little shorter than herself, had a thin face with a narrow nose, and had purple and green streaks in her short, black hair.

Camille handed the phone back to Sara.

Sanders said, "Sara, dear, be your usual talkative, do-gooder self but say nothing of importance for now. Flight connections between Brasília and Manaus are infrequent during nighttime hours. I'll get there when I can." He disconnected.

Sara said, "Let's go," as she slid her satellite phone into the side pocket of her torn slacks. She pulled a baseball cap over her blonde hair and picked up her suitcase. "I'm leaving the torn jacket here. It might make someone think I'm coming back."

Camille only nodded.

***

Hot, humid air enveloped Sara as they left a side door of the hotel. At home in the high desert of New Mexico, the temperatures dropped to the sixties in the evening on hot days. She'd forgotten nights in a jungle were hot and muggy.

Camille remained silent until they reached a gray sedan. "We'll drive a while to be sure no one is following us, except my aide in the black vehicle."

A black SUV pulled from the lot onto the street. Camille followed but quickly passed the black SUV. After a minute, Camille sighed. "You must have high clearance. Sanders is letting you stay at the condo he uses when in Manaus. It's not much to look at but it has all the electronic bells and whistles available."

"He likes his toys."

Camille frowned. "Do you... know... Sanders well?"

　　　　　　　　　　　　　　　　　　　　

Sara was surprised by the gutsiness of Camille's question and remembered Sanders's instructions to reveal nothing. "Enough to know he's worked security at a few embassies in Latin America, including Cuba. You know the embassy in Cuba was a security nightmare." Sara thought she'd covered for her flippant, perhaps too personal, comment on his toys. It was time to change the topic and meet Sanders's expectation of her. "Are you interested in scientific topics—like this conference?"

"Only to a limited extent. My B.S. is in journalism." Camille read a text.

Sara was surprised because government policy was clear. Embassy personnel were not to text while driving. Sara guessed Camille was not into rules.

"My aide in the black SUV thinks there's a white car on his tail."

"So, we'll be wandering for a while longer?" Sara didn't wait for a reply and tried to continue to project the image Sanders wanted for her. "You know this conference is a dream for a medical epidemiologist, like me. Mosquitos are vectors for tropical diseases like malaria and dengue fever. It's a real opportunity to talk to the agricultural specialists who found ways to prevent mosquitos from breeding successfully. I'm so glad the World Health Organization and the U.S. embassy sponsored this conference."

Camille seemed to stare in disbelief at Sara. Sara feared she'd overacted.

"The last ambassador didn't want to rile the Brazilian president, so he never supported any scientific or ecological conferences or inquiries. Of course, Brazil has a new president now." Camille didn't comment on the text she sent.

Sara tried to coax Camille to say more. "How did people in the embassy react to Sanders's decision to co-sponsor the conference? Or maybe I should say ask whether the embassy staff are pleased with Sanders's approach?"

"I don't know about the embassy staff. Most in the consular office in Manaus are ecstatic. He's been here four times since he was appointed. As a public relations officer, I dislike the way he seldom warns me when he's coming. Of course, his trip into the northern area of the Amazon with the scientists studying the effects of climate change on amphibians was a publicist's dream. The Brazilian press called the trip 'symbolic' and noted the President of Brazil hadn't visited the area in years."

Sara thought she heard a tone of disapproval in Camille's voice. "Isn't that good?"

"Only if he follows the symbolism with action. Most Brazilians are too poor to care about intent; they want results. The rich are profiting by current policies. They like the glamour of embassy parties. Sanders hasn't thrown any bashes yet."

Sara guessed Camille didn't especially like Sanders or his views. She wasn't surprised. Sanders could be prickly. She needed to change the topic again. "Don't big events, like this conference, mean a lot of work for you? What was the biggest problem so far?"

Camille glanced at Sara. "You're the most talkative scientist I've met. Sanders warned me not to be annoyed by your constant questions."

"That's why I left academia and went into consulting. I don't fit most people's image of a scientist."

Camille didn't even glance at Sara but focused on the road. "Are you saying you got tired of sexist comments and actions by your colleagues?"

"Being a woman scientist is not easy. I've learned to emphasize the positive and ignore the negatives."

Camille checked texts on her phone. "You're tactful."

"Let's get back to this conference. What's been the toughest part so far?"

Camille chuckled. "The conference organizer is a problem. He's been slow to update me as people registered for the conference. I didn't learn until three this afternoon he'd invited all the faculty and staff at the Federal University of Amazonas and at the National Institute for Amazonian Research to the opening reception. I only learned then because a friend told me she'd been invited to what she called a 'glam' reception."

Sara thought she should try to gain Camille's trust. "Camille, I may have something you'll find useful. I announced the U.S. embassy will sponsor several students to get further training in the U.S. at the reception. About twenty signed sheets and gave their email addresses. You can make a copy of my lists. It may augment your list of the attendees."

Camille slowed the car. "Who gave you the authority to make the offer?"

Sara was surprised Camille suddenly was interested in following the rules. "Sanders will find a way."

Camille turned into a lane, produced a pass card, and shoved it into a monitor at the gate. "Are you sure? You've got a lot to learn about how things are done in *this* consulate." She waited for the black SUV to pass her. Both vehicles parked in a garage underneath a small condominium complex.

The aide jumped from the black SUV, opened a locked door, and climbed stairs to the safe house. When he returned, he nodded to Camille who had said nothing the whole time.

***

The condo was sparsely furnished with what looked to Sara like a variant of mid-century furniture. The settee and two chairs would fit into Sanders's condo in Washington, D.C. She touched the upholstery on the settee. It was a red and white striped duck cloth. The fabric wasn't typical of Sanders's taste, but the settee's bent teak frame was. Sanders had mentioned in one of his daily phone calls that he'd met a talented architect and furniture designer at a reception in Brasília and purchased a couple pieces of the designer's furniture.

Sara noted the condo was devoid of photographs of his daughter—a young lawyer—or her. Several small Brazilian paintings adorned the walls. Although the Brazilian art wouldn't fit with the Persian rugs in the living room of his Washington townhouse, they'd meld well with the Cuban paintings in Sanders's bedroom in Washington.

Sara wasn't surprised when Camille said, "Sanders has never allowed anyone to stay here before."

Camille must have expected Sara to show surprise because Camille continued, "You know Sanders is a puzzle. All the women flirt with him because he's considered an eligible bachelor. He's charming but never shows any real interest in them. However, I noticed he often rubs a ring of twisted yellow and white gold on his left hand at receptions." She pointed to Sara's right hand. "His ring looks like yours."

CHAPTER 5: A Surprise on Day 2

Sara awoke as Sanders kissed her cheek. His dark hair was slicked back more than usual which accented his receding hairline and the worry lines on his brow. "What time is it?"

"Around two. Get dressed. We can't stay here."

Sara noted his tense tone. This was not a time for questions. "I didn't expect you until six or seven." She pulled on cargo pants and a zippered hoodie over her pajama shorts and T-shirt.

"Apparently, neither did anyone else. There was no guard on duty downstairs."

"Camille said the guard would regularly wander around the complex." Sara carefully tied her walking shoes because she'd learned nothing slowed down a fast escape more than inadequate or loose shoes.

"According to our protocol, the guard is to leave a note in the vehicle and lock it if he is on surveillance outside the garage. There was no note in the unlocked SUV. Good thing I had two security team members from the Manaus consular office meet my flight. This looks like a set up by local gangs." As he spoke, Sanders grabbed two blankets from the closet. "The gangs here like bombs. There's another blanket in the closet by the stairs to the garage."

Sara ran to the closet at the head of the stairs. It looked the same as it had last night when she checked all the closets before retiring—except a white shoe box now sat on the floor of the closet. She assumed the worse, slammed the door shut, and screamed, "Bomb in the closet at the top of the stairs!"

She sped down the stairs, opened the garage door, and ran into the alley behind the condo. A thin man with his graying black hair cut in a crew cut stepped out of the black SUV idling there. Another man—tall, blond, probably in his late twenties—ran from the side of the condo toward her. She didn't know if they were Sanders's security or potential attackers. She didn't have time to assess the situation before a nightmare unfolded in front of her.

Sanders had not cleared the garage when an explosion sent a fireball down the stairs. He kept running until he stumbled onto the alley and began to roll.

Sara ran forward hoping to beat the flames on the blanket he had over his head and shoulders.

Both men ran faster. The older one pulled off his jacket and covered Sanders with it to extinguish the flames on Sanders's shoulders.

The other grabbed Sara's arm. "I'm Paul." He pointed to his partner. "He's Jake. We're security for the U.S. consular office in Manaus."

Sara fought him off anyway and rushed to Sanders's side.

Blackened fabric covered Sanders's head and much of his body and he was moaning, "Get it off me." Jake peeled the fabric back.

The charred fabric crumbled in Jake's hand. Underneath what must have once been a blanket, a second blanket was heavily streaked with gray.

"Can't breathe."

Sara held her breath. She'd seen burn patients in intensive care units. They were ghastly. "Yell if it hurts." She gently began to lift the hot fabric upward.

"Hurry," Sanders moaned.

The hot fabric didn't adhere to Sanders's head or shoulders. She flung it aside.

Sanders's hair didn't appear singed. His face was flushed. "My neck... my neck hurts." He rolled onto his side. The back of his neck was bright red and smooth.

Sara was no expert on burns but thought the lack of blisters was a good sign. Of course, it might take time for them to develop. She resisted the urge to touch the back of his neck. "Is your neck hot?"

Sanders wheezed. "Yes."

Jake handed her a handkerchief. "Clean this morning." He waved to Paul. "Water."

Sanders wheezed more.

Sara poured water from the bottle Paul handed her onto the handkerchief. She laid the wet cloth over Sanders's neck and face.

Jake slit Sanders's jacket with a pocketknife. Sarah noted Sanders's navy jacket was sooty but didn't appear to have burned through or melted. As usual, Sanders had worn a light wool jacket lined with silk and an all-cotton shirt. He detested synthetic fabrics. She thought his idiosyncrasy may have saved him from severe injuries. Many synthetics would have melted, but the wool only smoldered.

Sara suddenly was pushed aside by an EMT. She had been so absorbed she had not noticed the arrival of an ambulance and fire trucks. Firemen were already dowsing the fire.

Paul pulled Sara back further. "Mr. Sanders would want you evacuated."

"I want to stay with him. Won't he be sent to an ICU? I'm used to medical jargon."

"You don't understand the situation. I found the guard who was supposed to be protecting you. His body was buried in leaves in at the side of the condo. I think he was killed only a few minutes before we arrived because his body was warm. My partner was calling the local police and a physician as you ran out of the garage."

Sara looked around. Two police cars were parked on the grass at the side of the condo. Two consulate vehicles, an ambulance, and two fire trucks filled the short driveway and the alley in front of the condo.

"Where's Camille Draco?"

"Good question. We couldn't reach her and had to leave a text message. Then she appeared while you were helping Jake tend to Mr. Sanders. She took one look at you and Mr. Sanders and tore out of here."

Sara looked toward Sanders. The EMT had connected an IV line to his arm and placed an oxygen mask on his face. Sara was distracted when a SUV roared to a stop behind the fire trucks. A gray-haired man jumped out with a medical bag and ran toward the EMT.

"I've got to talk to Jake. You stay here."

Sara ignored Paul's command and moved to stand not far from Sanders. She wanted to hear the conversation between the physician and EMT. Unfortunately, they spoke in Portuguese.

Jake whispered into the physician's ear.

The physician nodded and said clearly, "First-degree burns mainly. We need to get him to the hospital because he may have lung damage due to smoke inhalation."

Sara broke into the conversation. "I want to go with him to the hospital."

The physician nodded and then spoke in Portuguese to the EMT who was already rolling Sanders on a gurney toward the ambulance.

Jake was clearly annoyed when he stood. His voice was raspy. "This is a security nightmare. The Manaus consular office is not equipped to house you. We'll evacuate you to São Paulo."

"No, I'll stay here with Sanders."

He cursed quietly.

Sara ignored Jake's annoyance with her. "This probably won't be helpful, but the bomb was in a white container about the size of a shoe box in the closet at the top of the stairs. It wasn't there last night when I checked all the closets before retiring."

"You checked all the closets last night?" Jake's jaw hung slack.

"And the locks on all the windows and doors. I've been in tight spots before." She frowned. "When I saw the box this morning, I didn't stop to see if it was ticking." She thought a second. "So, the question is: who had keys to the condo, besides Camille?"

CHAPTER 6: What's Next?

A physician woke Sara by shaking her shoulder. She had fallen asleep on a chair in the alcove where Sanders lay in the emergency room of the hospital. "Mr. Sanders was lucky. A radiograph and CT scan revealed no lung damage. The first-degree burns on his head and shoulders are painful, but only a small streak on his neck is bad enough to be considered a second-degree burn. I gave him a painkiller, but he refused a sedative. He's authorized you to make all his medical decisions."

Sara nodded. "So, what do you advise?"

"Mr. Sanders doesn't need to be in a hospital."

Sara raised her wrist to look at her watch. "Guess I lost my watch, too, in the fire. What time is it?"

"About five."

"I hate to be taking up space in the emergency unit if Sanders doesn't need the care. Jake and I talked."

Jake must have heard his name because he pulled back the curtain at the rear of the cubicle. "Did I hear my name?"

"Yes." Sara smiled, but she was too weary to try hard to smile. "I was telling the doctor that we all fear another attack. Can Sanders be moved to a secure room in the consular office if a nurse is present?"

The doctor groaned. "Sanders asked the same question. It's not my first choice for his care, but..."

Jake tinkered with his phone. "We have a nurse on contract. She'll turn the sofa in our lounge into a bed in thirty minutes. Paul just called. The local police have finished their inspection of the site. We have a lot to discuss."

****

Sanders looked pale as he sat propped up in the makeshift bed in the consular office. White gauze bandages surrounded the back of his neck and forehead. "I apologize for my clothes, but collars aren't comfortable now."

Sara wanted to mention Sanders had fought with her over his clothes. He wanted to wear dress wool trousers and a shirt. She'd convinced him running pants and a hospital gown would be more comfortable. Besides all the clothes in his suitcase had burned. She figured that was too much info and said nothing.

Sanders seemed to study the three faces in front of him before he spoke. "Jake, let's start with the report from the local police department."

"Nothing official yet, but the guard who accompanied Camille and Sara to the condo was found with a single bullet in the back of his head. He'd been shot at close range. There was no evidence he'd been bound. The police are guessing he knew his assailant because his gun was in its holster. The coroner determined the time of death was between one and two in the morning—shortly after your plane from Brasília landed. Either someone was watching the airport or was expecting you." He stared at Sara.

Sara cleared her throat. "I didn't tell anyone. Camille Draco could have guessed Sanders would be arriving within three to five hours after my call to him around nine last night."

Evan Hinkley, the head of the Manaus office, had been sitting silently during the discussion, but his pale skin had gotten redder as the conversation progressed. His lips trembled after Sara's last comment. "Camille is a trusted employee. I...."

Jake didn't wait for him to finish. "I agree with Sara." His voice was raspy. "Camille's actions are suspicious. She pulled up to the safehouse less than two minutes after the explosion, took one look at Sara and Mr. Sanders on the driveway, and sped away." He coughed repeatedly. "I should stop smoking." More loudly, he said, "I didn't want to ask the local police to search for Camille until we assessed the situation."

Sanders raised his hand a few inches. "Enough on Camille for now. Do we need to protect the contacts Sara made last night? Has anyone checked on the Andersons?"

Jake pulled out his phone and checked his texts. "Sara, Paul, and I discussed them because it is possible the Andersons were part of the attack on Sara around eight last night in the Hotel Ramada's parking lot. Sara feared they would disappear when they learned of the bombing. I agreed because the mother is an indigenous person and their father had extensive connections throughout the region. Paul and I were shorthanded, so I had a friend from the local police bring the Andersons here an hour ago. I'm reading my friend's text now. It seems the Andersons were overjoyed to be brought here." Jake shook his head. "Weird. Sara, do you have anything to add?"

"I'm sure the Anderson want to go to the U.S., but I'm not sure they've been honest about their motives. But I think we should try to find the diary that they mentioned. The kids suggested their father had identified 'bad' people—probably key people in the local drug gangs—in his diary. They also thought his drowning in the Amazon wasn't an accident."

Evan Hinkley stood and waved his arms. "Nonsense. These concerns are misplaced. Lots of people drown in the Amazon—like the American collecting frogs for a zoo."

Sanders waved his right hand slightly. "I doubt Al Caputo—the man you described as an American collecting frogs for a zoo—drowned a year ago. FBI agents arrested a drug kingpin from Colombia as he brought a rare toxin into Florida a month ago. The arrest was based on a tip I received from a competing drug cabal and data I got on the golden poison dart frog while on my Amazon trip with scientists who are experts on amphibians. Caputo is one of the few experts worldwide with the ability to raise these frogs in captivity. We think those frogs were the source of the toxin seized in Florida a month ago. It seems unlikely Caputo drowned a year ago."

Hinkley trembled as he sat down. "Why wasn't I told?"

Sanders studied the obese Hinkley for almost a minute. "I knew there was a leak—a high level one—in this office. The Undersecretary was aware of our plan."

Evan Hinkley became even redder as he pointed at Sara. "Why is she allowed to hear this discussion?"

"She's got higher clearance than you do, and her scientific expertise is relevant to this case. She's the one who pointed out that golden poison dart frogs have some of the most toxic natural compounds known in their skin."

Sara thought Sanders was goading Hinkley. She decided she might as well help him. "Sanders left out a few details. We think the source of the toxin in the frog's skin is...."

"Sara, these men don't need to hear scientific details now. The point is Sara and Jake need to have a long discussion with the Andersons. Evan, you should devote your efforts to helping security staff who will be arriving from Rio shortly. They will be reviewing the backgrounds of your staff, especially anyone with ties to the people on this list." He handed a list to Hinkley that Sara had prepared based on what she had learned at the conference.

Jake stood and whispered in Sanders's ear. The lines on Sanders faced lightened and he looked ten years younger. Sara knew backup FBI agents had arrived.

"Sara, you'd better get ready for your speech at the conference. Aren't you scheduled to speak at ten?"

***

Sara interrupted Sanders's conversation with Jake. "I look like I'm ready for an evening party, not a conference, with these black palazzo pants and silk shawl. Your staff must have been worried about finding clothes which would fit and chose ones that could be described as 'one-size-fits-all.'" She bit her lip. "I don't mean to be bossy, but are you sure you should have shared my list of people to investigate with Evan Hinkley? Since he's annoyed with you, isn't he more apt to share those names with the wrong people?"

Jake muttered, "I didn't coach her to ask the question."

"Sara needs no encouragement to speak her mind." Sanders winked at her.

"You're acting too confident." Sara shook her head in mock disgust at Sanders. "Did you leave at least one name off the list *or* add one to confuse Hinkley?"

"Both. I didn't include the name of the conference organizer Dr. Braga on the list because, like you, I think he's the most likely contact for a drug kingpin."

"What name did you add to the list as a red herring?"

He coughed. "Our friend, Carlos Moreno, from Cuba."

Sara raised an eyebrow in disbelief. "Is that wise?"

"You and I might dislike Carlos but I'm sure he'd never make private deals with drug dealers. The Cuban government executes officials who sell out to drug dealers."

"I hope you and Carlos don't step on each other's toes."

"We won't because you're going to have drinks with Carlos later today to explain the situation."

"Have you told him yet?"

"No, you can make the arrangements. He'll jump at your invitation. Paul can be your guard."

Sara turned to go and then turned again. "In all the excitement, I forgot to tell you one detail. At the reception last night, I announced the U.S. embassy would help several students go to the U.S. for training. About twenty individuals gave me their names and emails on sign-up lists." She noted Sanders didn't stop scanning his tablet. "When I told Camille…"

"What? Why did you tell her?"

"I was trying to build a bond with her. I offered to make a copy of the list for her, but she didn't want it. It was the only thing she did that made me think she wasn't in league with the drug dealers or politicians spying on the consular offices."

"How so?"

"I told her the list had info on how to locate the Andersons." She thought a second. "I don't suppose my purse was found intact in the condo's rubble?"

"Did you put it in the safe as you usually do when you went to bed in a hotel?"

"Yes."

"Paul is with the arson investigators now. He can bring your purse when he returns to the consulate."

"One more question. Have the Anderson kids said anything about the diary?"

"No, but they gushed to the security staff about your generous offer." He stretched out his hand to Sara. "Thanks. I think you'll dazzle the conference attendees with your speech today." He shook his head. "I really planned to make last night romantic. I had roses and champagne in the SUV."

Sara leaned over his bed and kissed his cheek.

CHAPTER 7: Paul Royer Is Bored

Paul Royer chose a seat at the end of a row of chairs so he could stretch out his long legs. He might as well be comfortable while he was bored out of his gourd. This would be the first lecture on a scientific topic he listened to since completing college six years ago. He didn't like science, especially when delivered by an aging baby boomer like Sara Almquist.

It was annoying how she bustled around the consulate this morning. She was a nobody; except she was the boss's mistress. Paul thought Mr. Sanders should not have invited his girlfriend to play such a key role in this conference or this investigation, but no one had asked his opinion. He was surprised Jake hadn't complained about Sara's bossiness. Maybe it was because Jake had taken a real chewing out from another bossy woman. Paul shook his head. *That was Jake's problem.*

The session began worse than he expected. Sara climbed the stairs to the platform like an old woman, pulling her pant legs up as she took each step. Manuel Braga, the chairman of this session of the conference, awkwardly tried to clamp the lavalier mike to her shawl as she laid her notes on the podium. The mike fell to the ground. Sara almost bumped her head with Braga's head as both reached for the mike on the floor. Sara won and straightened immediately, clipped the tiny mike to the neck of her black top, and tossed one end of the black shawl over her shoulder. "Thank you, Dr. Braga, for the warm welcome."

Braga retreated from the podium.

"In 1901, Walter Reed confirmed the hypothesis of the Cuban medical scientist, Carlos Finlay, that yellow fever was transmitted by the *Aedes* mosquito. Despite extensive research, vector-borne diseases still account for seventeen percent of infectious diseases worldwide." Sara's first slide appeared. The slide outlined major epidemiological studies on malaria.

Boring.

Paul found himself getting into the swing of the talk after few minutes. The science details were tedious, but the topic was more important than he had thought. He slowly realized Sara must have spoken to large groups many times. Her presentation was clear and occasionally funny. He guessed the time Sara spent this morning extracting her slides from internet storage was worthwhile. The slides focused the audience on key points. However, he didn't understand her insistence on also extracting her presentation notes from storage; she seldom looked at them as she spoke.

During the question-and-answer period, Sara stepped from behind the podium and seemed to chat with the audience. Judging by their questions, the audience accepted her as a logical choice as the opening speaker—an experienced medical epidemiologist.

The question-and-answer period was useful for Paul. It gave him a chance to look around the room and learn names as people introduced themselves before asking a question. He spotted two embassy staff members from the Rio consulate with Maria and Juan Silva Anderson. That was another way Sara was annoying. She called the Andersons "kids," even though they were probably eighteen and twenty-three.

He wondered why Sanders was attracted to Sara. Sanders was old—in his early fifties—but the ladies liked him because he "came from old money" and he hadn't developed the paunch of most ambassadors. The older men in security at the embassy were in awe of him. Jake said, "Sanders practically wrote the book on modern data collection." It was funny how absolutely no one ever said *spying* around Sanders. He insisted they refer to their work as "data collection" and "information dissemination."

Paul analyzed Sara as she stood at the podium. She was tall, but not as tall as Sanders at six feet. She was no longer slender but looked okay in clothes. At least as well as you could expect for an aging baby boomer. He'd noticed that her face had no real wrinkles, except laugh lines around her mouth, when he drove her to the conference. Her chin-length, blonde hair which she casually tucked behind her ear gave her a playful look. A least, it might seem playful to men of Sanders's age. Paul hated to admit it, but she'd kept her cool during the emergency this morning.

He guessed Sanders had made a logical choice of a partner, but maybe not. Some of the gals who threw themselves at Sanders were drop dead gorgeous. Paul had not realized there were so many hot babes in South America before he was posted to Brazil a year ago. It was one of the perks of the job.

Sara lifted her pant legs awkwardly as she left the stage. It ruined her improved image in Paul's mind.

Sara didn't return to her seat near the stage but sat down by Paul. "Let's step out of this session so we can talk."

***

"Did the local bomb squad say anything useful? Did they find Camille?"

Paul was surprised Sara expected a full update. He called Jake to see whether she was cleared for a complete update.

Jake laughed. "Stop thinking of her as the boss's gal. She's got higher clearance than you or I. Moreover, she's known for recognizing the guilty and trapping them. I'd hate to see your hide drying in the sun."

Paul turned to face Sara.

"Well, now that you've established my clearance, what do we know about Camille?"

"Police found her car in an airport parking lot. Her apartment looked as if she had just left it to go to work. There didn't appear to be a missing suitcase and her parrot had been fed."

"Any news from the fire department?"

"Nothing unusual about the bomb, except how primitive it was. The time of detonation was set when it was placed in Mr. Sanders's condo." He paused. "It would have killed both of you if you hadn't spotted it this morning."

"So, the condo was completely gutted?"

"Yes. Nothing, but the contents within the fireproof safe, survived." He noted Sara shivered slightly. "The Rio security staff are already checking the names on the sign-up sheets in your purse. Two of the security officers—a blonde named Kelly and an African American named Latoya—accompanied Maria and Juan Anderson to the conference."

"I saw them. They were in the middle of the audience on the left."

Paul was surprised she had studied her audience during her speech. "Those two women are under strict orders to never let the Andersons out of their sight."

"Good, but the Andersons won't disappear voluntarily without their mother who is at the consulate." Sara shrugged. "I probably should talk to them on the q.t. after the coffee break. It would be best if they weren't seen with me. Can you arrange it?"

Paul thought, *Q.t. Who uses that expression anymore?* He nodded.

"I'll spend most of the coffee break with Carlos Moreno from Cuba. Don't worry about my safety. We'd better get back to the session. I need to bone up on the technologies used to control *Aedes* mosquitos."

Paul thought Sara had done it again. *Who says "bone up" or thinks mosquito nets and sprays are interesting?*

***

Paul was amazed when Carlos Moreno ambled over to Sara during the coffee break. The short, bald Cuban gave a slight bow as he approached her. "Dr. Almquist, you're looking elegant today. You must not have been staying at the ambassador's hideaway. I understand it was demolished."

Paul noticed Sara stiffened and then flashed a broad smile. "News spreads fast here." Paul faded into the crowd. He could hear the conversation in his earpiece because Sara was wearing a wire.

Moreno nodded. "Crime is high here, not like in my beloved Cuba. But even in Manaus an explosion in a wealthy neighborhood is news."

Sara opened her mouth to speak and then closed it. Paul thought she looked like a guppy gasping for air.

Carlos smiled and waved his hand slightly. "Are you surprised I knew the location of Sanders's secret getaway?" He sipped his coffee. "I noticed the ring on your right hand as you spoke. I assume you two are what Americans call an *item*? Which one of you had cold feet about marriage?"

Sara took a swig from her can of diet cola. "I see you're on top of all the news, but I think our discussions would be better held in a quiet place. However, it's a long walk to any bar from

J. L. Greger

here. Maybe we should walk to the university's bosque. It's quiet there and we can talk about a mutual problem."

"Perhaps that is wise. Besides, none of the bars here have the atmosphere of El Floridita where we first talked in Havana."

Sara ignored his leer. "Let's meet around four when most at the conference will be listening to the last speaker of the day."

"I had thought you'd given up on international information collection during the last couple of years and focused on public health problems in the U.S. Now I think you were just sharpening your claws. You'll need them. I'm told the U.S. office in Manaus needs a house cleaning. I'm surprised Sanders didn't bring you here sooner."

Paul choked on his soda. Moreno certainly knew about Sara and Mr. Sanders.

Sara winked at Moreno. "You'll have to give me more advice at four. I may have a bit for you, too."

***

The Andersons and Kelly appeared in a small conference room where Paul was waiting. Sara had shooed him out of the lecture hall when the Andersons had left in the middle of a talk and claimed she would follow them. Now he was worried about Sara as he walked back into the hallway. She was talking to the Andersons' second escort, Latoya, who looked like a real Amazon—tall, muscular, with short curly hair.

Sara stopped in mid-sentence when she saw Paul. "Paul is finding it hard to adjust to a talkative, middle-aged woman."

Latoya chuckled. "Nothing but young blondes for him."

Sara winked at Latoya. "Showtime. By now, the Andersons should be nervous with anticipation but not hysterical." She strode rapidly into the small room and asked, "Juan and Maria, are you enjoying the conference?"

Paul followed Sara, leaving Latoya on guard at the door.

Maria said, "I'm glad I got to come to this conference. Technicians, like me, usually don't get to go to events."

Sara sat down at a long table and motioned for the Andersons to be seated. "I wanted to talk to you about Al Caputo. Details you know could be important in determining who killed your father. Can you remember what Caputo asked you?"

Juan shrugged. "On the first day, he mumbled some gibberish about the St. Louis Zoo having problems keeping their collections of *Melyridae* family beetles alive." Juan shook his head. "It was nonsense. They thrive on a variety of flowers. Either he was dumb or fishing. I told him I no longer worked with the entomology department's collections and sent him to Maria. On the second day, he came back with more sophisticated questions."

Sara nodded. "Let's keep things in order and reconstruct the conversation with Maria on the first day before you continue."

Maria folded her hands in front of herself on the table. "He was jumpy." She looked at her brother.

"You mean nervous?"

"Yes." Maria smiled. "I was surprised when he asked, 'Do you wear gloves when you work with the beetles?' When I said of course, he asked, 'What happens if you don't?' and then other odd questions." She leaned forward on her elbows. "Finally, I understood. He thought the beetles were dangerous to touch. I told him, 'The beetles aren't bad. I wear gloves because it's the rule in the lab.' He seemed sad and started to walk away. Then he asked me to show him all the beetles in our insect farm." She smiled. "The entomology department has dozens of types of beetles living somewhere in the Amazon. We're proud of our collection."

"Nothing else happened on the first day?"

Juan nodded.

Maria bounced in her chair. "I showed him our beetles and told him the names of the species. Usually, I told him what we fed them. Would you like to see them?"

"No, I saw university insect collections when I was an undergrad."

Paul noticed Sara shifted her shoulders and wriggled her nose. He guessed Sara didn't like remembering the bug collections.

"Were you surprised when Caputo came back on the second day?"

Juan nodded.

Maria said, "No. When he left the first day, he told me he needed to talk to someone and might need to study one type of beetle more."

"Who did Caputo talk to first on the second day?"

Juan nodded. "He interrupted my lunch break. He told me how scientists from the U.S. had extracted batrachotoxins from a little-studied group of beetles—genus *Choresine*, family *Melyridae*—from New Guinea. The scientists hypothesized the poison in the skin of the golden poison dart frog came from similar beetles in the Amazon." Juan shook his head. "I remember because it was hard to believe the man who asked the stupid questions the day before was now asking such complex ones."

"And what did you say?"

"The obvious. Golden poison dart frogs are from jungles along the Pacific in Colombia. I doubted any of the beetles in our Amazonian collection could produce the toxin or substances that could be turned into toxins by frogs. We had plenty of beetles in our collection from the *Melyridae* family but none of the genus *Choresine*. He. argued with me and went away in a huff saying he had to find the right beetles."

"That's it?"

Maria was bouncing in her chair. "I saw Caputo on the second day, too—just before I went home. He asked me if anyone from Colombia ever worked with our beetles. I said yes. A chef at a local restaurant was interested in how our beetles tasted when roasted." She shrugged. "They eat them in Colombia. Caputo seemed annoyed and left quickly."

Paul hoped Sara was through with her questions. The last fifteen minutes had been some of the most boring in his life. Who cared about poison bugs?

Sara prolonged his agony and asked another question. "Did Caputo ask if anyone else had asked about the beetles?"

There was a knock on the door. Paul rose reaching for his gun.

Latoya stepped in. "Someone needs to use this room now."

Sara pushed Kelly and the Andersons out a side door. She whispered to Latoya, "Set up another meeting for us around two." She turned to Paul. "Not every problem is solved with a gun."

CHAPTER 8: Sara Is Surprised

Sara slipped into the back row of the conference hall. No one seemed to notice, except Carlos Moreno who was sitting in the next to the last row. The speaker was talking about the toxicity of various insecticides. Sara looked at the program and saw she'd missed a talk on the effectiveness of mosquito netting. *Nothing interesting.*

Sara pulled out her laptop. Although Sanders and Jake had heard everything, she'd said this morning, she'd not heard from them. The lack of feedback was her own fault. She had decided not to wear an earbud because she thought it made her look sinister—like an FBI agent.

She decided to continue her one-way communications with them anyway:

> *I'm set to meet with Moreno today at four. We'll skip the bar and walk to the university's bosque. Paul's bored with this assignment and too quick to pull a gun for my taste. Latoya would be a better guard for me.*

> *Here's the recap of my discussion with Juan and Maria. We were right in our guesses about Caputo. EXCEPT he wasn't looking for the golden poison dart frog but for the beetles they ate. That's why the FBI confiscated such a large quantity of batrachotoxins in Florida. It would be a lot faster to grow beetles and extract toxin or a precursor of the toxin from them than to find the rare frogs, grow them, and extract the toxin from their skin.*

She leaned back and looked around the room. The woman guards from Rio had been smart. Juan had entered the room alone a couple of minutes before. Now Maria and Latoya entered the room and sat by him. It was doubtful anyone, but Moreno, would have guessed Sara had been meeting with them.

A new message appeared on her screen. She read it slowly twice:

> *We found a name tag under the seat in Camille's car—the one found at the airport. The badge has Camille's name, but the photo is not of Camille. It has the embassy's official stamp.*
>
> *Look at the attachments. Did you see either of these women? One is of the real Camille Draco. We haven't identified the other woman, yet.*

Sara had a sickening feeling before she opened the attachments The feeling increased as she looked at the two photos. Both had short, black hair with green and purple streaks and were in their late thirties. The one on the badge had a thin face with a narrow nose. The streaks of color in her hair were bright. The woman in the file photo had a fuller face, subtle purple and green highlights in her hair, and a fleshier nose. Sara emailed Sanders:

> *The woman I saw last night looked like the picture on the badge, sorta. How did the fake Camille get your message to take me to your condo?*

***

Sara didn't want to show her panic. *Where was Paul?* She walked to the door of the session and opened it. Paul was standing nearby talking to a woman wearing tight pink shorts and an even tighter pink top. He didn't seem to notice Sara. "Paul, we need to talk."

The woman said, "Give me a call," and sashayed down the hall.

"Paul, check your phone for texts and emails."

He casually pulled out his phone.

"I think you missed an important one."

He gulped as he stared at his phone. "We've got to get out of here." He grabbed her arm.

"First, I think you'd better locate Kelly after I find out whether Latoya knows Kelly's location."

Sara hoped whoever was monitoring her mike feed had notified Jake or Sanders. Her phone pinged and she checked the text:

Paul, listen to Sara. Sara, stay in lecture hall at the back. Help is coming.

It felt good to know Jake or Sanders were monitoring her conversations closely. She showed Paul the message. Before he could ignore it, Sara grabbed his sleeve. "Wait while I ask Latoya if she knows Kelly's location."

"You shouldn't be seen talking to Latoya or the Andersons."

Sara stifled a cough. "My cover is blown. So, is theirs. You guard this door and listen for instruction through the feed from my mike."

Latoya rose and met Sara at the refreshment table at the back of the room. "Kelly should be back by now. She was going to stay in the washroom only a minute or so after Maria and I left."

Sara tried to stay calm. "Did you leave Kelly in the washroom next to the small conference room we were in?"

Latoya nodded and poured herself a glass of water but kept glancing at the front and back entrances of the conference room.

"Paul, are you listening? Be cautious when enter the bathroom. Don't flash your gun unless necessary. The four of us will stay by the refreshment table at the back." She didn't add *and don't flirt with anyone.*

Latoya sipped her water but stayed close enough to speak to Sara. "I asked Paul to check on Kelly a couple of minutes ago,

                                   J. L. Greger

but he must not have seen my text or listened to me on the feed in his ear."

"He was flirting with a blonde in the hall."

"Was she short and full chested? All in pink?

"Yes."

Latoya put her glass down. "That's the blonde who entered the washroom as Maria and I walked out. We may have a problem. I don't want to leave you three unprotected but I'm going to check the hallway on the north side of the room." She nodded in the direction of where Sara had sat.

Sara turned to the table, so it was less obvious she was talking into her mike. "Jake, send an ambulance. Paul is apt to find a problem in the woman's bathroom by the small conference room on the second floor."

Sara tried to act nonchalant as she ambled to the door on the south wall. It was a few yards behind where the Andersons sat. She quietly pushed the door open.

A long gray service hallway stretched along the conference room. At one end was an external exit. Facing the conference room were accordion doors leading to a service or storage area. At the other end of the hall, a door was propped open to an area with black floor tiles. She was about to close the door when she saw part of the profile of a man standing on the black tiles. His right hand hung at his side. A gun was in his hand.

Sara closed the door and whispered, "Man with a gun at west end of the hall. He's standing at the entrance to the service hallway on the southside of the conference room." She hoped both Latoya and Jake heard the feed from her mike. "He's thin, dark haired, and probably under thirty. He has on a white shirt and jeans."

As soon as the speaker had finished his talk, the lights in the audience were turned up. A man approached the standing microphone in the middle of the audience to ask the speaker a question. Sara couldn't discretely approach the Andersons, but they had to be warned.

Before she'd taken a step, Moreno rushed to the standing microphone. He pushed the man aside. "Dr. Almquist has published a paper on the epidemiology of an accident where large quantities of a pesticide entered the food supply in the Middle East. Perhaps she'd give us a summary?"

Sara was totally caught off guard. She forced herself to remember the study from early in her career. She couldn't decide if being the center of attention would protect her from attack or focus a gunman. She was sure it prevented her from protecting the Andersons. She stumbled to the microphone wishing she had listened more carefully to the previous speaker.

"Our speaker did a good job of explaining how pesticides can leach into rivers and pollute the surrounding land."

In her peripheral vision, Sara saw the rear door on the south side of the lecture hall open. It slammed shut. She heard a groan and then another. The door seemed to shake as if something had been slammed against it. More groans.

Sara debated what to do. It was probably best if no one tried to investigate the rumpus in the service hallway.

Juan stood and moved toward the door.

Sara was sure she didn't want him in the hallway. Most likely he was the target—if she wasn't—of any attacker. Secrecy was a secondary concern now. "Will the Andersons please meet their party at the north rear entrance?"

Maria looked confused. Juan went back to Maria, pulled her out of her chair, and dragged her along the back of the room to the north rear door.

Sara tried to keep her voice calm. "I'm sorry I interrupted my answer to Dr. Moreno, but I was asked to make the announcement before Dr. Moreno called me to the microphone." She decided it was best to go on as if nothing had happened. "Dr. Moreno wants me to mention a situation I studied more than twenty years ago in which seed grains treated with pesticides were eaten during a famine. There were warnings about the toxicity on the bags of seed grain, but the warnings were in English."

She heard a thump and then another against the wall near the rear door on the south wall. The door shook and a crashing sound reverberated from the hallway. Most of the audience was staring at the door. Several men were moving toward the door.

Sara tried to distract the audience. She spoke more loudly in as smooth a voice as she could muster. "Sounds like the staff are having trouble moving bulky items. To sum up my answer to Dr. Moreno's question, the seemingly minor precaution of labeling chemicals in local languages, not just English and

Spanish, is often forgotten *and* indigenous people are endangered."

The noise from the service hallway stopped. The door opened.

Sara instinctively dropped to a chair. *No need to be an easy target.*

Sanders stood in the doorway. He studied the audience and smiled when he spotted Sara.

As he stood there, Sara noted he had removed the bandage from his forehead and his tie and collar were askew. He must have gotten a larger shirt to accommodate the bandages on his neck. The shirt wasn't his choice. It was pink. He never wore pink. Otherwise, he looked okay—maybe a bit disheveled.

Sara thought the best way to conceal the situation was to not try to hide the obvious. She stood and spoke into the microphone. "The Acting U.S. Ambassador to Brazil meant to join the group for lunch today inconspicuously. I guess he bumped into staff moving equipment in the hallway."

Only a few members of the audience laughed.

Sanders joined Sara at the standing microphone. "I sincerely apologize for the disruption, but I want to note the U.S. embassy intends to honor the promise Dr. Almquist made at the reception last night. We will find scholarships for at least five attendees at the reception to receive more scientific training in the U.S."

As the group applauded, he lightly tapped Sara's elbow and guided her to the north rear door. Moreno almost ran after them.

***

Sara was surprised when Sanders stopped about twenty feet past the doorway and turned to Moreno. "Thank you, Carlos, for keeping Sara out of the service hallway until I could get reinforcements here. It seems..." Attendees began to pour out of the lecture hall. "...she'll have to explain the situation this afternoon when you meet." Sanders nudged Sara's elbow and guided her to where Jake was waiting.

"Well?"

Sanders turned so he prevented anyone from seeing Jake's face as Jake spoke.

"Both were stabbed. Kelly is dead. Paul's injuries aren't bad, but he appears to be in shock."

Sanders grimaced. "It often happens the first time a man sees his own blood. Did he say anything useful?"

"Not really. He just kept muttering 'pink' and 'boobs.'"

"I can identify the woman he's talking about. After I questioned the Andersons...."

"Sara, stop," said Sanders. "Latoya gave us the basics on everyone's actions but thought you got a better look at the woman in pink. What can you tell us about her?"

"Short—five-two with a solid build. Muscular shoulders and arms. Not pretty but I suspect all Paul saw was the pink T-shirt stretched across her large breasts. Her hair was heavily streaked with blonde. Too much to fit with her dark skin tones. Her eyebrows were overplucked. I'd guess she was in her forties."

"Makes sense," said Jake. "The stab wounds on Paul's hips are lower than I would have expected if a man had stabbed him."

Sanders winked at Sara. "Did you dislike the woman in pink because she looked shifty or because you were annoyed with Paul for being inattentive to you this morning?"

Sara straightened and stepped back. "I won't honor your question with an answer. So, did local police arrest the guy in the service hallway? He sure seemed to put up a fight."

Sanders said, "There were two men. After Latoya kicked the gun out of the hand of one man and kicked the other in his groin, I collected their guns Before we could handcuff them, the men regained steam. Then the local police arrived."

Sara sighed, "I'm glad I missed the action."

"You did a good job controlling the conference crowd." Sanders squeezed her elbow. "However, you should take lessons from Latoya. She's an expert at Brazilian jiu-jitsu."

"You can take the lessons. I just want to get this mission over. By the way, where is Latoya?"

"She's checking out the luncheon room. I think she's the most logical backup for me as I take your place at the luncheon here. You and the Andersons will have a private lunch at the consulate. Have the staff at the consulate find a pair of slacks that aren't too long for you." More softly, he said, "Love you."

Sara wiped the tears from her eyes, squeezed Sanders's hand, and followed Jake.

CHAPTER 9: A Message from a Dead Man

"Tell me about the man your Pai called the Spider."

Juan frowned. "I never saw him. Pai never described Spider to me."

By the time they'd returned to the consulate, Sara had been tired of hearing Maria's continual chirps and had selected a small, quiet room in which to interview Juan. Now she wondered whether she could pull much out of the young man without his sister's constant goading. "What do you know?"

"Mãe and Pai argued constantly during the week after Pai saw the man he called Spider. Maria and I didn't know what they were arguing about. They always became silent when either Maria or I entered the room. Most of what I know—or at least think I know—is based on what Mãe told me after Pai was killed."

"So, these arguments occurred about thirteen months ago?"

"Yes. About then, Pai started to visit the U.S. consular office in Manaus daily. All he talked about was immigrating to the U.S. When Pai wasn't around, Mãe would say he was hopeless dreamer. She said people in the office would not value his diary enough to process our papers to immigrate to the U.S."

"I don't understand. He was a U.S. citizen. Getting green cards for family members might be a slow process but not an impossible one. There is no need to trade his diary for visas."

Juan shook his head. "You don't understand how your office in Manaus works." He paused in thought. "Have you ever heard of *superfaturamento?* It translates to 'super invoicing' and is common in Brazilian government agencies. Employees at the U.S. consular office in Manaus have adopted the Brazilian custom."

Sara was glad she was recording this discussion. It looked like the problems in the Manaus consular office were much deeper than Sanders even imagined. Maybe not—Sanders had complained of nightmares since arriving in Brazil. "Did your Pai ever mention to whom he spoke at the consular office?"

"I think at least two different people, but he didn't name them to me. Mãe told us later Camille Draco laughed at him."

"What happened to the diary?"

"Mãe said Pai thought someone in the consular office might steal the diary, so he hid it. I would have thought Pai was crazy, but our house was broken into twice. The most expensive item in our house is our TV but they didn't take the TV. Only Pai's computer was stolen the first time and my computer the second time."

"Where is the diary?"

"It's all we've got. We really need it to emigrate." The look in Juan's eyes was hauntingly pathetic.

"You don't have bribe me or anyone at U.S. embassies for a green card. However, I think the diary will help us identify key drug kingpins and maybe bring Dr. Caputo home. Please trust me. Besides Mr. Sanders has already gotten approval of your visa request. It's an essential part of the process to grant you a scholarship to study in the U.S." She didn't add processing paperwork for Juan's mother and sister would be more complicated.

Juan closed his eyes. "It is in a display case in the social science department at the university. Pai was a lecturer on anthropology at the university and put his diary on display as an example of written Tupi. He knew almost no one could read it. He had learned Tupi at Yale almost thirty years ago while preparing for his dissertation research on cannibalism among the indigenous tribes in Brazil."

Sara was flummoxed. She wanted to ask, *why did your father choose such a strange topic to study*? She decided it would be impolite. She had wondered from the start why Will Anderson had only lived with his family in the summer when he was a guest lecturer in Manaus. The rest of the year he was a lecturer in linguistics at Yale. She now concluded Will Anderson was a kook and accordingly his assessment of the man he called

Spider could be misleading. But then again, Will seemed clever. She said, "So, your father hid the diary in plain sight."

Sara thought Sanders was still at lunch at the conference and texted Jake:

> *HELP. We need to go the university's social science department ASAP.*

***

Juan led the way into the building housing the social sciences programs at the Federal University of Amazonas. On the outside it was just another plain, modern, concrete box with a wide bamboo veranda. The inside wasn't any more interesting, but Maria excitedly pointed out the lecture room her father had used, his office, and the departmental office.

By the departmental office was a small display. Juan and Jake went into the office to get the key to the display case. Sara, Maria, and a consulate guard remained by the case.

Maria pointed to the sign in Portuguese at the top of the locked wooden case with glass sides. "It says: *What Brazil Is Losing*. See the beautiful feather work."

Sara saw a large headpiece of red, green, and yellow feathers at the back of the case. She guessed the feathers were old; they were faded and many of the side veins had been pulled off.

"You can also see our wonderful beadwork and weaving."

Sara had seen elaborate beaded necklaces and beautiful baskets in the gift shops at the airport. This necklace was a simple strand of stained red seeds interspersed with darker seeds. The basket was small and frayed. Whoever had lent the items for the display must not have wanted to display valuable pieces in the unprotected case.

"Most of the languages spoken by the indigenous peoples of Brazil have never been written down. The Jesuits in the 1500s began to write the language spoken by the Tupi who lived on the coast of Brazil."

Sara noticed Maria's speech pattern and tone of voice became less childlike as she spoke about the Tupi language. Sara wondered whether Maria was parroting her father's comments about the language.

Maria continued, "Tupi was widely used throughout Brazil until the Portuguese expelled the Jesuits in the 1700s. It's Brazil's first national language."

Sara tuned out Maria's comments and concentrated on the documents in the case. She saw three torn pages. They were yellow and cracked with age. The writing was in a graceful, looped script peppered with accents and diacritical marks like those used in Portuguese. Someone had drawn a cross at each corner of the pages. She guessed they were pages from a Bible.

Next to the old pages was a small notebook with a green cover. It was held open to a page with recognizable letters printed by hand on the lined paper. Sara assumed a translator could read the printed Tupi easier than the script.

Sara gradually realized Maria was still extolling the materials in the case. "Pai was proud of those pages. He found them many years ago in a wooden box when a church in Barcelos was remodeled. He couldn't save the rest of the pages of the Bible."

As Jake tinkered with the lock at the back of the case, Juan said, "My sister wants to become an anthropologist like Pai but the only job she could find was in the entomology department."

Maria gave a shrug. "I do not like the bug farm, but this department..." She pointed to the nearby office door. "... wouldn't hire me. They said I wasn't qualified to even be a secretary. They laughed when I said I could translate Tupi for them." She shook her head. "Although few write in Tupi today, it is the key to much of Brazil's colonial history. I can also speak three languages derived from Tupi."

Juan put his arm on her shoulder "Maria never liked math or science in school but every night she studied Tupi. Even Pai told her she was foolish. He said, 'No one will pay you to read Tupi. You must study science to go to the U.S.'" Juan pointed at Sara. "Even you will only give her a scholarship if she agrees to study science in the U.S."

Sara flinched. She had assumed Maria wanted to study entomology.

Jake broke the awkward silence. "This case is rickety. You'd better stabilize the glass sides as I slide the plywood sheet aside at the back of the case."

Juan and Sara held the sides of the case as Jake slid the plywood sheet. The sheet stopped sliding when a wood peg on the plywood hit the glass side. Juan reached into the partially open case and removed the feather headdress and the peg it hung on from the back of the case. Then Jake could slide the plywood sheet away.

Juan snorted as he examined the feather headdress. "No one wants this junk. The head of the department was glad we stopped by. He wanted to get rid of the display but hadn't gotten around to calling us. We can have everything in the case."

Maria looked angrily at her brother before she kissed the beads and carefully lowered them into the decrepit basket, which she put in a small tote. "I brought folders for the historic pages." She pulled manilla folders from her tote. She gently lifted an old page and put it into a folder. She repeated the process for the two other torn pages. She backed the folders with two heavy pieces of cardboard, clamped the packet together with rubber bands, and lowered the packet into the tote with the basket. She handed a second tote to Juan. "This should be large enough to hold the headdress. Please remove the tape from the sign. I'll take it, too."

Sara had leaned into the case late in the dissembling process and pulled out the small notebook with the green cover. It fit perfectly in one of the small plastic bags she kept in her purse for emergencies. "This display was a real testament to your father. I'm glad you got a chance to claim these mementos." Sara said it loud enough so the students standing nearby could hear. She hoped it would dispel any rumors and make this process look inconsequential to observers.

"Juan, help me slide the plywood back in place. Then you can return the key to the office." As Juan departed, Jake whispered into Sara's ear. "I hope the diary was worth the effort. Maria never stopped talking in that high pitched voice of hers. Good luck finding any university in the U.S. that will take her."

Sara whispered back. "I don't think we can rely on Maria alone to translate the diary from Tupi. You've got to find someone—besides a Brazilian—who can read this diary. Maybe in a university linguistics or anthropology department? I think Will trained at Yale. They may still have an expert there on Tupi. I also think any translator should only see a copy of the notebook. The original should go into a safe in the consulate."

Sara looked around a reception room now serving as her office. It looked like a workshop. Mãe—Sara knew that wasn't her name, but she and her children had never said her first name—sat on a bench making what Juan called "wish bracelets" out of brightly colored ribbons. Juan had said his mother sometimes sat on a street corner and sold these bracelets to tourist directly, but usually she sold her items to tourist shops because she didn't like to be photographed.

Maria sat cross-legged on a bench pulled up close to the room's long library table. She alternately hummed or repeated phrases in Tupi and then Portuguese as she traced her finger along lines on the xeroxed pages of the diary. Frequently, she muttered "no" or "not right" and repeated phrases to her mother. After a short discussion with her mother, Maria would write in English onto on a yellow pad. When she finished struggling with a page, she read it to her mother in Tupi and then Portuguese.

After a half hour, Sara realized Mrs. Anderson could recognize at least certain written words in Tupi. So, Sara assigned Mãe to scan the two hundred xeroxed pages of the diary and circle words that might translate to evil, drugs, spider, Cuba, and government house. Maria and her mother thought "government house" in Tupi was what Will would have called the consular office in Manaus. Sara also suggested Mãe start checking the last page of the diary first and work backward. Maria resisted but finally agreed to translate only pages on which her mother had found a key word.

Sara had decided Juan might be more comfortable with Ray because he was closer to Juan's age than her age. Thus, she'd asked Ray to interview Juan.

As Ray questioned Juan Anderson in another room, Sara studied the list she'd gathered at the reception the night before. Ray had already emailed the twenty students and requested they send him their official transcript and a short essay on what, why, and where they wanted to study in the U.S. Several essays, including Juan's, had already been returned with notations that transcripts would follow.

Sara noted Juan wanted to earn an M.D. and specialize in tropical medicine. His essay was a cross between idealism and practicality. He had said he didn't want to be stuck like his father

                                             J. L. Greger

in an esoteric academic field but wanted to help the indigenous people of Brazil. She wrote letters to the deans at Tulane and Johns Hopkins to consider Juan's request for admission. Sanders could sign them later. She then prepared a short list of characteristics she was looking for in the applications. A secretary could now complete the screening of the applications.

Maria's voice became shriller as she argued with her mother in Portuguese. She switched to English when she walked over to Sara's desk. "Excuse me? We have a problem. A page is missing. Pai mentioned meeting Spider on the previous page."

"Are you sure?"

"The pages are numbered."

"So, someone removed the page while the diary was stored in the display case?"

"I don't know."

Sara wanted to scream. Someone, who read Tupi, might know all the Andersons' secrets already. She emailed Ray and asked if Juan could provide any insights.

***

"Got a minute?" Jake stopped when he saw Mrs. Anderson. "What's the mother doing here?"

"Keeping Maria calm and quiet... Well, quieter."

"Mr. Sanders is back from lunch. He decided he needed a nap."

"Is he okay?" Sara turned off her computer and jumped from her chair.

"Evidently the pink dress shirt really rubbed his neck even though it was two sizes larger than the size he usually wears. Latoya said the lunch also tired him. He had to do a lot of glad-handing because many of the scientists at the conference were impressed by his trip with ecologists to the northern reaches of the Amazon."

Sara sighed. "This is a rough assignment."

"Let's talk in my office."

***

Jake closed the door. He motioned Sara to a chair upholstered in a green jungle print. He took off his jacket and sat in the matching chair. "Mr. Sanders told me to update you. The guard killed at Mr. Sanders's condo oversaw this unit's records, including security badges."

"I didn't think such an individual would do field work."

"They don't." He scowled. "Based on fingerprints on the ID badge found in Camille's car, we think the woman who assumed Camille Draco's identity was a former employee in this office. She was fired six months ago for insolence. We assume she and the guard who was killed were recruited by a drug gang."

Sara didn't think insolence was a reason for firing a federal employee under the Equal Employment Opportunity Act. She decided the point was not important enough to question at this time. "Have you identified others who are on the payroll of the gangs?"

"We think Hinkley was ratting on us to Brazilian politicians, but we have no concrete evidence."

Sara noticed Jake was scratching a spot on his right arm. The area was a bright red spot on his hairy arm. "Mosquitos are a problem here."

He stopped scratching and seemed to look over her head as he spoke. "The U.S. diplomatic presence in Brazil is a mess. The last ambassador was a political hack. Discipline at all the consulates, especially this office in Manaus, is lax. You see this office really should be a consulate or at least branch consulate. We have a relatively large security staff in this office because so many Americans are affected by crimes while in the Amazon region. Besides replacing hundreds of passports annually, we end up helping to investigate crimes against Americans."

"Why?"

"The local police aren't up to the job, and insurance companies demand certain assurance before they'll recognize claims by traveling Americans here." He coughed. "Now where was I? He paused. Oh yes. Unfortunately, Will Anderson's treatment by the staff here was not unique. Considering all the problems, I was shocked when Mr. Sanders mentioned in the car after the luncheon that you were here to help him with a special assignment." He stopped and stared at her expectantly.

Sara was surprised by Jake's speech. It didn't sound sincere. His speech sounded memorized. *Was Jake trying to impress her?* She cynically thought he was fishing for information on Sanders's special assignments. If Sanders had wanted Jake to know more details, he would have told him about the secret assignment. Furthermore, Jake seemed to be addressing problems beyond the scope of work of a security officer. "How did you become the chief security officer here?"

Jake flushed and pulled a cigarette from his pocket. He lit it and took a long drag. Sara decided her question had been too blunt.

"My current job title doesn't really describe what I do." He pulled at his tie and seemed to gulp for air. "While I studied at Harvard, I took advantage of their Brazilian studies program because I wanted to eventually live in Brazil. I guess because my family is Portuguese." He shook his head. "But the only job I could get in South America was as a security officer for a firm in Argentina. After I worked various security assignments in South America, I joined the DSS—you know the Diplomatic Security Service program in the State Department."

"When did you come to Manaus?"

"About ten years ago." He sat us straighter. "That makes me the senior staff member here. Evan Hinkley uses me as his chief of staff."

Sara stared at the man silently. Sanders might appreciate Jake's unique training in Brazilian culture. In their daily phone calls since arriving in Brazil, Sanders had not painted a pretty picture of U.S. and Brazilian relations. He had theorized part of the problem was the U.S. didn't understand Brazil. Although U.S. universities had many experts on the Spanish colonization of Latin America, really few had expertise on the Portuguese colonization of Brazil. *But* Sanders had not mentioned Jake as a resource in any of their conversations or in the briefing documents.

Sara decided—as she usually did when uncertain—to change the topic and not even acknowledge the secret assignment. "Have you made progress in finding a U.S. citizen who could translate Anderson's diary?"

Jake frowned. "You're testing me. You know most experts on Tupi are European or Brazilian. However, I found a semi-retired instructor at Brown University and sent him a copy of the text. He thought he could have answers for us in two days."

"Did you warn him about confidentiality? I may be a bit of a nervous Nellie but Will Anderson's comments on the man he called Spider could identify a major drug figure. Such knowledge can be dangerous."

Jake's frown deepened. "I'm no beginner. Neither is this instructor. I sent the pages on a secure line to the FBI office in Providence. They're being delivered now to his home. None of us wanted the pages lying around a departmental office with talkative secretaries, jealous colleagues, and nosy graduate students."

Sara decided not to mention the missing page in Will's diary to Jake yet. "Well, you just proved you understand university politics. I think I'll check on Sanders now."

CHAPTER 10: Latoya's Nightmare

Latoya was pleased when Mr. Sanders brought his foot into the black car, and she could slam the car door shut. He had been a nightmare to protect during the luncheon. Many of the conference participants had approached him in groups or individually to thank him for bringing attention to the ecological disaster facing Amazonia if Brazilian and world policies did not change. Many others had asked about the noises coming from the hallway.

It was Latoya's job to protect—not analyze—senior embassy staff, but she knew they were easier to protect if she understood their motives. The previous ambassador had been easy. He liked the glamour of the job and took no chances, except drinking too much.

Sanders was disciplined. He'd collected the weapons in the hallway as soon as she'd kicked the guns from the attackers' hands. She suspected Sanders would have been more hands-on if he hadn't been injured in the explosion earlier in the day. His bravado made him harder to protect. Sanders also was hard to predict. He'd asked her during lunch what she thought about global warming, listened to part of her answer, and said, "You sound like Sara."

Latoya was glad when they reached the consular office and Sanders became someone else's responsibility. Sanders's last order to her was to report to Ray Curtis who was at the conference. That was strange because Ray Curtis was the new science attaché from the Brasília embassy, but he seemed to be functioning as an information specialist.

She'd never met Ray before but somehow his name resonated in her memory. She didn't know why. He certainly didn't look like someone she would have met during her FBI training. He was only five-six, too skinny to have much athletic training, and wore glasses. No FBI agent would willingly be caught in his badly fitting, tan jacket, and non-matching khaki pants. This nerd would not be helpful in an attack, but he seemed more pleasant than Paul Royer. That wasn't much of a compliment to Ray.

What could she say about Paul? Kelly would not have bled out on the restroom floor if Paul hadn't allowed himself to be distracted by the woman in pink. He was the type of guard who put everyone near him at risk. He was also an arrogant sexist wrapped in what he thought was a perfect body. She thought he was too lazy to really exercise. She was sure, although he was a couple of inches taller than her at six feet, she could beat him in a fair fight.

***

Latoya found Juan and Ray sitting in the middle of the crowd in the lecture hall. Ray had emailed her that this session on "Bacterial Control of Tropical Vectors" was the most interesting session so far. She doubted she'd find the session interesting and assessed the difficulty of protecting the two men. Their position would be hard for an attacker or her to reach. It was okay.

She poured herself a glass of acai juice and thought of the lunch she'd missed. She'd been able to get only a few mouthfuls of the prawn stew. However, she'd eaten enough to know she'd missed something special. It was less spicy and richer than the shrimp étouffée, which her mother made, because this stew contained coconut milk. She smiled as she pulled a brigadeiro, a Brazilian version of a chocolate truffle, from her purse and popped it into her mouth. She had had enough brigadeiros to sustain her through the afternoon because she'd taken not only her own dessert from the luncheon but Sanders's, too.

***

Before Sara slipped into a chair in the last row, she tapped Latoya's left shoulder. "Read my email to you."

The guard who brought me is parking the car and walking the perimeter of the building before he joins the session. He'll take over as the

Latoya thought Sara was organized, communicated clearly, and believed in the importance of the conference. It was easy to see why Mr. Sanders asked her to represent the U.S. at this conference. Latoya was less sure how Sara would act in an emergency. However, Paul had admired her "coolness" this morning after the bombing. Still, Latoya was nervous about Sara's planned stroll along Avendio January Marihno with Moreno to the university's bosque at four. It was too open.

For the next half hour, Latoya learned how scientists infected mosquitos in the laboratory with *Wolbachia* bacteria. When male mosquitos infected with *Wolbachia* mated with wild female mosquitos, their eggs didn't hatch. The scientists at the conference were now laboriously reviewing trials, which had evaluated the effectiveness of this method of mosquito birth control to prevent the spread of tropical viral diseases, like dengue fever. Although Sara indicated this was to be an interesting session, she seemed to study her laptop throughout the session.

At three, Latoya's boredom was broken in a bad way. Jake texted her and Sara. The body of the fake Camille Draco had been found. He wanted Sara to report to the morgue immediately to see if the body was the woman she'd met yesterday. Sara had up to now been cooperative, but she refused Jake's request. She said she would stop by the morgue after her meeting at four. Jake had protested, but Sara was adamant.

At fifteen after three, Sara and Ray had both ambled to the back of the room and chatted as they sipped colas. Latoya thought it odd Sara chose to drink a cola when she was leaving for essentially a coffee break in another half hour. Latoya guessed Sara must be pumping up on caffeine to be sharp for her discussion with Moreno. This Moreno character certainly made Sara nervous.

At ten to four, Sara grabbed two cans of club soda from the back table, stuffed them in her tote, and left the session. Latoya texted Ray and the guard that she and Sara were leaving.

***

Moreno was waiting at the front of the building. He quickly turned Sara's handshake into a lingering hug and awkward kiss on the cheek. They then ambled slowly toward the university's so-called *bosque*. The only good thing about the blazing sunlight was few people were walking around the campus. Thankfully, the two displayed some sense and settled on a bench under a large tree after a few minutes. The only good thing about blazing sunlight was few people were walking around the campus. Thus, watching Sara and Moreno was easy. Latoya noted Sara had been considerate. There was a tree and another shady bench nearby from where Latoya could watch the couple.

As soon as they were seated, Sara dug into her tote, seemed to sort through its contents, and handed a can of soda to Moreno. He studied the can and traced his finger along something on the label. They laughed and then appeared to settle into a true head-to-head discussion as both slouched forward. Anyone watching might think it was two scientists talking about their laboratory data. Latoya doubted they were talking about scientific data.

Sara checked her phone around four-thirty. Both immediately stood. Moreno walked toward a black car idling nearby. Sara tinkered with her phone and walked slowly toward Latoya. "Better check your phone for messages."

Latoya did. She gulped as she read the text Sara had forwarded from the guard at the conference:

> *Juan & Ray went to the can. Can't find them now.*

The guard should not have sent the message to Sara and expected Sara to forward it. Latoya chalked up the mistake to the inexperience of the guard.

J. L. Greger

Latoya also thought it odd Sara was walking more slowly than usual. Nothing Latoya said or did, increased Sara's pace. Finally, they saw the guard uselessly pacing at the front of the building where the conference was being held.

Sara stopped as soon as she saw the guard and made a call. "Jake, who needs drug gangs and political enemies when we're blessed with inexperienced guards? Juan and Ray have disappeared. Pick up the guard at the front of the building where the conference is being held. He's waiting to see if Juan and Ray return. He'll know where to meet Latoya and me." She was silent as she listened. "No. I'll give you the details after you pick up the guard." She placed the phone in her tote. "Latoya let's go. Just remember I'm not in as good condition as you."

***

Sara made Latoya sit with her under the veranda of the social science building and wait for Jake and the guard to arrive. Their fifteen-minute walk in the brutal heat had been senseless. The guard had wanted to get the car and to drive them to the building, but Sara had insisted she and Latoya would walk while the guard stayed at the conference waiting for Jake. Latoya hadn't argued because Sara seemed too determined.

A red mini convertible screeched to a stop. Jake jumped from the car and ran to Sara with the guard trailing. "Damn Moreno. He stopped me and wouldn't stop talking. I could have gotten here five minutes sooner." He gasped for breath. "Where do we go?"

"Don't have a heart attack. Get your breath first." Sara pulled him onto a bench.

"Maria also slowed me down, too. She had no idea where her brother would go but wouldn't stop talking about her useless notes in Tupi."

Latoya thought Sara seemed awfully calm considering the potential gravity of the situation.

Sara said, "This is not the time to look panicked, we're probably being watched. Juan is with Ray Curtis and they're probably safe. Juan may have gone to his father's old office to find something...."

"Like what?" Sweat was beading up on Jake's forehead.

"The missing page in Will's diary."

"What missing page?" Jake seemed to calm himself slightly. "I need to get the key to Will Anderson's old office from the social science department office."

Sara grabbed Jake's arm before he could sprint off.

"I can do it faster without you."

"But Juan is more apt to hide from you than me." They entered the building arm in arm.

The young guard looked at Latoya. She shrugged. "Sara's in charge... I guess."

***

A young secretary in halting English said as she opened the door. "This room is used by our visiting faculty." She pointed to an old, mid-century modern style desk with an orange fiberglass reinforced chair. "Dr. Anderson used that desk."

Jake slammed open the drawer above the knee space. It was empty. He pulled the drawer out and felt around the casing. Nothing. He didn't bother to put the drawer in place and let it clatter on the floor before he pulled open the drawer on the left.

Latoya was confused. Jake was more interested in finding a missing page than in finding two missing men. And Sara seemed too calm.

"Let's not be destructive." Sara picked up the drawer and pushed Jake aside as she shoved the original drawer back into place.

He cursed and removed the drawer on the left. It was full of papers which he handed to the young guard. He checked the casing rapidly but jammed the drawer back in place before he searched the right drawer.

Sara turned to the secretary whose eyes were wide with surprise bordering on fear. "I'm sorry he's being so wild. He's looking for a special document. Would anyone mind if we took these pages?" She searched in her tote and pulled out Brazilian currency for a hundred reals. "Would this reimburse the department for the paper?"

"You don't need to bribe her," snapped Jake.

"It's not a bribe. One hundred Brazilian reals is only twenty dollars."

The young woman blushed. "I will not keep it. The money goes in our department's—how you say it—petty cash fund."

"Good." Sara grabbed Jake's arm. "The other place to look for Juan is in his office. Perhaps, your driver can drive us all there?"

"Five of us won't fit in the mini convertible."

Sara grabbed Jake's arm before he could run. "Then we'll all have to walk back to the conference and retrieve the consulate car."

The walk and then the drive was tense. The parade to the entomology department office and then to the office used by ten research assistants was a frantic race. No one in the main office of the entomology department had seen Juan today or knew which desk was his. They thought it was one of two on the back wall. No one was in the research assistants' office to provide information.

Sara made Jake stand aside as she searched the two old metal desks to determine which was Juan Anderson's desk. One was completely empty. The other one had pencils, markers, tape, and files. Jake yelled at Latoya to help Sara search through the files. Finally, Sara pulled a yellow page from a yellow file.

Jake snatched the page from Sara's hands, read it, crumpled it into a ball, and threw it on the floor.

"Let's not lose our temper." Sara took the ball, smoothed the page out, and laid it on the desk. The page read:

> *Got it.*
> *Ray*

Latoya heard rapid footsteps in the hallway. They were coming closer and closer. Agents with navy nylon jackets emblazoned with "FBI" in yellow raced into the small room. She didn't know any of them, but she knew a contingency of agents from outside Brazil had arrived this morning. The last person to enter the room was Mr. Sanders.

CHAPTER 11: Sara Turns the Tables

Sara felt relief rush through her when she saw Sanders. He winked at her, and she knew their scheme had worked. She sank onto a metal chair at another desk and watched the scene unfold.

The agents had entered with their guns out. They instructed Jake, Latoya, and the young guard to put their hands in the air. Latoya raised her hands immediately. The young guard looked expectantly at Jake.

Jake had stood defiantly staring back at the officers until he saw Sanders. "Don't make a scene, kid. I'll clear this up." He lifted his hands slowly. So did the young guard.

"Jake, I hope you can clear this up." Sanders nodded to the officers.

Two agents kept their guns directed at Jake, Latoya, and the guard while a woman agent patted the three down and pulled their guns from their shoulder holster. Sanders placed a box on the desk in front of Sara. The woman agent carefully placed each gun in the box.

Sara was prepared and donned a pair of plastic gloves. First, she picked up Latoya's gun, emptied it of bullets, and put it in a labeled bag from her purse. She unloaded the two other guns and placed them in separate labeled bags.

Sara was surprised when the woman agent pulled another gun from a holster on Jake's lower left leg. Sara noticed the slight sneer on Jake's face disappeared as the woman agent put the last gun on the desk.

Sanders must have noticed Jake's change of expression because he sighed. "I had hoped you weren't involved in the problems in the Manaus office, but I have proof now you were. Where's Camille Draco?"

Jake looked about the room. "I doubt your evidence."

Sara couldn't resist. "Then why were you so frantic in our search of Will's and Juan's desks? I know Maria told you her father's diary had gotten interesting as he described Spider, but a key page was missing. I think she told you at four-thirty. Am I right?"

Jake trembled slightly but regained his confidence quickly. "Latoya, you emailed me Sara was acting odd this afternoon. You can see I'm being framed. Sara's in league with that communist Moreno from Cuba."

Sara wanted to say: *Yes, Moreno is part of the communist regime in Cuba and has many undesirable traits, but he doesn't make deals with drug gangs.* She knew it was best to let Sanders have the last word.

"Latoya, as far as I can tell you were not involved with the drug gangs, but Maria has not finished translating her father's diary." Sanders's voice softened. "Have you heard any comments on Camille Draco's location? Or whether she is alive? Please recognize I have staff checking all your calls, emails, texts, and social media entries for the last month."

Latoya had turned gray when Sanders entered the room, but she replied confidently to his questions. "Mr. Sanders, you know I'm from the Rio consulate. I've never been to Manaus before yesterday." She paused. "I did meet Camille once in Brasília at a meeting of FBI agents, information specialists, and public relations officers posted to consulates in Brazil." She paled. "OMG. I thought I'd heard Ray Curtis's name before. Now I remember...."

Sanders smiled. "What do you remember?"

"I don't think I should say more."

"What about you?" Sanders pointed at the young guard who was literally quaking in his shoes.

"This is my first international assignment. I don't know what's happening here. I was surprised when Jake hired me two months ago. My old boss said I wasn't ready for Manaus, but I figured how hard could it be to work in a relatively small consular office?"

***

Sara was used to Sanders's approach to complex cases. He would not rush even though he feared delays were bad news for

Camille. He would start with the weakest link and offer him or her sympathy—maybe even enticements—for everything they knew, guessed, or feared. He would leave the primary culprit alone for at least an hour. Each suspect would, if possible, be put in a room with a two-way mirror with plenty of beverages. He'd call Sara when he wanted her help.

Sara hadn't understood all Sanders's actions during the arrest of Jake, Latoya, and the guard. She assumed Maria and her mother must have uncovered a lot after she'd left for the afternoon sessions at the conference and decided it was time for a talk with the two women.

Sara found them working at the library table in Sara's makeshift office. "Maria, besides being a talented translator, you're quite an actress. Jake believed you were incapable of translating your father's diary."

Sara suspected Maria had been acting for years—always hiding her sharp mind with simpering, childlike comments. Why? Then she recognized Maria's mother was also an actress. She had said fewer than ten words to Sara so far. Her son had claimed his mother could neither read nor write. However, she apparently could read at least some Tupi. She had also written occasional words in English—like yes and no—on the pages of Maria's translation of her husband's diary even though she spoke to her children in Portuguese. Did their reticence reflect acceptance of gender and cultural roles or distrust?

Maria uncrossed her legs and stood when Sara spoke. "It was scary, but you were clear about what I had to do."

Her mother said, "Thanks. We... fear Mr. Tarantino."

Sara almost asked her to say Jake's last name again. It sounded different the way she pronounced it and rang a bell in the back of her mind.

Maria interrupted Sara's thoughts. "You gave Juan and Ray Curtis harder parts to play."

"Yes, and they had to act quickly." Sara thought about the plan she and Ray had contrived. Ray and Juan had picked up Carlos Moreno after she'd talked to Carlos in the university bosque. They had dropped him at a back entrance to the conference before they changed into their disguises at the consular offices. Then they had gone to Juan's office in the entomology department to retrieve the missing page of the diary.

J. L. Greger

Maria giggled. "They were too busy to talk to me when they came here to put on their costumes. Ray and Juan put dark makeup on their faces, arms, and hands, and darkened their hair. In jeans and T-shirts with their hair slicked back they looked like bad boys when they left. I wanted to go along. I like costumes. But Ray wouldn't take me along with them."

Mrs. Anderson put her hand on Maria's shoulder. "Quiet, child." There were tears in her eyes when she looked at Sara. "I fear for Juan now."

Sara patted Mrs. Anderson's shoulder. "Ray Curtis is talented. I'm sure Juan is safe. They've got others with them." Sara didn't know the details, but Sanders had told her two staff members would go with Ray and Juan on their last errand in the deception. She imagined by now Sanders had utilized every staff member in the office whom he trusted.

It was time to change the subject. "How much of the translation have you finished?"

"Pieces." Mrs. Anderson was quiet for a few seconds. "My husband... had fears... for a long time."

"We read part of the missing page." Maria pointed to her pad of yellow lined paper. Sara noted many words were crossed out on the page. "Some words are hard to translate. I translated 'member of your tribe' as 'a friend.' I didn't know what to call a person you know but who is not in your tribe. I called him 'a man' unless Pai described him as evil. Then I called him 'an enemy.' I think Pai wrote 'killing tribes' when he meant 'drug gangs.'"

Sara read the lines on the yellow page slowly realizing the imprecision of the translation:

> *Important enemies work for the drug gangs. A man asked my friend about insects that eat the bark of trees. This man had dark hair on his arms. I call him Spider. My friend said Spider asked strange questions.*
>
> *It is not safe for Juan to work at the bug farm.*

Sara stopped reading. "Is there any mention of a Cuban?"

Mrs. Anderson shook her head. "Not on this page."

"Fine. Maria, take your time. I know this is hard. Who do you think is your father's friend?"

"I think he is my boss. That's why he hired me in the bug farm and made Juan his research assistant."

"Okay. Why would he tell your father about this visit by a man interested in beetles. It seems innocent to me."

Maria shrugged. "Mãe and I don't know."

"Did you show your translation to Mr. Sanders?"

Maria looked surprised. "Yes. Wasn't it okay? He only glanced at my first few lines and told me to show my notes to anyone but you."

This is the proof Sanders mentioned to Jake. He was faster than I was in recognizing Jake as the Spider. She hadn't recognized "Tarantino" sounded like "tarantula," until Mrs. Anderson said the name. She'd certainly noticed Jake had dark hairy arms. Tarantulas were hairy spiders. Simple but clear. Sara smiled to herself. She was glad she'd told Sanders to check on Maria's progress before he left the consulate.

"Maria, just a few more question before I let you get back to work. Are you sure Spider is a man? Was there any mention of a black spider or a non-hairy spider on any of the pages?"

Mrs. Anderson shook her head. Maria said, "I don't understand."

"Did you father mention another spider—a lady?"

Maria pouted. "One spider is enough."

Sara felt relieved as she emailed Sanders. She knew why Sanders was questioning Latoya's loyalty. Her middle name was Arianna. The Portuguese word for spider—*aranha*—was similar. But she doubted Latoya was compromised.

*****

"I want to talk to you about... what we did today."

Sara studied Ray Curtis. Maria was right. Ray with his hair and skin darkened and his hair slicked back did look like a boy from the streets of Manaus. "Do you think Moreno recognized you today?"

"Of course. I picked him up in my usual garb as a science nerd."

"So, he knows you're a master of disguises?"

"No, I was careful in Cuba. I only introduced myself to him when I was acting as a nerdy, blond science attaché who constantly chewed gum."

"Let's hope you're right."

Ray nodded. "One thing bothers me. Do you think it was smart to promise you'd share any pages in the diary mentioning Cubans involved in the Brazilian drug trade with Moreno?"

Sara shrugged. "I needed Moreno's help today to keep Jake running in circles long enough for you to complete your mission. It would have been easier if Juan had admitted sooner that his father had ripped one page from the diary and told Juan to hide it outside their house."

"Juan confided to me his father had made him promise to not tell his mother or sister about the missing page. He only admitted the truth after we returned to the conference this afternoon." Ray shook his head. "You don't know how close we came to being discovered."

"Oh?"

"Juan had trouble finding the missing page in his office files. We saw you getting out of a black car, as we left the entomology building."

"I certainly did everything I could think of to slow Jake." Sara sighed. "Now on to the next worry. Do you think anyone recognized you or Juan in the entomology department?"

"The two agents with us have Hispanic backgrounds. The four of us together looked like Brazilian hoodlums. We let the tires really squeal when we pulled away in the gold Chevrolet Opala. It looked like a car that drug smugglers would use with all its oomph. The only problem was being inconspicuous when we dropped off Juan and one agent a block from the consulate. Then the driver I went to the Anderson house."

"Did you spot anyone near the house?"

"It was under surveillance. Could have been drug gangs. More likely it was Cubans sent there by Moreno. It was sad what we had to do. The house was a wreck when we left. All I could save for the Andersons were a few of Will's mementoes that Mrs. Anderson wanted and one change of clothes for each of them. Taking more would have been too obvious. We ditched the car on a country road. Too bad. It was a beauty."

CHAPTER 12: Party Time for Sara?

Sara was so tired she couldn't concentrate on the screen in front of her. She really hadn't been physically active today— only short spurts of intense activity. Even so, she was mentally and emotionally exhausted. The good news was she was sure Sanders would be equally tired and not want to do anything special tonight.

Sara heard the door to the office open. Maria stopped her constant dialog to herself and started to giggle.

Sara gasped. A woman, who usually served as the receptionist in the Manaus consular office, was pushing a clothes rack into the office. There were black and ecru slacks, black and ecru sleeveless and short-sleeved tops, linen jackets, khaki Bermuda shorts, and two brightly printed scarves. "Since your clothes were all destroyed in the fire, Mr. Sanders ordered me to shop for you. You do know... you and Mr. Sanders are going to big event at the Amazon Theater tonight? Don't you?"

"You're kidding?"

The young woman's lips quivered. "He said to play it safe and give you choices in black and ecru with splashes of color. He seemed sure."

Sara stood and pulled the hangers along the rack. The clothes were exactly what she would have chosen—black trousers and a linen jacket for the conference, khaki Bermuda shorts for around the consular offices, and simple interchangeable tops. The cotton scarves would vary her look just enough.

"I brought everything in two sizes. I'll return those that don't fit. I also had the palazzo pants you wore earlier cleaned and shortened so you can wear them tonight."

Sara stroked the silk shawl draped on one hanger and traced her finger along the swirls of pinks, roses, and lavenders. "Did he tell you the colors to look for in the shawl?"

"Yes, he said you liked pastels, particularly pinks and roses. I thought bright colors would be better, but he insisted."

Sara smiled. "He's right. When I was young, bold reds were my favorite. Now I don't feel the need to look strong and prefer the soft warmth of pinks and roses. My problem is I'm not sure I'm up to an event tonight. I'm surprised he is."

"Oh, I forgot to tell you. He said he hoped you wouldn't mind if you two slipped out of the concert at the Amazon Theater at the intermission and missed the post-concert dinner, but the Mayor of Manaus would be disappointed if you didn't at least attend the opening. Mr. Sanders also wants to dispel rumors that he was seriously injured in the fire this morning."

***

Sara hated to be critical but the dome in yellow, green, and blue tiles glistening in the setting sun didn't match the architecture of the rest of the Amazon Theater—a three-story, pink Renaissance Revival building. It looked like an elegant pink birthday cake with white frosting trim and then one big, fat non-matching candle on top. However, she couldn't deny the building demanded attention, and the Brazilians had a right to make the dome reflect their country's aesthetic.

The driver stopped the consulate car in front of the elegant curving stairway to the main entrance of the opera house. It was nice not to have to wait in line to climb the stairs. However, it was embarrassing, too. She was sure those waiting in the plaza were hot and thirsty, including the ten or so protestors carrying signs at the edge of the crowd. This was not the time to worry about anything that was not essential. She gritted her teeth, sucked in her gut, and despite her aching muscles turned with Sanders to face the crowd. They both plastered smiles on their faces as they waved to the crowd.

When he nudged her elbow, they turned and climbed the stairs slowly. She figured it was safe to speak—the nearest person was six feet away. "I always knew glitz and glamour were overrated. We'd both be happier using a back entrance and sitting in good, but not prime, seats."

"We'll leave in about an hour."

They were greeted inside the marble entrance by the Mayor, his spouse, and local dignitaries. Sara, who had no facility for foreign languages, uttered *"Olá"* and offered her hand to each person in the reception line. If they responded by kissing her on the cheek, she responded in kind and said "Muito prazer." If they replied in English, she commented on the splendor of the opera house. Sanders—who spoke passable Portuguese—talked briefly with the Mayor and his wife while Sara moved down the line.

The general manager of a local radio and TV station laughed after he heard Sara's comment on the impressiveness of the opera house. "What do you really think of our dome?"

Sara didn't want to hear her comments discussed tomorrow on TV or radio. "I think it is wonderful that Brazilians at the end of the nineteenth century found a way to highlight their country while building an opera house as grand as any in the world."

The man's eyes narrowed. "I thought you were a scientist and would not be interested in our culture and history."

Sara sucked in her breath. It would be easy to annoy this man. "Being a scientist doesn't mean I don't enjoy the arts. In fact, one of the perks of scientific consulting is I've had a chance to visit many exciting cultural sites." She thought for a second about a way to show awareness of cultures other than European ones. "In New Mexico, I live only a couple of miles from several of resorts built by Native Americans. I find the mix of indigenous and Western cultures in the resorts to be fascinating."

He stared at her blankly.

She'd given a poor example and needed to extract herself before she created a scene. "Of course, the pueblos are not elegant like your opera house."

His face was red, and his voice was loud. "Are you saying this opera house is too sophisticated to be sitting in the middle of a jungle?"

"Oh, no. It's a wonderful statement of pride by Brazilians." Sara noticed several people in the reception line were now staring at her.

The Mayor spoke first. "Senhor Braga was not expecting you to have such wide interests."

Sara had a sickening feeling when she heard the station manager's name clearly. "Are you related to Dr. Manuel Castro

                                                J. L. Greger

Braga?" Sara thought the question alerted Sanders and Ray Curtis, who was listening via the hidden microphone she wore, that this man could have ties to the drug cartels. Earlier they'd agreed Dr. Manuel Braga—of the people she'd met at the conference—was the most likely link to the drug cartels.

The man's face remained flushed.

She tried to be inoffensive. "I know Braga is a common name in Brazil. But I enjoyed meeting Dr. Manuel Braga yesterday at the reception before the conference."

Senhor Braga sniffed. "Yes, our Mayor is right. You are not what I expected." He paused. "Manuel is my brother."

Sara felt Sanders nudging her elbow. She guessed he didn't want to be embarrassed by any more of her comments, but she didn't know how she could have avoided this mess. It certainly was an inauspicious introduction of her in the role of a diplomat's wife or significant other. She hoped they would laugh about this incident later. But she couldn't help thinking. *You can't make a silk purse out of a sow's ear. You don't belong here.*

***

Sara noticed the Mayor's wife rearranged the seating as the VIP party entered the first balcony. Sara was assigned a seat between the rector of the Federal University of Amazonas and his wife, while Sanders was seated between the mayor and the archbishop for the Catholic Church in Manaus. Senhor Braga was seated on the far side of the Mayor's wife.

The rector was eager to talk. He pointed out a large contingent—about thirty scholars—from the conference were seated in the floor below. Sara spotted Ray Curtis in his nerdy science disguise in the group.

The rector was a good conversationalist, but Sara wanted to gawk at the auditorium. From her first balcony seat, Sara could see the full stage, the flamboyant paintings with green backgrounds on the ceiling of the large auditorium, all the gilding surrounding the paintings on the three tiers of balconies, and the glittering chandeliers.

Sara really didn't feel like talking and was glad when the lights were dimmed. The concert featured a Brazilian singer-songwriter famous for his protest songs. Sara thought he sounded like a folk singer with a bossa nova beat in the background. She didn't really listen to the concert because she was too busy worrying.

Eventually, the concert halted for the intermission. Sanders looked haggard. Red swelling extended beyond the bandages on his neck. Sara apologized profusely for their early exit to everyone. All were gracious and wished Sanders a quick recovery. Senhor Braga disappeared before Sara reached him to apologize.

Their car was waiting for them at a side entrance of the opera house. Ray Curtis was already sitting in the front seat.

Ray chomped on his gum like an old cow chewing her cud as he turned to look at the back seat. "Boss, you looked fine. Not like the walking wounded as you feared."

Sanders slumped in his seat and then straightened. "The collar chafes more when I slump." He removed his tie and unbuttoned his collar. After he got into a presumably comfortable position, he patted Sara's hand. "I'm glad you wore a wire. I think Jorge Braga confirmed our worst fears. Ray, did you catch and record our entrance?"

Ray grinned. "Sara's better than a bloodhound in tracking a scent."

"You mean I'm better than rotten meat at attracting flies. I'm afraid what Jorge might air tomorrow on a radio talk show."

"Nothing. It would only embarrass him. The Mayor was furious at Jorge." Sanders patted her hand. "I'm sorry. This is another night that's lost its romantic potential."

CHAPTER 13: Day 3 Has to Be Better

Sara awoke early in a guest room in the consul's house. Everyone called this house—the "consul's house"—but it was technically not true. The previous ambassador had wanted to raise the status of the Manaus consular agency to that of a consulate. As a first step, he had gotten the State Department to purchase this house for the chief of the Manaus consular office. The ambassador and Evan Hinkley had claimed it was cheaper to maintain a consul's house and staff than to rent hotel rooms and dining facilities for the many "official" guests coming to Manaus. However, Sanders had stayed in the house only once and purchased his hideaway with his own funds because he distrusted Evan Hinkley.

The house was silent even though there were supposed to be a couple of security people present. A light was streaming from around the partially open door to the adjoining room. Through the narrow view, she saw Sanders slouched in a chair scanning his laptop.

The explosion at Sanders's private hideaway yesterday morning had been the last straw. Sanders was convinced Hinkley's poor management of the consular office was the ultimate cause of the attack. Sanders talked to the Undersecretary and sent Hinkley to an emergency meeting in Washington. Hinkley had resisted, but a call from the Undersecretary had been effective. Hinkley and his wife had flown from Manaus to Rio in the early afternoon and caught a red eye to Washington, D.C.

Sanders had not told Sara the details, but she suspected Evan Hinkley and his wife would not enjoy their meetings today with FBI agents and State Department analysts.

Sara watched Sanders. He seldom slouched, but he usually chose to sit at a desk not in an easy chair. She arose and tiptoed to the door. Sanders's head jerked toward her. She never seemed to move quietly enough not to disturb him.

He motioned for her to come closer. "I couldn't get comfortable last night. I ached all over. The skin on my back and neck didn't hurt per se but felt hot, tight, and slightly itchy. I was also worried. Do you realize the security gap created when the head of security, like Jake, in a consulate goes rogue? Washington analysts are now scrutinizing the background of everyone who had even slight contacts with Jake for suspicious activities."

She kissed the top of his head. He pulled her down onto his lap. His tongue flicked her cheek, and his arms surrounded her. She thought this was going to be a better day than yesterday. She shifted her weight to face him and nuzzled his mouth.

"Ouch." He sighed as he pushed her away. "My skin is sorer than I thought."

She figured she must have brushed the bandages on his neck. She leaned forward and kissed his lips and awkwardly turned to stand. In the process, she fell back onto his lap. "I had bad feeling about Brazil before you took this assignment."

He kissed her and pushed her upward. "We both had bad feelings about this assignment, but I had to do it."

Sara knew the Secretary of State and Sanders's direct boss, the Undersecretary, had made promises to him. All were contingent on solving supposedly two problems in Brazil. From what she'd seen so far, she wondered how they'd chosen only two problems. One she knew was related to the recovering Al Caputo and reducing the movement of drugs from Brazil to the U.S.

"So, what's on the docket for today?" She sank in a matching easy chair facing Sanders.

"I know you think the best sessions of the conference occur today."

"Yes. The first session today will focus on new biotechnology methods for altering the genetics of *Aedes* mosquitos so they can't reproduce. Thus, they spread dengue and other viral diseases less. However, the techniques used to reduce *Aedes* mosquitos have been less successful with *Anopheles* mosquitos."

He shook his head and in a dead pan voice said, "Sounds fascinating."

"Don't be so blasé. It's essential info for those interested in tropical medicine."

"I get the message. You want to hear those presentations. Can you meet with all three Andersons this morning and learn the nuances of their translation of Will's diary? Ray said they were working on the translation when he checked on them at midnight."

"So, they might have finished translating the diary. Is there a reason to hurry?"

Sanders's jaw dropped.

"Well, besides the obvious one—to identify employees in the consulate who've sold out to the drug cartels?" Sara arose and began tinkering with the coffee machine on the wet bar.

"I'd like to get the whole Anderson family out of Brazil today. The U.S. Citizenship and Immigration Services has agreed to my request to grant them asylum in the U.S. because they will be killed if they remain in Brazil. Otherwise, I could only get Juan out on a student visa. I don't want to tell the Andersons yet because they might make comments. Then Jake or someone else might alert the drug cartels."

"You assume Maria is too talkative to keep a secret. I think everyone underestimates her." Sara opened the under-the-counter refrigerator under the bar and studied the choices. She shook her head "The Hinkleys assumed their guests wanted only booze. The coffee machine appears to be broken and the choices in the refrigerator are limited." She selected two cans of tomato juice and handed one to Sanders.

He studied the can, frowned, but drank its contents. "I also want to send Will's diary back to analysts in Washington, but I can't find it."

"What? I thought you locked the missing page with the diary in the safe in Evan Hinkley's office. Isn't that where Jake left the diary after he gave copies to Maria and to his friend at Brown University to translate?"

That's what Jake claimed, but the diary was missing when I tried to hide the lost page before we went to the theater. Since then, Ray searched Jake's and Hinkley's offices but couldn't find the diary. I checked the safe here, too. I think the diary must be in the consulate because Jake was under surveillance constantly by FBI agents. They kept him in a locked room in the consulate last night with only a cot and no phone." He paused. "I'm glad the FBI legal attaché in Brasília arranged to import agents from outside Brazil for this operation."

"Why?"

"We both feared the potential corruption among DSS guards, like Jake, could have spread to even FBI agents in Brazil. This way I can at least trust the new agents."

"So, you think Latoya, as an FBI agent based in Brazil, might have gotten the diary from Jake and passed it on?"

"I have no evidence against her and I'm short on staff. I had to let her work security at the Amazon Theater last night..." He sighed. "...with two FBI agents usually stationed in Peru monitoring her."

Sara hated to allow herself to be as paranoid as Sanders seemed. "Let's explore your fears. Did Latoya ever get close to Jorge Braga last night?"

"I was reading the Peruvian agents' report when you came in. They don't think Latoya had a chance to pass off anything to Braga because she never spoke to him." Sanders shook his head. "Problem is a good pickpocket in the crowd could have lifted the diary from a pocket in her suit jacket without even an observant FBI agent noticing."

"My other question is who besides Ray heard my conversation with Braga last night."

"No others at the time. Only Ray knew you were wearing a mike and knew the frequency of the transmission. Several by now have heard it. By the way, no one can figure what set Jorge Braga off last night. Ray's guessing Braga was nervous because he was hiding something, and you threatened him."

"More likely, he assumed I'd be an easy source of info and I disappointed him."

"Hmm. Ray was going to have agents investigate more thoroughly the background of both Bragas today."

She swallowed a slug of tomato juice. "Hate to ask this, but are there any State Department security officers or FBI agents left in Brazil outside Manaus?"

Sanders scowled. "It's not funny. Eight more FBI agents arrived in Rio at five this morning. They're on their way here now. Two will escort the Andersons to the Washington area."

"Why don't you send Jake back to Washington for questioning, too? Then you wouldn't have to waste guards on him."

"I'm still hoping he'll lead me to others in this or other U.S. consulates in Brazil who are on the payroll of the drug cartels. The possibility is gone once he leaves Brazil."

"Is Camille one of your suspects?"

"No... well, perhaps. All I'm sure about is Camille alerted me to the problems here and Jake wants to find her. He claims Camille was a major leak from this consulate to the drug gangs."

"A real 'he said, she said' situation. And you think Camille is still alive?"

"Yes, for two reasons. When I worried about her safety before you arrived, she assured me she had the perfect escape plan."

"Do you know what she meant?"

"No, she claimed if I knew, I'd write it down and then it could be discovered by others."

Sara shook her head and touched his shoulder. "That's more an example of hope than of evidence."

He handed Sara a card. 'This was delivered here by an urchin about an hour ago. Agents questioned the boy, but he claimed he'd been given the card by another boy to deliver. Although he said he didn't know the boy who gave him the card, he knew enough to ask for a meal. The agents still have him here. He's eaten three eggs and two slices of toast already."

Sara saw the card was a prayer card. It had a stylized image of the Virgin Mary on one side. A few lines in Portuguese script were on the back. Someone had written with a marker across the back:

Don't trust guards recruited by Jake. CDr

"Anyone could have sent the card."

"Camille always signed her emails to me with CDr."

"I assume you're checking to see if she took sanctuary in a Catholic church. Were there fingerprints?"

"Lots of prints. All hopelessly smudged. I'm told this is a depiction of Our Lady of Aparecida, the patron saint of Brazil. The script quotes Matthew 19:14. 'Let the little children....'"

"I didn't realize you had gotten so good at reading Portuguese."

"This was easy." He tapped the card on his computer. "A nun at the Catholic diocese office here told agents that the diocese in Manaus had printed tens of thousands of this card for Children's Day last October."

"Interesting. Nuns, not priests, answer calls at weird hours." Sara took another slug of tomato juice. "That reminds me. Do I still need to see the Camille-look-alike in the morgue? Jake ordered me to go to the morgue yesterday just to prevent me from talking to Moreno."

"There may have been another reason why he wanted you to view the body."

"Yeah, to scare the hell out of me." She stood. "Enough lolling around. Time to take a shower." As she walked out the door, she added, "If I were Jake and thought my boss was watching me, I would have hidden the diary in an easily assessable spot. A spot outsiders could get to if I couldn't get to them. Isn't there a cooler with water bottles in the waiting room near the front entrance of the consulate? By the way, may I have a xeroxed copy of the prayer card?"

***

They pulled back the cloth covering the body. Sara stared. The corpse had a thin face and narrow nose. Sara had seen enough dead bodies to know people often looked different in death than in life. This woman had been dead for several days. However, the placement of color streaks in hair wouldn't change. The streaks extended into this woman's bangs. Sara tried to reimagine the face of the woman she'd met. She remembered that she'd thought it was odd. The color streaks didn't frame the live woman's face.

She studied the face more. The eyebrows might be different. The corpse had more natural-looking eyebrows. The woman she'd seen had thin—highly plucked—eyebrows. The corpse had no freckles. She remembered the woman had freckles because it caused Sara to assume the woman's hair wasn't naturally dark.

She found on her phone the photo of the badge found in Camille's car. A photo of the dead woman had been used to make the fake badge.

"She looks like the photo on the badge."

The police officer sighed. "Senhora, is this the woman you saw? I don't care if she resembles the woman in a photo."

"No."

***

Maria jumped from the bench at the library table when Sara entered her office. "We've finished the translation. I was up most of the night."

Juan also stood. "Mãe and I together checked my sister's translation of important pages. Mãe gave an exact translation of sections and I tried to put them into typical English. We found Maria hadn't mistranslated anything, but we thought she misinterpreted a couple of sentences. One area is particularly important, I think."

Maria looked as if she might cry. "I'm sorry. I tried."

Juan pointed to a section of Maria's notes on the yellow pad of paper. "We both think Maria was right when she translated this:

> *Camille Draco laughed at me. She said, "Do not return."*

But Maria was confused by the next words. Here is the correct translation:

> *Enemies are here. Get out fast. Go to the consulate in Rio.*

"Maria translated it originally as, 'I am not your friend. Run to the consulate in Rio.' Now we all agree that Pai didn't think Camille was an enemy but others in the consulate were."

Maria nodded.

Juan continued, "It makes sense because I found an airline reservation for a flight to Rio on Pai's computer after he died. I didn't tell Mãe or Maria because they were grieving." He gulped. "There was no return ticket. Mãe and Pai had argued a lot during the week prior to his death. I didn't want Mãe and

Maria to think he might leave them." He bowed his head. "I am sorry."

Sara studied the notes. "Are you sure the diary said, 'enemies' and not 'an enemy?'"

"Yes, well maybe." Juan looked at the ceiling. "Tupi is a polysynthetic language. There are limits."

Sara had read enough about Amazonian languages, like Tupi, during the last day to know she would never understand linguistics jargon. The translation of so-called "non-rich," or polysynthetic, languages to English was complex and imprecise.

"I have only a few more questions for you." Sara focused on the descriptions of several people mentioned in the diary. Then she held up the missing page and the diary. "Look at these. Are these documents in your father's handwriting?"

She noted the surprise on the Andersons' faces. She didn't want to admit the diary had been lost and Ray had found the diary in a plastic bag wedged in the bottom of the cooler in the consulate's waiting room only ten minutes earlier.

Juan said, "Why are the pages so cold? Are you storing the diary in a refrigerator?"

Maria traced her fingers along lines on the diary. "It is good to touch my father's real words."

Sara texted Ray and almost immediately received a response:

I'd rather be lucky than smart. Today we're both.

Sara felt muscles throughout her body screaming with weariness. She sank into a chair. The last two days had been stressful. For every gain, there had been a loss. Now it appeared one section of the puzzle was almost complete, and she had found a working partner in Ray. He was easier to work with than Paul.

Just thinking about Paul was depressing. She had an idea. Maybe she could use Paul's weaknesses to gain insights into Jake's motivations. Moreover, if Sanders was true to form, he'd kept Paul isolated from knowing Jake was basically under house arrest.

Sara suddenly realized the Andersons were studying her. Juan had stopped counting pages. Mrs. Anderson was no longer sorting items in her purse. Maria had ceased bouncing and had a perplexed look on her face. Sara wondered how long she'd been thinking about Paul.

"Are you okay?" asked Juan.

"Sorry, I was thinking." She flashed a smile. "Have you ever flown on a private jet? Well, you are now."

***

Sara found the talks at the conference interesting. Both irradiation of male mosquitos and genetic modification of female mosquitos had been used to successfully reduce *Aedes* mosquito populations and the incidence of viral diseases that they spread. However, the problems were the same as with the use of the *Wolbachia* bacteria. These procedures required long-term planning, didn't provide immediate control of mosquito populations, and lost their effectiveness with time. Unfortunately, these techniques had not successfully reduced the incidence of malaria spread by *Anopheles* mosquitos.

She could guess what the reports from the breakout sessions during the afternoon would say: The control of dengue fever and other tropical viral diseases requires a multi-faceted approach which combines long-term control of *Aedes* mosquitos—by use of *Wolbachia* bacteria, irradiation, or genetic modification—and short-term destruction of *Aedes* larvae without harming other insects using environmentally-friendly insecticides. The control of vectors carrying malaria parasites requires further research. Thus, the need for an effective malaria vaccine is paramount.

In other words, there were no silver bullets in the control of malaria. Sara guessed there were no silver bullets for gaining control of the Manaus consular office either. It would take a multi-pronged approach. She decided it was time to shape another prong.

She left the conference at ten-thirty to go to a candy shop to buy a box of brigadeiros. She'd been told these chocolate truffles were the most popular dessert in Brazil.

***

The nurse said Paul was lucky. Evidently, the woman in pink missed both Paul's gut and femoral artery, but she had cut tenons and ligaments in his right hip. The nurse guessed Paul would need a boot for weeks and the therapy required to walk normally again would be long and arduous.

Sara found Paul sitting in bed watching cartoons because he wasn't allowed access to phones, newspapers, or television news programs. The FBI agent on duty was disgusted with Paul. Although Paul had moaned about the woman in pink before his surgery, he now claimed he had no idea who stabbed him.

Sara concluded Paul was a jerk with everyone *and* was afraid of someone in the gangs. "Paul, I brought you a gift." Sara handed him a box of brigadeiros with a big pink bow. "It's better than the last gift you got from a woman."

He looked at her blankly.

"You know, the woman in pink?"

She thought she saw a bit of recognition in his eyes before he tore the bow off the box. "I may not be as attractive to you as she was, but I won't stab you."

Paul didn't say thank you as he eagerly opened the box.

"I was told you like chocolate. You may not see much chocolate in the future. Prisons often don't serve desserts."

He'd bitten into one piece but stopped chewing and stared at her. "You can't scare me."

Sara liked finding clues and fitting the pieces together. She hated pretending to be tough, but the FBI agents were stretched thin investigating clues and the clock was ticking for Camille. And Ray and Sanders had agreed that she might be able to elicit more from Paul than they could. She had resisted the urge to call Ray and Sanders *chickens*.

Sara focused on Paul's face. "I'm not trying to scare you. I'm reviewing the facts with you. We know Jake was on the gang's payroll. We also know Jake had an accomplice—more like an underling. The drug gang Jake worked for might want to silence that underling." Sara frowned. "A competing drug gang might want the underling to talk. I suspect it would be better to be caught by the first group. They'd just kill the underling. The second group would torture him first."

Paul shrugged. "I'm no underling."

"I won't argue the point. I'm here to give you options. You could be shipped back to the U.S. for good medical care and a

                                      J. L. Greger

light sentence if you cooperate. Otherwise, you'd better really savor this candy."

She thought she'd finally caught his attention. He was looking at her and not the candy. She opted to start with an easy yes-no question. "Did Jake warn you not to enter Sanders's condo or garage before the bomb went off yesterday morning?"

CHAPTER 14: Forgotten Clues

Sanders and Ray had been wrong. Sara didn't get anywhere with Paul. He began his answers to all her questions the same way: "You sure are a dumb broad."

After ten minutes, she gave up and negotiated Paul's release from the hospital. Sara figured Paul could be provided a hospital bed in a spare bedroom in the Hinkley's home. Then the agents stationed in the house to protect Sanders could also monitor Paul, and the agents at the hospital could be released for other activities. It wasn't much of an idea, but it was the best she could do.

Suddenly. Sara remembered Gabriela González Gómez. Sara had been so immersed in the Andersons' problems that she'd forgotten part of her original assignment. She had not spoken to Gabriela, the third person on Camille's list.

***

Sara wished she was the proverbial *fly on the wall* and could hear Gabriela's and Manuel Braga's conversation over lunch. They were seated at a large round table at the luncheon with six others attending the conference, but they appeared oblivious to others. Sara assigned an agent to watch them while she tried to learn more about Gabriela scientific expertise.

Sara found online a manuscript Gabriela had co-authored with Manuel Braga. They had reported two species of woody vines growing in the jungle undergrowth produced more extractable curare when exposed to more sunlight and when grown in less acidic soil. Sara thought the research was rather esoteric because synthetic muscle relaxants had replaced curare for medical purposes. There wasn't much of a market for raw curare. It didn't matter. The information Sara wanted from Gabriela wasn't scientific.

As soon as Manuel left the table, Sara greeted Gabriela. "I've read several of your interesting papers." Sara hoped the lie sounded sincere. "I'm puzzled. What would you gain from another postdoctoral experience?"

Gabriela's brown eyes flashed her annoyance. "I made a strategic decision to gain firsthand experience in the Amazon when I took my current position in tropical forestry. My long-term goals are to develop drugs and useful products from the jungle flora and fauna and to get out of Manaus."

Sara was caught off guard. This woman was easy to annoy. "So, you want to work for a major pharmaceutical company?"

"Of course. I'm more apt to be noticed by a big pharma firm if I'm working in a major research lab in the U.S., not stuck here in the jungle."

"Have you identified plants in Amazonia deserving further study?"

The woman looked around her. "I'd rather discuss this in a more private place." She lowered her voice to a breathy whisper. "Unlike my mentors here, I think the fauna of the jungle undergrowth are more promising than the flora."

Sara thought she'd have a heart attack. No wonder Caputo had wanted to talk to Gabriela. Sara conferred with her guard, texted Ray Curtis, and led Gabriela to the second floor.

The guard had just found an unlocked room when Ray bounded in. "I was about to go to a breakout session when I got your message." Ray flashed a toothy smile at the gorgeous Gabriela. She ignored him. Sara wasn't surprised. He looked like a sixteen-year-old as he ogled her.

"Gabriela just told me she is interested in the fauna of the jungle undergrowth as a source of valuable drugs and compounds. I thought you'd like to hear more of her ideas." Sara turned to Gabriela. "Have you spoken to others about your research interests?"

"Yes, I wrote to several scientists in the U.S. One from the St. Louis Zoo even came here a year ago to interview me."

"What happened?"

"He was a real CDF."

"A what?"

"A *cabeça de fero.*"

Ray must have noticed the blank look on Sara's face. "A nerd."

"Yes," said Gabriela. "He promised me big money from the drug cabals if I helped him extract batrachotoxins from the insects eaten by the golden poison dart frog. What a fool. The frogs don't live in the Amazon. I doubt the insects that the poison dart frogs eat live in the Amazon."

"What did you tell him?"

"To go home. I didn't want to talk to him."

Sara wondered if Gabriela had been as blunt as she claimed. She debated internally how to assess Gabriela's honesty. "You know, when you work for big pharmaceutical companies, they own your ideas. It's not a good place for idealists to work."

Gabriela snorted. "I lost my idealism when I was fourteen and my father, a drug trafficker, and my mother, his mule, were killed. My grandmother forced her brother to pay my tuition at Florida State as an undergrad. I never asked her what she had to do to get the money. Then I got a research assistantship during graduate school."

"Is your grandmother still in Colombia?"

Gabriela's voice became less strident. "She's dead. There's no one I care about in Colombia now." She lowered her head. "I know the drug lords may pay you big money, but you disappear when you are no longer useful to them. Just like the fool from the St. Louis Zoo and my poor grandmother."

Sara didn't think Gabriela would appreciate a sympathetic hug. "Okay, enough about your past. Let's talk about your future."

Gabriela nodded.

"Where do you want to do postdoctoral research in the U.S.? I'd suggest you go somewhere besides Florida."

"Of course, I think a lab in a top-notch school of pharmacy would be right." She named professors with strong industry ties at the University of California-San Francisco and the University of Michigan.

Gabriela had certainly done her homework, but her answers were too good. She might be a talented actress. "Why don't you send your resume and a two- or three-page letter on your research objectives to Chargé d' Affaires Sanders in care of Ray? Ray will call you for an interview at the consulate."

Gabriela's eyes narrowed. "You're already through with me. Why won't you process my request?"

Sara tried to hide her surprise. "I'm here on a short-term assignment—only to represent the U.S. at this conference. Ray is the permanent science attaché."

"Rumor has it you're the ambassador's... friend and here to help him clean up this so-called consulate in Manaus."

"Yes, I am Mr. Sanders's partner, but where did you hear the rest?"

"Everyone knows the ambassador's hide-out in Manaus was blown up yesterday. And the woman killed down the hall was an FBI agent, presumably here to protect you."

Sara saw no reason to deny the truth but wanted to correct the inaccurate part of Gabriela's statement. "No, the agent was here to protect the attendees of this conference because we had reason to believe several might be targeted by drug gangs."

"Mere semantics. Dr. Braga said Carlos Moreno ceased doing research or seeing patients many years ago and is the chief of the group preventing the importation of drugs into Cuba. I saw you talking to him several times." She smiled almost sheepishly. "Dr. Braga knows I hate it in Manaus. He told me you were my way out."

Gabriela turned to Ray. "I'll deliver my application to you at the consulate tomorrow morning." She stood. "I'm sure you'll want to check out my statement. My grandmother's name was Gabriela Escobar González. You'll have no problem locating her obituary." She walked out without looking back.

Ray whispered, "Forget the rest of the conference. I'm checking Gabriela out."

Sara wanted to ask Ray how he planned to check Gabriela out but decided it might be too personal.

He must have noticed her lips twitching in amusement. "I mean... the State Department will get her what she wants if she knows half as much as I think."

"Looks can be deceiving."

***

Sara was too tired to stay at the conference and monitor the breakout sessions. Besides she was needed to review the reports she'd requested—the financial, personnel, and travel records of all the key suspects. When she had told Sanders about her requests last night, he had sighed and said, "Jake, or even Hinkley, should have done that weeks ago. I'm sorry you're stuck with routine analyses which don't utilize your science background." He smiled. "But thanks. It just proves how much I need you."

Sara thought it was nice to be needed but not like this. Looking for tiny irregularities in dumps of computer files was tedious. It was like looking for needles in haystacks.

She started with Paul's records because she hoped to gain info that would help *others* question him. She pitied them.

Paul didn't have excessive amounts of money in his bank accounts, but he had made three trips to the Cayman Islands in the last year. Each time he'd flown to from Rio to Miami and then to the Cayman Islands. His flight patterns didn't prove he was getting payments in Miami. There were no cheap direct flights from Rio to George Town, the capital of the Cayman Islands. There was also no way to learn about his investments in protected Cayman accounts.

She read Jake's six-month evaluation of Paul incredulously:

> *Paul not only performs surveillance activities but orients new guards. I've hired several from a private detective agency rather than wait for the State Department to send guards already in the Diplomatic Security Service. These guards need intensive onboarding. Paul's a super trainer and a good team player.*

Sara had never heard the term "onboarding" before. Paul was right. She wasn't *with it*. It didn't matter. Those contract guards might be able to provide insights into Paul's behavior. She also thought of the warning on the prayer card. The files on contract guards had to be reviewed, and she couldn't face more boring files. She emailed an analyst in Washington whose specialty was doing security clearances.

She climbed up the food chain and began to examine Jake's records. Jake had visited Zurich twice a year for the last five years. Zurich wasn't Sara's idea of a great travel destination, but it was the home of many secret bank accounts. This info wouldn't be enough to make Jake talkative, but such info might make his ex-wife talk if she felt he hadn't shared his earnings *fairly* with her. She requested the FBI legal attaché for Brazil locate Jake's ex-wife.

The Andersons' only asset was their house and they had not traveled outside Brazil in the last five years. Similarly, Gabriela hadn't flown anywhere outside Brazil since she arrived two years ago. There was one interesting aspect to Gabriela's financial records. She'd received the equivalent of a couple hundred dollars a month from Jorge Braga during the last year.

Sara found only one interesting note in Camille's personnel and travel records. Although Camille had great work evaluations from Consul Hinkley, Jake had inserted a note in her file six months ago:

> *Camille is having difficulty working with several new staff members. When I suggested she modernize her views, she went to an upscale beauty shop near campus and had green and purple stripes put into her hair. That defiant act is typical of her attitude.*

Sara wondered whether Camille had refused to work with Paul and the new guards because she thought they were taking payments from the drug cartel. It was a nice idea but was based completely on guesses.

Then Sara had a weird idea. Women were often talkative at beauty shops. She found a salon online fitting Jake's description—an upscale beauty shop almost on the university campus.

Sara emailed a summary of her findings to Sanders and set off to the beauty shop with Jane Ellis, an FBI agent who spoke passable Portuguese. She would have preferred having Latoya as her guard, but Latoya was at the conference with Ray. Sara also took along three Kevlar vests.

CHAPTER 15: Sara Adds Color to Her Life

"Do you speak English?"

The matronly woman with purple streaks in her gray hair at the front desk of the beauty salon looked confused. Jane Ellis, the FBI agent accompanying Sara, repeated the question in halting Portuguese.

The matron sighed and pointed to a woman with long pink hair streaked with lavender at the back of the shop.

Sara waited until the woman with the pink hair had finished cutting another customer's hair before she repeated her question and added, "Several of my friends added green and purple streaks to their black hair. I was thinking about adding pink streaks to my hair. They said they came here." Sara showed the woman pictures of Camille and the fake Camille from the ID badge. "Do you remember doing the hair of either of these women?"

They woman pointed to Camille's picture. "I do Camille's *haw* regularly, but she was a no-show yesterday." She shrugged when she looked at the other picture.

Sara pulled out a photo of the woman in the morgue. It was the most attractive one Sara could find, but it was still eerie. "How about this one?"

The woman gasped. "What happened to her?"

"Good question. Do you recognize her?"

"Show me the other photo again." The stylist studied the picture. "Now I remember. I did her *haw* last week. She showed me a photo of Camille and said she wanted to look like her. I had to dye her brown hair black and then put in the streaks." She looked Sara up and down. "Can't let my boss see me talking to anyone but a client."

"Could you give my hair pink streaks? What's your name?'

"Call me Jo. I'll be done with my current customer in fifteen minutes."

As she waited, Sara thought about the woman's voice. It was strident like those of many who came from New York City. But the pronunciation wasn't right. The r's were dropped. So, "hair" sounded like "haw." Sara guessed Jo was most likely from Boston.

***

Sara negotiated with Jo to add a few pink streaks to the hair around her face. As Jo prepared the chemicals, Sara asked. "Jo, how did you come to work here? Your English sounds like you grew up around Boston."

"I came from Rhode Island with a boyfriend who wanted to study international law ten year ago. We split, but I'm still stuck here."

Sara thought Jo's timeline might fit Jake's scenario. He said he came to Manaus ten years ago, but he never mentioned studying law here. Sara decided it was just a coincidence and focused on Camille. "What is Camille like? Has she seemed more nervous lately?"

Jo turned the chair around so she could look Sara in the face. "Who are you? I don't want to be dragged in by the local police."

"Got it. Maybe I can help you if you help me. Tell me about Camille."

"She first came here six months ago. All she said was her boss was an 'ass who said she was stuck in a time warp of fifty years ago.' Said she wanted to look fire."

Sara assumed "fire" was slang for "modern." "What did she talk about?"

"Not much." She paused. "I guess mainly about an orphanage run by a church a couple of blocks from here. She volunteered there." Jo finished applying pieces of foil around sections of Sara's hair. "Are you ready for the color?"

Sara gulped. "I guess."

Jo applied one color of pink. "Now I'll add a darker pink on other sections. Do you want to see it?"

"No, just tell me what shampoos are best for removing the color."

Jo laughed.

"Do you know the name of the woman in the other two pictures?"

"She came off the street like you did. Never talked."

When Jo was finished, she turned Sara to face the mirror. Sara gasped. The pink and rose streaks weren't bad and did give her a more modern look.

Sara suddenly realized she may have endangered Jo. She might have been followed when she left the consular offices even though Jane hadn't spotted a tail. Sara handed Jo a generous tip and Ray Curtis's and her own business cards. "We can suggest ways you can speed up your return to the U.S. Why don't you see us later today or tomorrow?" Sara had handwritten on her card:

Staff should allow Jo immediate access to the consular offices at any hour. SA c/o Sanders

***

As they left the shop, Jane said, "My boyfriend wouldn't be upset if I streaked my hair like you did, but I think my dad would hit the roof if my mother put pink streaks in her hair."

"I guess we'll have to see how modern Sanders is. I suspect he won't like it, b*ut* he'll be glad I did it if Jo's tip pans out. Now we've got to find the orphanage near here."

"I should phone in where we're going."

"I agree, but I don't think I trust all the guards from the consular offices. Why don't I text Sanders and mark it urgent? I'll tell him someone needs to meet us at this address in an hour."

"Are you sure?"

"Yes." Sara realized her transmission could be intercepted. She and Sanders had certain phrases they used as code in the past, but they hadn't discussed codes to use in Brazil. She realized that was a mistake. Based on this morning's conversation, she thought he would recognize Our Lady of Aparecida as Camille. Sara checked the Web. There was only one children's shelter run by the Catholic Church near the university. Sara texted:

Our Lady of Aparecida will be at the orphanage near the campus. Will need help in an hour.

Jane drove in silence for several minutes. "I don't mean to be nosy but your arrangement with Mr. Sanders seems unusual. They say you two are... *partners,* but you don't act it. Why don't you call him by his first name?"

Sara decided to ignore the comment and only respond to the question. "He doesn't like to be called Eric. He usually wants everyone to call him Sanders. I notice most of you call him Mr. Sanders. I guess because he's the acting ambassador." Sara noticed a sign. "Is this the place?"

The building looked like another one-story, box made of concrete. Pre-school children were playing noisily under a wide bamboo veranda at front of the building. On one side, several old cars and bicycles were parked under the veranda.

***

Inside the orphanage, children were sitting on benches and leaning over books on a long table. Sara found it hard to judge their age. Several were working on long division problems, but they seemed smaller than ten- to twelve-year-olds in the U.S.

Sara noted each book appeared to be shared by two children. The books looked old with torn covers and frayed bindings. Similarly, the children's T-shirts and shorts looked worn and often grimy.

The teacher had on a blue blouse and black skirt with a short, black wimple over her hair. Her only jewelry was a large silver cross on a silver chain.

Sara guessed she was in right place and pulled a sheet of paper from her purse. "Does your religious order hand out prayer cards like this?"

The woman looked at the xeroxed copy of the card presumably sent by Camille. She shook her head. "*No Inglês.*" She pointed to a door at the back of the room.

Sara shook her head when Jane stepped forward to translate. "Let's find the main office and the mother superior or whatever they call the boss here."

The door opened to a dark hallway lined with three more classrooms and a room with a sign, *ESCRITÓRIO,* on its door.

Jane whispered "office," pushed Sara toward the door, and knocked. There was no reply. Sara and Jane entered anyway. A teenage girl, apparently engrossed in the music streaming from her earbuds, sat behind a wood counter. The door behind her was closed.

"*Olá.* Do you speak English?"

The teenager didn't look up. "*No Inglês.*"

Jane spoke in Portuguese. The teenager pressed a buzzer without looking up.

Sara heard a chair sliding on the tile floor behind the door. A short, slender woman with a wrinkle-free complexion appeared. She had on a black skirt and wimple, but her blouse was pink. Judging, by the woman's appearance, Sara guessed she had a Filipino background and was in her forties, but that was a wild guess.

She extended her hand. "I'm Sister Rose, the principal here. May I have help you?"

Sara thought it would be unwise to ask immediately about Camille. She started with a non-threatening question. "Did your order distribute prayer cards like this?" Sara showed Sister Rose the copy of the card.

"Yes, all the churches in Manaus did in October for Children's Day." She pointed to Camille's handwritten note. "How did you get this card?"

Sara said, "Can we discuss this in your private office. We're with the U.S. embassy."

Sister Rose's light tan color grayed slightly. "Yes, of course."

When the inner door was closed, Sara said, "The card was sent to Acting U.S. Ambassador Sanders last night." Sara was about to say she was his significant other but decided it was best not to get into that discussion with a nun. "He asked me to inquire if you might know who sent him this card."

Sister Rose kept her eyes fixed on Sara's face and gulped.

Sara figured Sister Rose knew the answer but didn't want to endanger Camille. "We think Camille Draco sent it. We also think the security in our office in Manaus has been breached. That's why I'm here." *There was no way around it.* "Sanders and I were almost killed yesterday. Perhaps you heard a condo on the north side of Manaus was bombed."

Sister Rose nodded. "I am happy you were not injured."

"Sanders has placed Jake Tarantino, the head of security at the consular office, and his assistant Paul Royer under house arrest. But he's needs Camille's testimony to speed the arrest of others who may be involved. Camille also needs to know I was lured to the bombed house by a woman attempting to look like her."

Sister Rose cleared her throat. "We had feared...." She must have thought it unwise to complete her sentence. "I'm not sure what you want. Do you suspect Camille tried to trick you?"

"No." Sara bit her lip. "I think Camille would be safer if she was sent to Rio or back to Washington. Can you help us?"

Sister Rose looked at Jane.

"Oh, I'm sorry this is FBI agent Jane Ellis." Sara decided it was best not to admit Jane could speak some Portuguese. "She's assigned to protect me."

Sister Rose just continued to stare at Jane.

"She was sent here three days ago from Chicago and has never worked with Jake."

Sister Rose spoke slowly. "It is not a secret that guards at the U.S. office in Manaus have close contacts with the drug gangs. I'm surprised it took your government so long to discover the problem."

Sister Rose had backed Sara into a corner. Sara decided to become more proactive. "I believe the U.S. government is like the Catholic Church. It's hard for large bureaucracies to know what is happening in all their units. Just like I suspect, the Archbishop of Manaus doesn't know the names of everyone given sanctuary in churches, monasteries, and convents in Manaus. Thus, I didn't ask him about Camille's location."

Sister Rose frowned. "Bureaucracies can be frustrating and are easy to criticize but they prevent mistakes due to haste." She stood and motioned Sara toward the door.

Sara figured she'd blown the interview. Sister Rose might look sweet, but she was tough.

"I think we should take a walk in our garden after I make a call. You can wait in front."

***

Sara and Jane waited for ten minutes in the anteroom of Sister Rose's office. The teenage girl never spoke or looked at them, but her head nodded rhythmically in time to the tunes she was listening to on her earbuds. Jane sent several emails and then paced the narrow waiting area. Sara tried to look calm, but she suspected Sister Rose had made several calls. She hoped if anyone dashed into the room it would be Sanders or Ray—not gang members or the consulate's contract guards.

Sister Rose seemed more relaxed when she emerged from her office. "The sister who teaches applied biology offers her classes early in the morning and in the evening because the garden is too hot midday. She and her assistant like to sit in the shade and study the garden after the rush at lunch is over. I think they can answer your questions."

Sister Rose led Sara and Jane out the side of the building, and through the passageway where cars, scooters, and bikes were parked. She opened the gate in a high chain-link fence covered with vines dripping with green and yellow oval fruits.

A row of tall plants with huge leaves were about five feet from the fence. Sara asked, "What types of bananas do you grow?"

Sister Rose smiled. "These are plantains. We find they are a more practical source of food for the children."

Sara recognized tomato, watermelon, bean, and onion plants in the core of the garden. She pointed to rows of tall shrubs which looked like house plants with large palm-shaped leaves. They had been planted around three sides of the garden, "What are those?"

"Manioc. You might call them cassava. We grow it around the outer perimeter of our garden because it doesn't produce fruit that tempts children to steal." She gave a tired smile. "Theft is a problem here with thousands of hungry children on the streets. We also think our students should learn to prepare cassava properly to remove the poison in their roots."

They walked into the center of the garden. Sister Rose pointed to two women sitting on a bench in the shade of the cassava. "Our applied biology teacher and her helper don't wear our standard garb of a black skirt and wimple when working in the garden." Both women wore straw hats with floppy brims, ivory blouses, and khaki pants. Sara thought the pants could best described be as baggy cropped pants. Both women stood as Sister Rose walked toward them.

                                          J. L. Greger

The taller woman, who was about Sara's height, walked forward and peered at Sara. "You must be Mr. Sanders's Sara" She continued to stare. "But you changed your hair. It didn't have pink streaks in any of the pictures I've seen."

Sara couldn't see the woman's face because of the large floppy brim on her hat. "That's how I found this children's shelter. Jake said you had your hair done at an upscale beauty shop near the campus. We found the shop. Jo there said she had streaked your hair."

The woman stepped back a step when Sara said "Jo" but said nothing.

Sara continued, "But Jo would only talk if I paid her to work on my hair. So, I had her add pink streaks to my hair."

The woman stared at Sara. "I'm surprised my hair stylist called herself Jo. She must have thought you were being followed."

Sara hoped she hadn't walked into a trap. "Would you mind removing your hat so I can see your face?"

"I suppose I have to." The woman removed her hat. Her hair was covered with a sweaty, yellow bandanna.

Sara noted the width of the woman's nose and her olive skin. She pulled a photo of Camille Draco from her purse. The features were right. "Camille?"

"I wish you hadn't found me. I'm happy and safe here."

"I doubt it would last."

"It might have if you hadn't come here. They're monitoring your emails and calls."

"Who is they?"

"Jake and Paul. Jake became grouchier after he learned you were attending the conference. He kept telling Paul, 'That nosy bitch is notorious.'"

Camille looked around the garden. "They'll be here soon."

Sara wanted to ask for more details about Jake and Paul but decided it was more important to calm Camille. "Jake and Paul are under house arrest. Hinkley and his wife by now are being questioned by FBI in Washington. We got the Andersons out, too."

"At least three good people may survive this blood bath. Jake will send in the gangs. They will shoot everyone."

Sara noticed Camille didn't look at her as she spoke. Both she and Jane were eyeing the perimeter of the garden.

Sara tried to sound confident. "I think Sanders will get here first." Sara turned to Sister Rose. "Can you and your applied biology teacher return to your office? Don't allow anyone but a thin man of six feet with a receding hairline back here. He'll call himself Sanders and will ask to see your Lady of Aparecida."

CHAPTER 16: Sara Is in a Tight Spot

"Where should we hide?"

Camille and Jane looked around the garden.

Sara added, "I'll text Sanders and Ray again." She hoped Ray would understand the text; she knew Sanders would:

> *HELP. Lady of Aparecida, Jane, & I are desperate at orphanage.*

Although Camille wasn't an FBI agent, she apparently had thought about security a lot. "There's a six-foot chain-link fence topped with razor wire around the property. It would take time for gang members to climb the fence. But they can shoot through the fence. In the back corner is our corrugated metal storage shed." She pointed to the back corner where the plantain plants merged with the cassava shrubs. "I think that's the best place to hide if we create a duck blind." She ran to the bench where she had been sitting and picked up two spades. She motioned to Sara as she ran into the tomato patch and began to dig up a large plant.

Sara ran to Camille, took the second spade, selected another large plant, and began to dig. While Camille dragged the tomato plants to the back corner, Sara dug up other plants. The women arranged the tomato plants to look like they were growing in front of the bare stems of the plantain trees and the cassava plants in the corner in front of the corrugated metal shed. Then they crouched behind their *hopefully* natural looking camouflage.

Meanwhile, Jane paced the perimeter of the garden and tried to peer through the foliage to the outside. When Jane joined the other two women in the corner, she said, "I couldn't see you behind the tomato plants. If you only take a quick look at this area, it looks logical."

"Did you see anything suspicious outside?"

Jane dropped to her knees besides Sara. "I spotted a gray BMW slowly drive past the garden and stop in front of the orphanage. No one got out. Otherwise, cars and people buzzed by normally." She tapped Camille on the shoulder. What is the building on the far side of this lot?"

"A produce market with a coffee shop. There are no doors on the side of the building facing our garden," said Camille. "Our weak spot security-wise is an alley—really a rutted gravel path—directly behind the orphanage and garden. There's a large warehouse on the other side of the alley. The sisters built the shed to provide privacy. It has three doors. One is into the garden. The second opens to the passageway between the orphanage's main building and the garden. The third opens to the alley and allows for easy delivery of goods."

Sara in her excitement hadn't even noticed a door in the shed. Now she saw a gray sliding door ten feet away.

Camille must have noted Sara's gaze. "It's padlocked. I have a key. So does Sister Rose."

Sara decided to see the glass as half full instead of half empty. "So, we have an escape route?"

Jane frowned. "Gang members also have an alternate entrance to the garden besides the front entrance."

Sara continued to think positively. "Would it be best to unlock the door now, so we can use it quickly or keep it locked to slow entry from the back?" She felt her phone vibrate. She read:

> *Is there a back entrance?*
> *S*

Jane glanced at the message. "Are you sure it's from Sanders."

"It sounds like Sanders." Sara texted:

> *Back alley. Locked corrugated metal shed.*

Jane turned to Sara. "This cheap corrugated metal would be reduced to shreds by repeating rifles. The gangs could quickly

                                                    J. L. Greger

shoot off the padlock on the back entrances to the shed, but we couldn't. If we enter the shed, we're trapped."

"Not necessarily." Camille ran to the shed before Jane could stop her, unlocked the padlock with the key hung around her neck on a cord, and disappeared inside the shed for sixty seconds before she returned to the hiding spot lugging a shotgun and a big burlap bag.

Camille was breathing heavily. "The sisters face huge problems with theft here. They padlocked the doors to the alley and the alley from the inside. I unlocked them so we can get out fast if we need to."

Sara pointed at the shotgun.

Camille shrugged. "None of the sisters wanted to use guns to protect the orphanage from theft. But Sister Rose knew I kept a double-barreled shotgun in a basket of brooms in a dark corner of the shed." Camille opened the bag. "One thing I learned from Jake is the importance of ammo. I have slugs for long range and buckshot for close up." She motioned to shell boxes of ammo in the bag and pulled out a shoebox.

When Camille opened the shoebox, Sara saw a big handgun. She had no idea what it was.

Jane gasped. "How did you get a 44 Magnum?"

"There are fewer restrictions on gun sales in Brazil than in the U.S. I asked the guards at the consulate which handgun was the most powerful."

"Have you ever tried to shoot it?" Jane continued, "I had difficulty handling guns that large during FBI shooting practice."

Camille shrugged. "It took a lot of practice, but yes."

Sara decided this was not the time for conversation. "Look I don't carry a gun, but I could use the shotgun if you remind me how to load it. I also must be in a kneeling position to shoot it."

Camille and Jane said together. "You'll be no help."

Sara shrugged. "I've killed a man at fairly short range and destroyed the hand of a hitwoman at very close range."

"You really misaimed." Jane shook her head.

"No, we had to take her alive. Sanders needed her testimony at trial. Both she and Sanders were injured and needed to reload. I had to destroy her shooting hand and give Sanders time to reload." Sara smiled. "Don't worry, I know enough to shoot for the chest unless they're wearing a vest. Then it's the head."

Jane whistled and pulled her gun from her shoulder holster.

Camille face was white as she showed Sara how to load the shotgun. Then she loaded the Magnum.

***

Street noises continued to filter into the garden from the front. Basically, no sounds came from the warehouse on the far side. In back, the noises were soft unless a truckle rumbled past in the alley or stopped at the loading dock of the warehouse. The loudest sounds were of children playing in the orphanage.

A new sound suddenly became obvious. Car doors were being slammed at the front of the orphanage. Sara whispered, "Would we buy some time if we opened the door to the shed? They might assume we used it to escape and not study the garden as much."

Camille ran to the shed door and slid it open about two feet. When she returned, no one spoke. They just waited.

Sara heard children screaming at the front of the orphanage. Next, she heard gunshots and louder screams. There was the sound of heavy footsteps on the concrete pathway between the orphanage and the garden. She prayed silently.

The sounds of curses and repeating gunshots came from the orphanage and then the front entrance to the garden. Sara figured Sister Rose must have padlocked it when she left earlier. She guessed the lock had been destroyed.

It was probably Sara's imagination, but she thought the background noises of city traffic and children playing had ceased. Then she heard the piercing sound of a siren. *Was someone coming to their rescue? Would it arrive soon enough?* The siren stopped. Sara guessed the ambulance or police car had gone to another location.

Time was moving slowly now. Sara thought once the padlock was destroyed, gang members would enter the garden quickly. But it seemed like a long time before there was a slight screech and then footsteps. Strangely the footsteps didn't seem to be rapid like those she had heard coming from the passageway between the orphanage and the garden. The footsteps seemed slow, even cautious. The gang members must be searching the bushes carefully. *Not a good sign.*

She hoped they'd notice the open door on the shed. She checked her shotgun and noticed Jane and Camille were similarly checking their weapons. They'd agreed not to shoot until the attackers were close. Sara's shotgun blast and Camille's Magnum shots would be first. Jane as the most experienced marksman would wait to catch anyone lurking on their right side. Four car doors had slammed. So there had to be at *least* four gunmen.

A grunt was followed by more low guttural sounds. The latter came fewer than ten feet from their hiding place. A man ran toward the door. Jane shook her head.

The man opened the door wider and stepped inside. He yelled to his compatriots. One ran in front of the others into the shed. Sara wished the banana plants were real trees. Then Jane could have been positioned in a tree with a real view. As it was, they had no idea where the presumed other attackers were stationed.

Sara heard a thump and then another as someone hit something on the shed wall behind her. The two men must be searching the shed thoroughly. Two more men slowly approached. They did not run straight to the open shed door but were walking in the dirt along the row of the banana plants.

The men soon might kick the tomato plants in the blind out of their way. Jane nodded to Sara. When both men were within six feet, Sara blasted her shotgun. Camille and Jane started shooting. Sara didn't take time to look, she reloaded her shotgun.

She heard a loud noise to her left. She thought it came from within the shed. Those men could begin shooting through the corrugated shed walls at any second. She decided nothing could be done to prevent that and focused on the scene in front of her. She heard gunshots also coming from the main orphanage building.

Three men ran into the garden. It was easier to see them now because several banana trees were on the ground. Suddenly guns began blasting from the entrance of the shed. She saw one gang member fall in the tomato patch. Sara figured the blasts from the shed were friendly fire for the women. The gang members thought the same and returned fire toward the shed door.

Sara looked to her right and motioned she had a clear shot at one gang member firing at the shed door. Camille pointed to a second man. Jane and Camille fired almost simultaneously. The gang members stopped firing. Jane stood to observe the scene.

There was a sudden burst of gunfire—probably from only one gun—to Sara's right. She felt a jolt of hot prickly pain in her right arm. Jane fell onto Sara's shoulder and then slid to the ground. Camille was firing her Magnum not far from Sara's head toward the right.

The gunfire stopped. Sara reloaded her shotgun. It was hard, but the fact she could reload her gun suggested the shot through her arm had not hit a bone.

She looked to her right. A body lay at the end of the stubble of what once had been a row of plantain trees. Two bloody bodies were stretched on the ground in front of what had been the tomato plant screen. Two more bodies lay close to the entrance to the shed. She stared into the tomato patch and saw movement. She aimed her shotgun and squeezed the trigger. Camille must have seen the movement because she fired, too. Nothing moved among the shredded tomato plants.

Sara heard a familiar voice. "Don't shoot! We've got two gang members tied up in the shed. Ray said he's subdued others out front." It was Sanders.

At Sara's feet, Jane was emitting a rattling sound. Jane's blouse was red and her face ashen.

Sara screamed, "Medic—fast!" She leaned over Jane and applied pressure on Jane's shoulder to slow the blood flow. It was impossible task because multiple wounds on Jane's right shoulder and arm were oozing blood.

***

Paramedics carrying stretchers raced from the shed. Within seconds, they had whisked Jane away.

Sara was having trouble focusing because her head throbbed, especially her left ear. It was as if the gunfire was reverberating in her head. She felt dizzy, nauseated, and in generally disoriented. Her arm hurt more now than before. She again recognized Sanders's voice in the background. He seemed to be acting more like a chief security officer than an ambassador. She gradually realized someone was examining her arm.

"You were lucky. The bullets went through the muscle. Your partner caught the brunt of the bullets."

Sara pointed to her left ear. "Hurts. Bad."

"You probably have a ruptured eardrum." The paramedic inserted an IV line and pulled Sara onto a waiting stretcher.

Sara saw Sanders's white face above her. "Hang in there, honey. I'll ride with you in the ambulance."

She squeezed his hand. "Jane?"

"Critical. An ambulance left with her already. Camille's fine but went with Jane."

"The early shots?'"

"Sister Rose is dead but no one else from the orphanage was shot."

Sara felt like she'd been kicked in the gut. She'd brought all this carnage to the orphanage and caused the nun's death.

Sanders continued, "The teenager at the front desk has internal injuries from being kicked repeatedly. She apparently tried to protect Sister Rose. Ray is overseeing the cleanup."

Medics picked up the stretcher and carried Sara through the shed to a waiting ambulance. Sara was surprised by the number of emergency vehicles. Sanders had come prepared.

A local police officer spoke to Sanders just before the paramedics shoved Sara's stretcher inside the ambulance. "Six dead in the garden. Three dead up front. The two you tied up in the shed have been sent to police holding along with the four drivers of the cars. We'll start removing the bodies now."

CHAPTER 17: Sanders's Perspective

Sara looked ghastly. Sanders assumed she had a head wound when he saw all the pink in her hair, but the physicians at the hospital assured him the pink color was from dye not blood. Her arm wounds were relatively minor with no bone damage. However, she might lose some feeling in her upper arm and would probably need plastic surgery on the skin of her upper arm after the underlying muscle and tendons had healed. They also advised she needed a small skin graft to her eardrum to speed the healing.

Jane had survived because she had worn a Kevlar vest, but her shoulder was shredded. Her right arm might have to be amputated. Surgeons wanted to transfer her to a medical center in São Paulo as soon as they stabilized her enough for a medical evacuation.

Sanders felt the U.S. embassy in Brazil should pay all the medical expenses for the teen who had been almost kicked to death while trying to protect Sister Rose. Together she and Sister Rose had slowed the entry of four carloads of gang members enough for Sanders and Ray to arrive with agents and police in time to save Sara, Camille, and Jane.

Sanders decided all three should be sent for better medical care in São Paulo. He kissed Sara just before the plane left for São Paulo and said, "I hope I can join you in a couple of days." As he expected, she was too sedated to reply. He'd pinned a handwritten note to her hospital gown.

***

As he sat in Hinkley's old office, Sanders reviewed the situation. It was dire. The battle at the orphanage had eliminated a small percentage of the gang members in the region, but no major drug leader had been killed or captured.

As soon as he arrived in Brasília three months ago, he began to receive letters, emails, and calls about corruption in the Manaus office. Several unsigned letters claimed members of the consulate's security staff were "in league" with Brazilian drug gangs. Several messages stated Evan Hinkley and his wife were illegally exporting cultural artifacts from Brazil. He guessed the accusations were true, but the informants provided insufficient details to be he helpful.

Accordingly, he had asked a personnel officer in the State Department in Washington to review the hiring practices at the consular office in Manaus. He didn't ask the embassy personnel officer because he feared individuals in Manaus would be notified.

The personnel officer in Washington reported Hinkley and Jake had complained to the previous ambassador that they needed more guards in crime-ridden Manaus. Their solution had been to replace two of the three vetted members of the State Department's Diplomatic Security Service—so called DSS guards—with cheaper, inexperienced "contract" guards hired from a private detective agency in Providence, Rhode Island. The only vetted member of DSS in Manaus would be Jake.

The previous ambassador had thought Hinkley's and Jake's scheme was logical because the office could employ more "contract" guards than vetted DSS members at the same cost. Besides, the detective agency guaranteed all the guards spoke Portuguese. Few members of the DSS knew any Portuguese.

Sanders had immediately requested a review of the detective agency in Rhode Island. He'd finally received a memo last week—more than two months after his inquiry. The FBI was currently investigating the head of the detective agency for potential ties to organized crime leaders in the U.S. but could supply no other details.

About a month after his arrival in Brazil, Sanders received his first letter from Camille Draco. She documented Jake had harassed her and other women at the Manaus office. She also hinted Jake had abetted the disappearance of Al Caputo. However, her hunch was backed by meager evidence.

In response, Sanders had agreed to accompany scientists on a fact-finding mission to the upper Amazon. While the scientists studied the effects of global warming on frogs, he looked for clues to explain Caputo's disappearance.

About the same time, Camille suggested the World Health Organization's conference on "Vector Control of Tropical Diseases" might provide Sanders a logical way to talk to people whom Camille was convinced knew more about Al Caputo's disappearance—specifically the Andersons and Gabriela González Gómez. Thus, Sanders had contacted the conference organizers and told them the U.S. would send an official delegate to the conference and make a hefty donation to support the conference as proof of the U.S.'s commitment to the eradication of malaria in Brazil. He furthered his investigation by recruiting Sara. First, he used Sara's expertise to trap a Brazilian drug trafficker who was importing potent batrachotoxins ostensibly isolated from the skins of golden dart frogs into the U.S. That had piqued Sara's interest and she'd agreed to be the U.S. representative to the World Health Organization conference in Manaus.

As Sanders expected, Sara had succeeded in breaking the stalemate in Manaus. He had enough evidence now to guarantee prison sentences for Jake and Paul.

The news from the Undersecretary was also good. Mrs. Hinkley had broken down in tears when the Undersecretary gave Mrs. Hinkley a ultimatum. She and her husband could remain safely in Washington while their belongings in Manaus were evaluated by the Brazilian National Historic and Artistic Heritage Institute. If any of the Hinkley's possessions were found to have been illegally obtained, the U.S. would turn Mrs. Hinkley over to Brazilian authorities, unless she cooperated with the FBI investigation of Jake.

Again, Sara had been helpful. She had found boxes of museum-quality artifacts in several closets in the consul's house.

There was another big problem—how to make Jake talk. Sanders knew no threat he could make to Jake would be as bad as what the gang leaders would do to him if he talked. Sara had advised him to focus on Paul and the recently hired contract guards. She'd even obtained help from an analyst in Washington.

So far, the analyst had identified one contract guard's file as interesting. A janitor at the Manaus office had reported to Jake and to the personnel officer in the embassy in Brasília that this guard was high on drugs twice in his presence. Jake said the janitor lied and fired him. Sanders asked two of the agents he'd brought from outside Brazil to grill this guard carefully.

Meanwhile, Sanders had also asked Camille to review files in the public relations office for details on the lives of the everyone in the office. Camille wasn't Sara and had noticed nothing of possible use in her old computer files.

In desperation, Sanders showed Camille a picture of the woman in the morgue and the picture on the fake badge. "Sara said the woman who identified herself as you had more highly plucked eyebrows than the woman in this picture. Her face was thin, and her nose narrow like those of the woman in the morgue. Sara also thought your impersonator might have originally been a blonde or redhead because she had freckles and a pale complexion. Do you know any past employee or frequent visitor to the consulate who might meet this description?"

Ten minutes later, Camille placed a photo on his desk. "This is photo of Jake and his wife taken eight years ago. His wife Bridgit is almost my height and has a thin face, freckles, a light complexion, and narrow nose. Then her red hair was beginning to turn gray. After she divorced Jake three years ago, she continued to work at a hair salon. The last time I saw her a couple of weeks ago, her hair was pink with lavender streaks and her eyebrows were plucked into thin arches."

Sanders couldn't decide if the photo scared or angered him. He tried to keep his voice calm as he asked, "How did you happen to see her?"

"She's the one who styles my hair every two weeks."

Sanders couldn't hide his annoyance. "Really?"

Camille gulped. "OMG. I should have realized." She gulped again. "I thought it strange when Bridgit told Sara her name was Jo. I figured she didn't trust Sara, but she could have been..."

"Hiding her identity from Sara." Sanders poked buttons on his phone. "Has the Jo who Sara mentioned entered the consulate?"

Camille dropped into a chair. Her voice was soft and sounded like she was in a trance. "Bridgit is my best—my only—friend. She doesn't like Jake and says he's dumb." Tears streamed down Camille's cheeks. "I trust her. She wouldn't hurt me."

Sanders handed Camille a tissue but appeared to be listening more to the person on the phone than to Camille. "Find her. She's Bridgit Tarantino, Jake's ex-wife. Assume she's armed and dangerous. She's the one who tipped off the gang to storm the orphanage.

CHAPTER 18: Sanders Searches for a Chameleon

"Jake, tell me about your ex-wife, Bridgit?"

Jake's lips tightened as he sneered at Sanders. "You're slow for such a big-time spymaster, but you're finally making progress." He chuckled. "Too late for you or your Sara."

Sanders studied Jake's shaking hands and forced himself to not respond to Jake's comment. "You must really be afraid of Bridgit. What does she have on you?"

Jake sneered. "Mind if I smoke?"

"Yes, I mind. Smoking is a disgusting habit."

Jake shrugged. "Got to die of something."

Sanders had thought Jake was a stereotypical security officer—a silent he-men who lacked empathy for others. Now Sanders recognized Jake's bravado was an attempt to hide his fears. "If you cooperate with me, you might not be charged with espionage. You might even end up in one of those country-club prisons for perpetrators of white-collar crime." Sanders doubted his last statement but was desperately wanted to gain Jake's cooperation.

Jake shook his head. "Don't try to snow me. I'll be tortured and killed here or left to rot in a Brazilian jail where I'll be molested daily by other inmates."

Sanders needed to convince Jake that the U.S. legal system was Jake's best hope. He repeated his question softly, "Tell me about Bridgit. You'll feel better if you vent your anger… your frustrations."

Jake sighed and leaned back. "Bridgit's father told me she was 'bright as a penny' when I married her. I thought he was referring to her bright red hair. I soon learned she was smart but didn't know how smart until we arrived in Brazil. Within six months, she was exporting Brazilian junk—supposed indigenous artifacts and art—illegally. She introduced me to a few of her business associates. After a couple of years, she dumped me for one of them. Since then, we've lost contact."

"Stop the act. You've remained close enough to refer Camille to the beauty salon where Bridgit works."

Sanders noticed Jake had closed his eyes when he spoke of Bridgit. He guessed Jake had strong emotions—love, hate, or both—for Bridgit. "Time for a little honesty. Why would you send a woman who was driving you crazy to another woman who drove you crazy?"

Jake seemed to go into another world and his eyes seemed unfocused. "You have no idea how creative Bridgit is in the sack." His eyes focused again. "I thought she could fix a problem for me."

Sanders studied a new text as he waited for Jake to continue. Finally, he said, "Did it work?"

"You saw the results, Camille went from being a quiet, graying fuddy-duddy to being a fit, ballbuster."

"Was Bridgit trying to make your life harder?"

Jake studied the floor. "Nah. Bridgit and I get along—as long as I do as I am told."

"Are you telling me Bridgit is your handler and contact to the drug gangs?"

"Nah." Jake spat on the floor, and he swiped his mouth with the back of his hand. "More like my boss's boss. Ever since she teamed up with the head honcho in Manaus, the gang's profits have soared."

"How do you know that?"

"Everyone knows it."

"How did she make money for the gangs?"

"Lots of ways. She understands the insatiable hunger of the rich for trinkets to make themselves look cultured—like those stupid artifacts made by the indigenous people of the Amazon region. You know she recruited Hinkley's wife to be a mule for artifacts." He smiled slightly as he shook his head. "Although the Consul's wife may have a stick up her ass, she's technically not a mule. She doesn't swallow artifacts or do anything interesting. She just packs them in carry-on bags and claims diplomatic immunity. Bridgit had high hopes for Camille. She thought

                                                    J. L. Greger

Camille had potential as a mule for South American religious relics, but Bridgit didn't realize Camille was a religious fanatic and loco besides."

Sanders thought Jake's ramblings were interesting but wanted to get back to the current problem. "How would making Camille a mule fix your problem?"

"Camille would stop ratting on me if I had a little leverage on her. But Camille goes crazy sometimes and is uncontrollable. Then Camille disappeared before Bridgit could eliminate Camille."

"Didn't Camille's disappearance embarrass Bridgit with her boss in the gangs?"

"Nah, he has confidence in Bridgit. Surprised Bridgit hasn't found Camille yet." He studied Sanders. "Damn. You're here because you think you can find Camille before Bridgit does. Forget it."

Sanders was pleased. The FBI agents had been successful in isolating Jake. He didn't appear to know about the raid on the orphanage. He texted Ray and waited for a response, figuring the pause might make Jake more nervous. "What do you think Bridgit would do if she felt herself in danger?"

Jake closed his eyes. "Hard to imagine Bridgit in a corner." He sighed. "She'd lash out."

"Let's suppose Camille was safely inside the consulate now. What would Bridgit do?"

"Easy She'd get inside and plant a bomb. Like she did at your safe house." Jake spat on the floor again. "More likely... She'd have someone else plant the bomb."

"Why a bomb?"

"Bridgit says making a bomb is like mixing up a hair dye solution. You just take your time and follow instructions. Then you walk away and wait."

Sanders choked at Bridgit's strange perspective. "What would Bridgit do to you if she heard we were talking?"

"Depends. If she was just annoyed or in a hurry, she'd plant a bomb near me. If I goofed and said something important... and she had the time, she'd perform a little surgery on me before she killed me."

"Do you think you've said anything important?"

Jake shrugged. "If Bridgit's in the consulate, I'm a dead man."

"How about Paul Royer and the contract guards you hired?"

"Depends on what they can deliver. Bridgit is good at making a man think he has a chance."

***

Sanders decided not to waste the time of FBI agents by making them take Jake back to the consul's house. Instead, he asked an agent to lock Jake in a large closet in the consul's private office with a chair and a couple of cans of soda. Sanders was sure his order was counter to human rights regulations, but he doubted Jake would be alive tomorrow to complain. For that matter, he gave himself at best a fifty percent chance of seeing tomorrow.

He read an email from Ray:

> *Agents at the consul's house had a breakthrough. One of the contract guards admitted he—on Paul's orders—convinced the file clerk in the consular offices to sit for the photo on the badge found in Camille's car. He also heard Paul order another contract guard to garrot the clerk two days later. It seems the murderer was the contract guard killed outside your safehouse.*
>
> *The agents failed to get Paul to talk. They're bringing him from the consul's house to our offices for you to question. I'll send Camille back with them to the house. Figured she could help the agents question the other contract guards. I was also tired of her whining.*

Sanders thought of Sara. He wouldn't have to do these interviews if she was present. Her folksy—or sometime motherly—manner often gave interviewees a false sense of security. Then she snapped the trap. He planned to use her techniques to engage Paul into a discussion. He reviewed Sara's notes on Paul for ideas:

J. L. Greger

***

"Paul, we're both men of the world. Don't you find it hard taking orders from a woman?" He watched Paul's smiling lips twitch. "We know about Bridgit Tarantino. The guards said you and Jake sat up and rolled over whenever a woman with a Boston accent called. She's your boss more than Jake, isn't she?"

Paul pupils dilated but he remained motionless in his chair. Sanders was not surprised. After all, Paul had been stabbed the day before and was tightly bandaged.

"I bet there was hell to pay when Sara and I weren't killed in the bombing yesterday morning."

Paul squirmed and as he massaged the thigh of his injured leg, but he never ceased smiling. "Not for me. Not my fault that Jake didn't have the guts to shoot your broad when she came running out of the garage."

Sanders had never heard anyone call Sara a "broad," but Sara sometimes did when she made a stupid mistake. He forced his jaw to stay clenched and not to chuckle.

"Far as it goes, it wasn't Jake's fault. He didn't plant the bomb. I ...." He paused obviously not wanting to incriminate himself.

"The contract guards all say you gave them their orders. One has signed a statement saying you ordered one of the guards to garrote the file clerk who looked like Bridgit after both she and Bridgit had their hair dyed black with streaks of purple and green.

"It's his word against mine. Besides—ask anyone—Bridgit had never dyed her hair black. She keeps it a hot pink shade."

Sanders suddenly recognized an obvious point. He was surprised Sara hadn't realized it. He texted Ray to have agents look for a black wig with purple and green streaks near Bridgit's station at the beauty salon. If found, the wig's interior should be tested for DNA. Normally, he'd ask the local police look for the wig. However, he couldn't guess how deeply the gangs had infiltrated the local police.

"You know the guard you're counting on to testify against me is a goner. The Manaus police even arrested him once for threatening a girlfriend. I had to fix it with the locals."

Paul seemed to move in his chair to rub his back and rear.

Sanders figured Paul's wounds were healing quickly and beginning to itch. Sanders sighed, "Ah to be young again" under his breath.

"Guess who the girlfriend was—the stupid file clerk lying in the morgue. Local police will assume he killed her after a lovers' quarrel."

Sanders realized he had underestimated Paul and needed to goad him. "How about the woman in pink at the conference? I was wrong before. The lady in pink had orders from Bridgit Tarantino, not Jake, to kill you. I bet the order still is in effect." Sanders stood. "While you think about where you saw the woman in pink before, I'm going to see if the consulate's cook has baked the chocolate chip cookies I requested."

***

Marty Santos, a DSS agent who Sanders had brought yesterday from the embassy in Brasília, was waiting in the observation room. He shoved a plate of cookies toward Sanders. "Should someone take a couple in to Paul?"

Sanders shook his head. "Let him stew for a while." He grabbed a cookie. "Besides I'm hungry and want to eat one without having to look at his smug face."

"You two put on a good show. You're both good at bluffing."

"I don't bluff."

"Really? How did you know about the fresh cookies?"

Sanders guessed the stress was getting to him, too. He shouldn't be grumpy with staff. "Sara was disgusted with the food choices in the consul's house this morning. It seems the Hinkleys liked mixed drinks and peanuts but not much else. Sara said she'd have the cook in the consul's house make cookies and something for sandwiches for tonight. I guessed she ordered my favorite—chocolate chip—cookies."

"Mmm."

Sanders knew why Marty was overweight as Marty inhaled two cookies in the time Sanders took to eat one.

The phone rang. It was Ray. Sanders put his phone into speaker mode.

Ray's voice boomed out. "We found the bomb. The Manaus bomb squad has already defused it."

"Where was it?"

"In a mop pail about where you predicted in Hinkley's office. We found a woman in the secret back passageway leading from the closet in Hinkley's office to a side door. I guess Jake was right when he said Bridgit would have a henchman kill him with a bomb. The maid who left the pail wasn't Bridgit. We're trying to question her now, but all she says are curse words in Portuguese."

"Any sign of Bridgit?"

"No, still looking."

"Have you sent the maid's picture to Sara?"

"Yes. Do you really think she's functioning already?"

"Unless they drugged her heavily, Sara will be functional by now. Bring the maid here."

Ray disconnected.

Marty stared at Sanders. "How did you know?'

Sanders grabbed another cookie. "Jake told me Bridgit had used a secret back exit through the closet in the consul's office to deliver artifacts to Hinkley and his wife. I also figured Jake knew his ex-wife well. Jake was sure Bridgit would kill him with a bomb if he was lucky. That's why I *accidentally* turned on the intercom system when I told an FBI agent to put Jake in the large closet in the consul's office and then take his dinner break."

"Ha. Some accident. Weren't you too obvious when you said the agent could take a dinner break."

"Perhaps. I'm in a hurry. I think the gangs will attack en masse soon."

"Then why the pause now?"

He looked at his phone. "I was waiting for this message."

CHAPTER 19: Sara Gets Busy

Sara awoke suddenly. *Where was she?* She was strapped on a stretcher and must be on a plane because she could hear the droning sound of its engines. At least, she could hear a dull sound in her right ear. It was less clear on her left side. Her upper right arm ached, but muscles all over her body were complaining.

A man with Nordic looks walked by. *A good sign.* He wasn't apt to be a member of a Brazilian drug gang. She could see a body strapped to a stretcher on the other side of the aisle. A woman was leaning over the body and adjusting an IV line. Sara thought there was as an IV line in her right arm but wasn't sure because her arms and shoulders were tied down. *Why?*

She remembered the gun fight at the orphanage, Sanders's arrival, and the ambulance ride to a hospital. *What else?* Sanders had told her she would be taken to São Paulo to get her eardrum repaired and maybe for surgery on her arm. Then nothing.

The woman leaned over. "Are you feeling better?"

"Are we going to a hospital in São Paulo?'

"Yes. I'll tell the doctor you're alert now."

"I'd rather not be strapped to this board. Is it necessary?"

The woman made no comment as she checked Sara's blood pressure.

Another woman appeared. "I'm Dr. Ravistan. You've been asleep for two hours and your vitals are now normal, except your blood pressure is elevated."

"Maybe because I don't know where I am. Or who's with me."

The doctor laughed. "I was told you were a civilian, but you sound like a police officer. They're often tense when they awake after surgery. You're safe now." She motioned to the man with Nordic looks. "Do you want to see his FBI badge?"

Sara knew a badge didn't prove much. A fake security badge had been her introduction to Manaus. She also knew she couldn't distinguish a real one from a fake. "What needs to be done to my arm?"

"We didn't find any bullet fragments in your arm, but we put in a few stitches to repair soft tissue damage. Other physicians will check it for problems in São Paulo, but you should be able to function normally. In a month, you may decide to have a little plastic surgery to reduce the scars on your arm."

"What about my ear?"

The doctor laughed and continued in her sing-song voice typical of Asian Indians. "You're all business. You must be feeling good. The ambassador pulled strings. You're set to fly to Washington early tomorrow and have surgery the next day."

Sara was terrified. Sanders was sending her away. She suspected he didn't expect to survive and wanted to protect her while he could. She knew she still could help him to protect the Bungle in the Jungle—that was their private name for the consular office in Manaus. "Please remove this IV line and let me sit like a regular passenger. Maybe let me walk the aisle a bit?"

"You're an assertive patient. I was warned you would be, but exercise would be good for you. We're more than two hours away from São Paulo."

Sara felt unsteady when she first stood. The plane's aisle wasn't the easiest path to walk. She was sure she'd not normally notice the engine vibrations so much.

She felt more confident after a walk to the cockpit, the restroom, and the galley. As she walked, she talked to the other passengers. She learned Jane Ellis was one of the unconscious patients on stretchers. The other was the teen from Sister's Rose's office in the orphanage. She saw Latoya asleep in the next row. However, no one answered her questions about the situation at the consulate. Finally, she said, "I want to talk to the boss here."

The Nordic-looking agent appeared in the aisle next to her seat. "Yes, ma'am?"

"Forget the protocol. I know many of those in the consulate may not survive the expected attacks. I might be able to help them. Please get me a computer. One with secure connections would be great, if possible.

The agent's jaw dropped. "The Ambassador was insistent. He wanted you safe."

"Fine, but I want him and the agents in Manaus to be safe, too. Don't argue with me." Sara knew she'd been snappier than usual, but it worked.

The agent brought her a laptop and pushed Latoya into the seat beside Sara. "Perhaps you'd be more comfortable if Latoya encoded and sent your messages, but I want to assure you of my credentials. Do you want to see my FBI badge?"

Sara stared at him. "Did Sanders give you a code phrase before we left?"

"You're a cautious one." He smiled. "Bug is number one."

Sara smiled. Bug was her Japanese Chin dog. She normally took him everywhere with her, but she had feared Brazil was too dangerous and had left him in a secure kennel where he was being pampered with massages daily. There was no time to think of Bug now. "Right." She turned to Latoya. "Let's get to work."

***

Sara checked for messages. There was one from Ray. He'd attached a picture of a short, muscular woman with her hair pulled back from her face. Her eyebrows were overplucked and her face had seen better days. The message was simple:

> *Who is she?*
> *PS. Your Jo was really Bridgit Tarantino—*
> *Jake's ex, the impersonator of Camille you met,*
> *and the mistress of the drug overlord of*
> *Manaus.*

Sara recognized the face immediately and quickly began to reply. Then she studied it more. Latoya sent the final coded message:

> *This is the woman in pink who stabbed Paul*
> *and probably killed Kelly yesterday. She also*
> *sat at the front of the beauty salon I visited.*

Sara decided one way to locate Bridgit and identify her probable partner might be to examine the real estate records for the salon. She typed rapidly and located a plat map of Manaus. The GPS technology was amazing. She was sure she had the right location when she saw the street view of the building. It was the beauty salon she'd visited. The building was owned by St. Bridgit Enterprises. *What an interesting name.*

Sara wandered through Manaus city and Amazonas state records looking for information on St. Bridgit Enterprises. She failed, but in the process was amazed by the thoroughness of the property records in Brazil. It appeared Brazil had invested in the development of a Manaus Free Trade Zone since the 1950s. Those regulations encouraged Manaus to retain the original and renovated architectural plans of commercial buildings. For example, she learned the building containing the beauty salon had two floors. The previous building on the site had been razed nine years ago and the current building erected eight years ago. The second floor was recorded as an unfinished storage area.

Lacking a better idea, Sara checked for other properties held by St. Bridgit Enterprises. She hit the jackpot. St. Bridgit Enterprises owned three warehouses in Manaus. Records indicated a casino and gentlemen's club had been added to one warehouse ten years ago. A fitness center had been added five years ago and apartments four years ago to a second warehouse. A third warehouse on a pier along the Amazon River appeared to not have been updated in the last twenty years.

Sara regretted in all the tizzy that she had not had a chance to explore the port of Manaus. The Amazon River was large enough for moderate-sized ocean-going vessels to dock there. Facilities along the piers allowed the shipment of containers, bulk grains, and petroleum products. The warehouses owned by St. Bridgit Enterprises seemed to be centers for the collection of goods to be loaded into containers. *A perfect way to ship drugs.*

St. Bridgit Enterprises also owned two houses. Bridgit and Jake had lived in one of the two houses owned by St. Bridgit Enterprises before they were divorced three years ago. Jake had continued to live in it for another six months. Sara noticed the last names of the persons who had signed the current rental leases for the two houses were Braga Duarte and Domingo Braga. They could be relatives of the Braga brothers, or it could be a coincidence.

Latoya transmitted the new data to both Sanders and Ray:

> *The salon is in a building owned by St. Bridgit Enterprises. The company also owns two homes in the suburbs of Manaus, three warehouses, and a condo complex not far from Sanders's safehouse. I can't find the identity the owners of St. Bridgit Enterprises in Brazilian records.*
>
> *According to the records, Jake and Paul both live in the condo complex owned by St. Bridgit Enterprises. I can't find anyone with the name of Bridgit living in the complex. So, I'm guessing Bridgit has a hideaway near the salon. One of the warehouses appears to have apartments on its fourth floor.*
>
> *I just remembered. There were lots of wigs on display around the beauty salon, especially at the back near Jo's station. If you find one with black hair and green and purple streaks, check its interior for DNA.*

Sara received a message less than a minute later:

> *We've already confiscated two wigs from the salon.*
> *Thanks for the real estate data.*
> *Did you get the note I pinned to your hospital gown?*
> *Love,*
> *S*

Sara turned to Latoya. "Did anyone find a note pinned to my clothes?"

Latoya gasped. "Was it important?' They probably discarded your blouse at the hospital once they cut the shreds off you."

"It might have been pinned to my hospital gown."

Latoya rose. "I'll check."

Dr. Ravistan sat down beside Sara less than two minutes later. "I should have given this note to you sooner. But I didn't want to upset you. The nurse gave it to me after we took off for São Paulo.

Sara read:

If this is goodbye, know that I love you. The Undersecretary promised to arrange a new identity for you, if necessary
Love,
S

CHAPTER 20: Sanders Makes Progress but Not Enough

The woman strutting down the hall was short. Ray had said she was extremely strong with a muscular torso and legs, but a loose-fitting blue shift hid everything but her lower arms, ankles, and feet. Her hair was covered by a scarf. The defiant look in her eyes and the sneer on her lips would have been frightening if two agents didn't have a firm grasp on her handcuffed arms.

Sanders was less afraid than he'd been two hours earlier. He reread the email from Sara, gulped, and said to Marty, "Showtime. Get me the name and background of the woman."

He opened the door to the interview room and waited while the agents seated the woman across the table from Paul. As expected, Paul gave her a quick glance. She wasn't pretty enough for him to study her.

Sanders closed the door after the two agents left to wait outside the room. He stepped behind the woman. "Paul, take a good look at her. You've seen her before. Think hard."

Paul didn't change from his position with his legs stretched out under the table, but he did look at her. "No idea."

"You flirted with her when she wore a blonde wig, plenty of makeup, and tight pink shorts and top."

"Couldn't be."

The woman spat at Paul, but only wet the table.

"Young man, do you notice anything about women except their bra size and maybe hair color?"

The woman emitted a hoarse laugh.

Sanders was sure she understood English, even though she had pretended not to.

Paul straightened in his chair as he stared at the woman. "I can't believe it."

The woman spat again. This time her aim was better, and she hit Paul's right hand.

Paul yelled, "Give me a tissue! She could infect me with something." Paul frantically grabbed the napkin from under the plate of cookies and wiped his hand.

"The agents and I would like to unlock her restraints and leave you with her for..." Sanders looked at his watch. "... a minute. But you might not be able to talk afterwards because of loss of blood."

Paul smiled. "You wouldn't do that because you follow the rules."

"You know less than you think." Sanders's phone vibrated, and he took his time reading a text from Ray. "I could put you in the big closet in the consul's office. Jake talked after only a half hour there. He was smart. That's where this lady..." Sanders pointed to the woman who continued to stare at Paul. "...placed enough explosives to wipe out several rooms. Her name is Lolita Valle. She's Bridgit's best assassin."

Paul's eyes narrowed and he looked away from the woman who suddenly flashed a smile. "Okay, I was wrong. Bridgit was annoyed at Jake, but she'll forgive me for the problems yesterday. I obeyed orders."

Sanders scanned his latest phone message. "Jake thought you'd spent time in what he called 'Bridgit's secret lair.' Why don't you tell me its location? Maybe then, we could move Lolita."

"Are you kidding? The bitch will get deets back to Bridgit if I talk."

Sanders had no idea what "deets" were but thought Marty in the observation room might know. "Fine. I'll let you two sit and talk. I wonder which of you will get your handcuffs loose first?" He stood and tried to walk briskly—even though the skin on his face, neck, and shoulders itched, <u>and</u> most of his muscles ached from yesterday's activities—into the observations room.

***

"'Deets' are detailed information." Marty studied Sanders. "You faked it well with Paul."

"He wasn't faking it for me. He's young and his injuries aren't bothering him much. Too bad Lolita didn't have time to make him a soprano when she stabbed him at the conference."

"Never saw you lose your cool before. When I get grouchy, my wife says I need to eat." He looked down at his bulging middle. "I guess I'm grouchy a lot." He slouched in his chair. I think Sara expected all of us to be grouchy today. This morning she ordered the cook to make enough barbecue, coleslaw, and cookies for fifty people. She must have anticipated our current situation."

Sanders gave a tired smile. "Her predictions are sometimes wrong, but they're always useful. I've come to depend on her."

"My wife and the gals in the embassy in Brasília all said the rumors about you two were true. I and most of the men at the embassy thought Sara was just a convenient cover for you."

Sanders didn't like what Marty was hinting but ignored the trivial comment. He sat down. "Any updates?"

"Yep. Sara convinced the Undersecretary, that she should return here. Of course, the four-hour flight can't take off until the plane is refueled in São Paulo and Jane Ellis and the teen from the orphanage are delivered to the hospital."

Sanders sighed. "You know, the Undersecretary might have Sara appointed to replace me if I was incapacitated. Then, Paul will know fear. I've never seen Sara write such a negative profile on a suspect."

"Paul knows how to irritate middle-aged women. After he accompanied Evan Hinkley to a party at the embassy in Brasília, my wife threatened to never go to another event if I left her again in his vicinity. She wouldn't even tell me what he said or did." He muttered more about his wife under his breath as he walked to the door. "By the way, Camille wants to talk to you."

***

Camille looked nervously around the observation room before she rolled in a cart with a plate of barbecue sandwiches, a bowl of potato chips, a bowl of coleslaw, and lots of napkins. She avoided eye contact with Sanders as she said, "Since I was delivering the food from the consul's house, Ray thought I might also deliver a message." She looked quickly at Sanders. "You sent the cook and all non-essential staff at the house but *me* home. The agents were all busy."

Sanders couldn't believe this woman had been a fierce fighter at the orphanage only a few hours before. "Did the consulate's physician or nurse talk to you? They can give you medicine to battle... your pains." He didn't want to say shock or depression.

"I'm fine. I just want to go to my apartment. I feel safe there."

Sanders almost snorted. This woman had hidden in the orphanage for days because she feared Jake and gang members. Now many gang members would have personal vendettas against her for killing their friends who attacked the orphanage. "I think you should stay in the consul's house. It's safer. Why don't you sit down and tell me about what the agents have learned from interviewing the guards?" He texted the physician on call for the consular offices.

"The contract guards became cooperative after the agents convinced them Paul would get all of them killed" She shrugged. "It didn't take much to convince them. All agreed, Paul was a difficult...."

"The word is *bastard*."

Camille blushed.

Sanders tried not to snicker and bit into his sandwich instead. "What did the contract guards say about Jake?"

"They liked Jake because he was fair to them."

"Explain?"

"Jake got them good rates on their apartments. He sometimes took them along when he went to play poker."

"So, he went to a casino regularly?"

"No, that's what Ray wanted me to tell you. Jake went to a club in the back of a warehouse. Ray says it's a warehouse on Sara's list. The one with a casino at its front. Anyway, the guards said Jake often lost a lot of money gambling, but his credit always seemed to be good in this private club."

"Is Ray following up on the gambling club?"

"He's following up on something better first. It seems all the guards had gone to a fitness center in another warehouse on Sara's list with Paul, but Paul seldom left with them. He usually stayed for a massage, a Brazilian wax job, or a pedicure. When he returned several hours later, he was always in a good mood."

"Why did Ray think this was important? We know Paul is a dandy."

"Ray thinks he may have finally located what Jake called 'Bridgit's love nest.'"

"Okay, now I understand Ray's latest text."

Camille shoulders sank. "Oh dear. Everyone is moving so fast. I could work at my own pace when I was accumulating the evidence on the conference and the Andersons. The rush today makes me forget important points. The agents sent to explore the penthouse apartments have already called in preliminary observations. There are three apartments on the fourth floor of the warehouse. One they believe is Lolita's apartment; the other large one is Bridgit's. And there's a smaller apartment which...."

"Looks like a love nest?"

Camille turned red. "Ray said it looked like a brothel. Agents are processing fingerprints and DNA from all three apartments."

"I assume they didn't find Bridgit?"

"No, but they found a burning cigarette in what they believed was Bridgit's apartment. Ray estimated he missed her by fewer than ten minutes." Camille stared at the clock on the wall. "I delivered the food and the messages. Can I go back to the consul's house now?"

CHAPTER 21: Sara Returns to Manaus on Day 4

As soon as the plane landed in São Paulo, ambulances rushed Jane and Sara to a hospital. Surgeons immediately began operations to save Jane's life, and if possible, reconstruct her shoulder. After two hours, they announced Jane should survive but they doubted they could save her arm.

Sara wasn't sure how the embassy performed the next miracle. An ear, nose, and throat specialist showed up at the hospital at two in the morning. He advised Sara that a tympanoplasty was generally done on an outpatient basis, but dizziness was a normal sequela of the surgery. He also noted surgical repair of the eardrum was often unnecessary because the eardrum usually healed without surgery. Sara opted to delay the surgery. The doctor packed her ear to prevent infection and warned her not to get her ear wet.

The net result was Sara's hearing was reduced but she was okay when the plane took off to return to Manaus with Latoya, her, and ten men at two-thirty in the morning. The new crew in camouflage uniforms looked ready for action. She was told they were a Navy SEAL team responding to a request by Mr. Sanders.

***

Sara tried to sleep but couldn't. She decided she might as well be useful and pulled out her laptop.

The same architectural and construction firms had built and renovated all the buildings now owned St. Bridgit Enterprises. The owner of both firms was Emilio Braga. *What a disturbing pattern.* The name Braga was common in Brazil, but the frequent appearance of the name in this case didn't seem like a coincidence.

Sara decided while she was in the Manaus property database, she'd look up the residence of Gabriela Gómez. Sara was surprised to see the postdoctoral researcher could afford to live in the condo complex owned by St. Bridgit Enterprises. Then she remembered Jorge Braga gave Gabriela monthly payments of a couple of hundred dollars.

Sara guessed Gabriela was Jorge's mistress, and Manuel was Bridgit's lover and co-owner of St. Bridgit Enterprises. Jake had said Bridgit had attached herself to his boss's boss. If true, Manuel was the chief drug lord of Manaus. *But* the conclusion was based on a lot of assumptions. After all, Gabriela had co-authored a scientific paper with Manuel. The lovers could be reversed.

Sara logged into a genealogical database and typed in the names of Jorge and Manuel Braga. As she expected, they were brothers. Emilio, their father, was in his late seventies. The residents of the two homes owned by St. Bridgit Enterprises were the families of the children of Jorge Braga. Manuel's only son had died ten years ago.

Sara looked up the home addresses of the Bragas. Jorge lived in Manaus. Manuel and Emilio appeared to live on a ranch more than thirty miles from Manaus on the Rio Negro River. An aerial photo suggested the ranch had multiple large buildings and a sizable wharf on the river. She'd bet Manuel didn't commute from the ranch to work daily and had a residence of some sort in Manaus, probably not far from the Federal University of Amazonas where he was the dean of the biological sciences. After another search, she found a M. Braga owned a condo in the same complex where Sanders's safehouse had been.

While Latoya encoded and emailed all the data which Sara collected on the Braga family to Ray and Sanders, Sara tried to think like Bridgit. *Where would she hide?* It depended on her relationship with Manuel Braga. Bridgit would be at his ranch if they had a stable relationship. She'd be in one of the warehouses, if not. Or Bridgit could be hiding in one of the warehouses because she hadn't yet had a chance to get to the ranch.

Neither Sanders nor Ray responded to the email. The crew at the back of the plane appeared to be sleeping. She decided they were smart. The plane probably was a safer place to sleep than anywhere in Manaus. Besides, she had no idea where to search next and drifted off to sleep.

***

Sara awoke slightly before five in the morning when the leader of the SEAL team handed her a phone. "I can't get through the switchboard at the Mayor's house. They'll recognize your name. Here are the names of three Manaus police officers known to be on the payroll of the drug gangs. The Mayor needs to get this information before the planned six a.m. raid." Barking orders, he immediately returned to the back of the plane.

The call to the Mayor was awkward. The staff person hesitated but finally recognized Sara's name and put her call through to a phone in the Mayor's bedroom. The Mayor was disoriented, and Sara had to repeat her name several times. Things became more coherent after Latoya entered the conversation and explained the situation in Portuguese.

When Sara gave the Mayor the names of three of his police officers with gang connections, he started to speak rapidly in Portuguese and hung up.

Sara stared at Latoya.

"If I understood him correctly, one of the three men on the list is in charge of the police operation at six. The mayor planned to call the police chief and the Governor of the State of Amazonas." She looked at her watch. "Our plane is due to land at six. We may be too late to be of help."

All the bustle at the back of the plane stopped when the SEAL team leader stood. "I've just learned the consulate is under attack by gangs under the direction of Manaus police officers. If they succeed, there will be no hostages."

Sara wanted to scream. She feared she'd have plenty of time to cry later.

The SEAL leader continued, "I've talked to the Commissioner of the Amazonas Military Police. He thinks he can prevent us from receiving a hostile reception at the airport. Sara and Latoya, put all consulates in Brazil on alert."

The pilot announced over the intercom he'd gotten clearance to land in Manaus ten minutes early.

The first pink streaks of dawn filtered through the plane's east windows as Sara and Latoya texted and called consulates. The team at the back of the plane spoke in whispers. Sara felt as if she was sitting on top of a powder keg and wondered whether Sanders was alive. She recognized texting or calling Sanders, anyone in the Manaus consular office, or even the

Undersecretary would only distract them from necessary actions. She prayed.

She turned to Latoya. "Better give me a gun and review how to load it. Guess I should have boned up before I came to Brazil."

"Perhaps...." Latoya didn't finish her sentence but demonstrated the basic technique.

CHAPTER 22: Sanders under Fire

Sanders got up from the reclining chair in Hinkley's old office, staggered to the attached bathroom, and stared in the mirror. He looked worse than he expected and pulled out a razor. He thought he'd look better after he shaved, but he didn't. He knew he needed a clean shirt, but he'd not brought one along from the consul's house to the consulate when he arrived twenty hours ago.

He checked his messages. A team of Navy SEALs was on its way to Manaus, but unexpected delays made it unlikely they'd arrive before six. He was alarmed. Six was the time Brazilian local, state, and federal police would descend on the four of the properties of St. Bridgit Enterprises—the three warehouses and the beauty salon.

One of the *delights* of Brazil was the complexity of it police system. There was of course local city police and the regular army but there were two types of state police. The state-administered civil police oversaw criminal law enforcement and forensics but generally didn't patrol streets or wear uniforms. The state military police were responsible for maintaining public order and were classified as reserve troops for the Brazilian army. Then there was also a federal police department responsible for combating international drug trafficking, terrorism, organized crime, and public corruption. Sanders thought the duties of the federal police closely paralleled the duties of the FBI in the U.S.

Sanders thought a moment and decided the Brazilian system of law enforcement was no more complex than the system in the U.S., but it was different. He found coordinating efforts with them stressful. Accordingly, he'd had the Manaus consular staff establish a hotline network last night to facilitate instantaneous communications among his office in the consulate, the consul's house, and the offices of the chief of Manaus Police Department, the commissioner of the Amazonas State Civil Police, the adjutant general of the Amazonas State Military Police, and the director of the Brazilian Federal Police.

Each member on the network had agreed to monitor the line continuously for the next twenty-four hours. Sanders figured by then either he'd be dead, or the crisis would be resolved. The leader of the incoming Navy SEAL unit had been added to the network when his plane left São Paulo at two-thirty.

He and Ray—with the help of all the core staff of the consulate and FBI agents—had thoroughly searched the consulate and consul's house last night after Lolita was captured. Jake had been cooperative and identified hiding spots and secret passages in both buildings because he knew he was dead man if Bridgit or her henchmen captured him. Paul—after a half hour in a room with Lolita with both handcuffed to their chairs—spouted fewer defiant taunts but offered minimal help. Sanders decided Paul knew less than he pretended. However, Sanders thought Paul's frequent refrain, "Bridgit will know about your unified attack and will strike first," was most likely true.

He felt worse when he learned Sara was on the flight with the Navy SEALs. He'd sent her to São Paul for treatment of minor injuries because he wanted her safe. And nowhere in Manaus was a haven for him or her now. However, Sanders had secretly known she wouldn't leave if she thought she could help him. He shook his head. Sara was too much of an optimist. Usually, he thought her optimism was one of her good characteristics, but not today.

A little before five, Ray reported the morning rush hour traffic near the consular offices seemed to have already begun. That was strange.

A couple of minutes later the Mayor of Manaus called. He hysterically explained Sara had called and given him the name of three ranking police officers on the Manaus police force with allegiance to the local drug gangs. The news was disastrous because the vice chief, who planned the mission, and the lieutenant and the sergeant, who were due to lead the raids on two of the warehouses, were the three individuals named.

Sanders activated his hot line network. The Manaus police chief, who the leader of the SEALs had alerted directly, had already arrested his vice chief, but he was too late to stop the movement of the other two officers. Both had left the police headquarters early with their detachments.

The Amazonas State Military Police had already been ordered to find what was feared to be two groups of renegade police officers. Sanders had staff added the Mayor to the hotline network.

Two minutes later, Ray entered Sanders's office with more grim news. Ray knew the location of one group of renegade police officers. They were infiltrating the crowd of armed men—presumably gang members—who had assembled a block away from the consulate. What Ray had thought previously was an early morning traffic jam was dozens of cars parked intentionally to stop traffic on all four sides of the building housing the consular offices as well as several other offices.

Even though Ray had already stationed the agents with the best shooting skills in strategic positions, Sanders convinced a major in the state military police to have a helicopter with trusted police snipers land on the building's roof. Sanders decided to not evacuate the consular offices because ground transportation was impossible and only one helicopter at a time could land on the roof. However, he had military police helicopter remove one computer technician from the core staff remaining at the consulate. She had two young children and no husband.

The situation evoked comments from those on the hotline. The most important came from the Manaus police chief. "I propose the state military police move in immediately to control the crowd of gang members and rogue police forming around the consular offices. The rogue police lieutenant who will lead the charge..." There was a long pause. "He's capable, and he's my nephew. I don't want to have to tell my sister I gave the order to shoot her son."

Coughs and groans could be heard from several sources on the line.

A major in the state military police said, "Two of my detachments can arrive at the south and west sides of the offices in ten minutes, but then the attacks on the warehouses at six will be understaffed."

"We'll group our agents at windows on the north and east side of our offices and create a ruckus to mislead the mob and give you a better chance to surprise them when you come from the south and the west," said Sanders. "Ray Curtis will deploy the agents to meet your specifications once you're established on the scene."

The Manaus police chief spoke hesitantly. "We—my staff—are transmitting photos of the twenty-three rogue officers we think will be participating in the raid on the U.S. offices and another, yet undetermined site. The rogue sergeant was assigned to lead the raid on the warehouse with the gym and Bridgit Tarantino's apartment. I think he will lead his men to that warehouse early and...."

"Rescue Bridgit Tarantino. He might be there already," said Sanders. "It's one location where the state military police were key."

"I'll fill in the gap and personally lead the attack on that warehouse," said the Manaus police chief. The Mayor has agreed. I've turned over the coordination of Manaus police to our most senior captain." He sighed. "It's better this way."

The commissioner of the federal police sighed, "We'll fill in another gap and send a few officers to the consul's home immediately."

***

At five-fifteen, shots rang out from buildings adjacent to the consular office. Shards of glass from shattered windows showered several rooms in the office. At the same time, repeating guns blasted the front and back doors of the building.

Sanders had anticipated the attacks at the doors. Agents with repeating rifles were ready to shoot at anyone trying to enter. Sanders hoped those agents could buy enough time for the military police to arrive.

Meanwhile, sharpshooters leaned from windows to target apparent leaders in the mob below and shooters in adjacent buildings. Those staff who were not experienced in handling guns dropped grenades on cars or groups surrounding the building. Ray had done a good job of training staff members to peer out cautiously, release the pin, throw the grenade quickly, and duck.

Sanders had announced on a bullhorn to the crowd, "All civilians should flee the vicinity." He noted sadly no one had left the area. Either the civilians were too frightened to move or the crowd of a couple hundred around the consulate were all gang members or rogue police. He chuckled to himself. He guessed *rogue police* was a redundancy for *gang members*.

Sanders recognized the horror of his gallows humor and checked with Camille. She was manning the hotline for the consul's house and was only semi-hysterical. He decided she'd need a six-month paid medical leave in a psych unit after today.

His next task was the worst. He checked on the agent who was guarding Lolita and Paul in a closet on the second floor. The agent knew what had to be done if the mob breached the walls and reached the second floor. Sanders had decided not to put Jake in the closet and trusted him to be among the group lobbing grenades on cars below. He hoped he'd not have to answer questions about his decisions at a future congressional hearing. A hearing was the least of his problems now. He gave the agent a signed note clearing him of responsibility for his potential actions.

The gunfire to the south and west of the consulate now was louder than the noise of exploding grenades on the north and east sides of the building. It could mean the staff had run out of makeshift grenades. Sanders hoped not. They'd used up the real grenades in the first ten minutes. Since then, they'd been dropping bottles—glass or plastic containers filled with alcohol from the consul's extensive liquor stock and containing a lit wick—at the mob below.

Sanders peered out a window facing south on the third floor of the consulate. Uniformed state military police had opened fire on the crowd. Members of the mob were dispersing and running like rats. He wondered how many families would claim later their loved ones were not gang members and just innocent victims caught in the crossfire. He hoped their stories wouldn't be true.

Suddenly the shots from the office stopped. Ray must have received a command from the state military police.

***

Sanders had mixed feeling as he and two FBI agents boarded a helicopter on the roof to take them to the consul's home at fifteen minutes before six in the morning. Most windows in the consulate were shattered. What had been the front door was now a pile of blackened rubble. The walls of most of the rooms on the first floor were peppered with bullet holes. The exterior walls on the north and east side of the building were singed in places and smoke filled the nearby rooms.

The attacking forces had been decimated. The rogue Manaus police lieutenant who had led the attack was dead. Sharpshooters had targeted him and his apparent second-in-command. Ten gang members and three more Manaus police officers were also dead. The state military police had arrested and turned over to the state civil police for incarceration forty-one civilians in the mob and five soon to be ex-police officers. The state military police had also sent thirty members of the mob to the hospital with a variety of wounds and burns. State civil police would process the injured for incarceration after their wounds were treated.

Sanders was pleased that morale among the consulate staff and agents was good. Only two had been critically wounded. Those two were already at the hospital being prepped for surgery. Ray Curtis had the full loyalty of the staff and admiration of the Amazonas State Military Police.

Sanders decided one—perhaps the last—way he could help Ray was to rid him of responsibility for Lolita and Paul. Lolita had been on the most-wanted list of the federal police for years. Early this morning, Sanders had sent the Manaus police key evidence incriminating Paul in the murders of the file clerk who had posed for Bridgit's fake ID badge and for the contract guard at Sanders's secret hideaway. Sanders had also indicated the U.S. would not extradite Paul. Sanders knew he was being sadistic, but he thought time in a Brazilian jail would be a learning experience for Paul Royer. Thus, just before he left the consular office, he ordered agents to deliver Lolita and Paul to the Brazilian authorities.

Sanders hoped he hadn't made a mistake in not sending Jake too, but Jake had fought well alongside his past colleagues during the attack on the consulate. Besides, Jake, with his extensive connections, could be a valuable witness against gang leaders in the U.S.

Now Sanders was ready for his next battle. He hoped he'd reach the consul's house in time. Two of the captured rogue Manaus police officers had bragged after they were arrested. "The battle isn't over yet."

***

The situation at the consul's house had remained stable throughout the attack on the consulate. Camille had not reported any accumulation of crowds near the consul's house, but she wasn't a trained observer like Ray. Although the four FBI agents there were less experienced than those at the consulate, Sanders had thought they were adequate. He thought the two contract guards, whom the agents were patrolling, could be trusted to not turn on the FBI agents. Although the contract guards knew they faced incarceration in U.S. federal prisons for drug smuggling and racketeering violations—RICO offenses, they also knew they'd probably not survive in Brazilian jails. Moreover, Sanders had told the contract guards they might receive shorter sentences in lower-security federal prisons if they cooperated fully.

When he heard Camille's voice on his earpiece, Sanders knew everything had changed. Her voice was sharp. "Two minutes ago, we saw two trucks park in the street in front of the house. Now the street in front of the consul's house is blocked off at both ends by cars."

Sanders heard a barrage of gunfire. More than two repeating guns were being discharged simultaneously from different directions.

CHAPTER 23: Sara Misses Her Target

Sara saw a large assemblage of vehicles and uniformed officers on the tarmac as the plane skidded to a stop. The SEALs' leader entered the cockpit within seconds of the plane's landing gear first touching the ground.

The pilot announced, "We won't be unloading into the terminal. Do not...."

The SEALs' leader interrupted, "As I understand the situation, Ambassador Sanders regained control of the consular office five minutes ago when state military police killed the leader of the raid on the office—a Manaus police lieutenant who was leading the collaborative action of drug gangs and renegade police. Ray Curtis is now in command at the consular office."

Why is Ray Curtis in charge? Where is Sanders? Sara decided to not interrupt the announcements.

The SEALs' leader yelled five names. "You five will be going to the consul's home where gang members have blocked off the street. Exit through the front and help the federal military police load all the ammo and guns from the plane's forward hold into the unmarked white vans. Three of us will ride in each van. I will join you in a minute."

Five men assembled their gear while the pilot turned off the engines.

The SEALs' leader yelled louder. "The rest of you will be going to a warehouse on a pier on the Amazon. It is a confused situation. The local and state civil police are trying to control the crowd while they search for Bridgit Tarantino. You'll oversee checking out the cargo on ships using this pier. Leave the plane by the rear exit and take the direction of the non-uniformed state civil police in the two Jeeps. Good luck."

Latoya grabbed Sara's arm. "You should stay here on the plane." Her phone beeped and Latoya scanned the text.

"Is Sanders, okay?"

"Yes, but too gutsy for his own good. Usually, ambassadors are the first ones out to a safe location, but he's on his way to the consul's house."

Sara wished Sanders felt less responsibility for the safety of his staff and more concern for his own safety. She knew nothing she could say would change him. Sara gulped. "I'll go where I can be most useful."

"Sanders figured you'd say that." Latoya pushed Sara forward off the plane and toward a waiting car. "Sanders wants you to review every woman found in the warehouses before they're released or sent to the hospital, if possible. He thinks Bridgit Tarantino will be disguised and you're more apt to recognize her than anyone else because you've studied her features."

***

Latoya shoved Sara into the back seat of an unmarked black car, nodded to the driver, and slid in next to Sara. "Pedro was the Hinkley's driver and knows Manaus well."

Pedro laughed. "Senhor and Senhora Hinkley made *manye* strange *tripse*. The old ambassador ignored me. Mr. Sanders didn't. I *coulde*...."

Sara had to concentrate to understand Pedro because he spoke English in the melodic way Portuguese is spoken. The accents were on the wrong syllables. And he added an "e" sound at the end of some words and pronounced m's as n's. Long words like "ambassador" required a major translation job to be understood, at least by Sara.

Latoya seemed annoyed with Pedro and interrupted, "I need to get Sara up to speed on our plans." She winked at Sara and said under his breath, "Don't get Pedro talking. I've been warned he's a great driver, but he never shuts up." Then she spoke loudly enough for Pedro to hear, "We think the most likely place to find Bridgit is in the warehouse with the gym and her apartment."

The driver almost sang, "To the warehouse we go."

Sara fingered her phone. "We should also look for these two men—Dr. Manuel Braga and his brother, Jorge Braga." She flashed their pictures at Latoya.

Pedro was obviously experienced at listening to private conversations in his car because he whistled. "You shoot for the stars."

Sara ignored Pedro and reminded Latoya, "One of the men pictured is apt to be Bridgit's lover and the chief of the drug gangs in Manaus. I'm just not sure which one."

The driver whistled again. "I don't know about Manuel, but I know about Jorge. I've tailed him for Senhora Hinkley. He likes the ladies and Senhora Hinkley liked him. *Mulher boba.* The stories I could tell."

Sara didn't know what the driver's words in Portuguese meant, but she decided it might be worthwhile to listen to him carefully. "What kind of stories?"

"A man who chases every woman he sees doesn't have the brains to be a gang leader, but his old man Emilio is another story. We don't see him in town any more since his accident a few years ago."

Sara jolted to attention when Pedro said Emilio. His name had been on the plans for all the buildings owned by St. Bridgit Enterprises. "Can you tell me more about Emilio?"

"Emilio controlled the construction industry in Manaus for thirty years and was responsible for cutting down trees in large areas of the Amazon. He had a freak car accident five years ago. His wife was killed, and a daughter-in-law and he were injured." Pedro's attention seemed to be focused on a side alley for a moment after a woman screamed. He continued, "There should be a detailed report in the police archive, but you might not find it. Seems to me, it was hushed up."

Latoya had seemed annoyed when Pedro started to reminisce but became interested after he mentioned a police coverup. She asked, "What was strange about the accident?"

"The roads out of Manaus, especially along the Rio Negro River, are *bed*."

Sara thought Pedro had said *bed,* but realized he'd said *bad* when he continued. She'd have to remember his unusual pronunciation of a's.

"The road when you are thirty miles out of the city, like around the Braga's ranch, are very bad. Speeding isn't a problem. But as I remember, it was reported the speeding car hit a rut, the driver lost control, and the car rolled."

"Who was the driver?"

"Strange—it was old Braga's wife."

"Why is that strange?"

"Old-style, proper donas don't drive." Pedro frowned. "And after the accident, Jorge and his wife moved out of their house at the ranch."

"They had a separate house?"

"Oh yes. The three donas did not get along, but Emilio liked to keep his family close."

Latoya tensed. "We don't have time for more reminiscences." She pointed to the warehouse. "Pedro, park a block away from the warehouse and keep the car idling. Sara and I may need to leave quickly."

***

Sara saw the street in front of the warehouse was blocked by police cars. Men were standing and sitting in a roped-off area. Four were in apparent uniforms of khaki shorts with red polo shirts; Sara assumed they were the gym staff. The other seven men were older and wore mismatched exercise shorts and faded T-shirts; Sara assumed they were clients who liked to exercise before work.

Latoya pulled at her earpiece, adjusted the attached microphone, and appeared to listen to someone. Then she pulled a bag from the front seat and handed Sara a shoulder holster and a navy windbreaker. "You need a way to carry the gun I gave you on the plane. The jacket will hide your shoulder holster."

As Sara struggled to put on the gear, she noticed a black car pulled up behind them. Two FBI agents jumped out and ran toward the police officers controlling the men in the roped-off area. The driver remained in the idling car.

Sara hesitated before leaving the car. She couldn't stop worrying about Sanders but knew it was important to concentrate on what she *could* do—even if the details she was responsible for were trivial. There was no time for emotions.

Latoya grabbed Sara's arm. "It's not too late to return to the plane. Uncontrolled street scenes make me nervous, too.

Random events can trigger attacks. I don't want anyone in the crowd to know your identity."

"Then let go of my arm. You wouldn't hold the arm of another agent."

Latoya flushed. "This is so *not* our usual protocol. The police claim they have cordoned off all those who were in the warehouse."

"Doesn't look right to me. Besides the employee and patrons in the men's club, there should be warehouse workers. I also know the men's club employed women as massage therapists." She shrugged. "At least that's what the women were called on the fitness center's webpage."

"I agree." Latoya stopped and whispered in her mouthpiece. Then her shoulders sagged as if she felt more relaxed. "The warehouse workers are being held on the side of the building. The massage therapists were allowed to remain inside."

"I want to see the women first. Can the two agents we just saw use the photos I provided to check out the men? Any man with the name Braga should be retained."

***

Sara carefully studied the faces of the four women waiting inside. None had Bridgit's thin face or narrow nose.

Latoya wanted to leave the building immediately. Sara knew time was important but so was thoroughness. She asked for a tour of the massage facilities with the therapists. A police sergeant who spoke barely understandable English led the massage therapist, Sara, Latoya, and another police officer to the elevator.

The massage therapy area on the second floor of the warehouse had a typical modern reception area. It was accessed by an elevator and stairs from the gym on the first floor. Sara smiled at the women. "How do your private guests enter? I'm sure all clients don't enter through the gym where everyone can see them."

Two women stared blankly. The other two pointed to a series of black panels on the wall behind the reception desk. The police sergeant looked confused. One of the therapists pushed a button under the counter. There was a click. One panel slid aside to reveal a steel door. Latoya pushed the door open. A marked off parking area on the second floor of the warehouse appeared.

The police sergeant gasped. "This door was not on the plan of the building in our files." He called his boss—the Manaus police chief—supervising the search of the building.

The police officer opened every door leading from the reception area. Four of the doors were to small windowless rooms. Each room contained a massage table, a counter with drawers for supplies underneath, and a closet for the client's clothes. The agents found no trick doors.

The fifth door led to a short hallway with three more doors. These three doors led to large rooms. The policemen snickered as they searched these rooms. Sara guessed they looked like rooms in a brothel to the men. Each contained a large bed, a reclining chair, a massage table, and a closet. The three rooms were the same except for the predominant color in each room differed. One was red, one was green, and one was purple. The agents found no trick doors in the red and green rooms. There was a sliding door in the back of the purple room's closet which led to a locked steel door.

Sara stared at the women. "Who has the key?"

One woman smiled, pulled a purple silk cord from around her neck, and unlocked the steel door. Not surprisingly a marked parking spot was nearby in the garage. The police sergeant called his boss again.

After a short conversation with his boss, the police sergeant spoke in Portuguese to Latoya. She quickly summarized the situation in the warehouse for Sara. "No one was found in the apartments on the fourth floor. None of the men detained were named Braga but one was a police officer. All were released." She added, "I think we should move on to the next warehouse."

"No, I think we should question the women massage therapists and uniformed men in the gym individually."

Latoya groaned, "That's what the police chief said, too."

Sara and Latoya, with the help of the police sergeant, quickly ascertained Jorge Braga, his son, and several senior Manaus police officers were frequent clients at the massage parlor. All the staff claimed they'd never seen Manuel Braga.

The ensuing discussions among the FBI agents, the police chief, and his officers were amusing in a cynical way. After the discussions, Sara was convinced of several points. The architectural plans of this warehouse and probably all the buildings owned by St. Bridgit Enterprises were missing hidden exits and secret closets. Any of the police officers who frequented the men's club should be checked for alliances with the drug gangs. The police chief had not been a client in the facility. Although prostitution had been legal in Brazil for years, the chief obviously considered it offensive to even be in the building.

The most important discoveries came last. After Sara promised to help the woman with the key on the purple silk cord immigrate to the U.S., the woman admitted one client had escaped the massage facility during the police raid. After considerable grilling, the police officer assigned to prevent anyone from leaving the warehouse by a side exit admitted a blue car had left while he stopped another car leaving the warehouse almost an hour ago. Two people with short hair were in the blue car. The woman in the detained car was the massage therapist with the purple silk cord and key.

The therapist with the purple silk cord and key answered Sara's follow-up questions calmly. "You didn't ask how the client escaped or who he was. He was Jorge Braga. He often comes in before he starts his day at the radio station. We were busy when he got a call a few minutes before six. As he got dressed, he ordered me to open the back exit of the purple room. A blue car was waiting for him. He told me to get my car and head for the side exit of the warehouse." She shrugged, "You know the rest. I was stopped at the exit. The blue car sped by. The guard told me to return to work."

Nothing Sara could promise changed the woman's answers. She claimed she had not seen who was in the blue car, but assumed it was Jorge Braga and a man dressed in workman's clothes.

***

Latoya seemed to give up on herding Sara halfway through the discussions with the police chief and read reports from the other sites.

The police and agents at the beauty salon had found no one present in the salon at six in the morning but discovered a woman and two children asleep in a small apartment on the

J. L. Greger

second floor of the building. The woman's black ancestry and youthfulness made it obvious: she wasn't Bridgit.

The agents and police at the warehouse with the casino had found only two janitors in the casino because it was closed from two to six in the morning. The janitors and all ten of the workers in the warehouse were of black or indigenous ancestry. None spoke English; all claimed they'd not seen any of the individuals in the photos shown them. They were allowed to return to work. The police and agents had discovered two secret exits from the poker room into the warehouse.

When the agents arrived at the warehouse on the pier on the Amazon River, it was packed with goods and people. All were intent on lading boats as quickly as possible before new shipments arrived. The local and state civil police had begun pleading for help by ten minutes before six. The reinforcements sent by the adjutant general of the state military police arrived at six.

CHAPTER 24: Is Sanders Too Late?

Sanders couldn't believe his eyes as he peered from a helicopter at the street in front of the consul's house. Two cars blocked each entrance onto the short street. Two trucks with tarps over their cargo were parked directly in front of the house.

A major in the Amazonas State Military Police sitting at the front of the helicopter handed Sanders a pair of binoculars so he could get a better view of the scene. Men with rifles and shotguns were herding men and women from the homes on either side of the consul's house. He noted several strange things about the people emerging from the houses. There were no children. Only one or two left each of the five houses on the street. All those leaving the homes were dressed in jogging outfits or work clothes, not nightwear or robes, even though it was only a few minutes after six.

A man's voice amplified by a sound system kept repeating several sentences. Sanders's Portuguese was insufficient, but he thought the man was announcing homes on the street would be destroyed if the U.S. did not do something.

The major must have noted Sanders's confusion. "He says his men will raze the consul's house in five minutes if those inside do not come out. Brazilians are being evacuated from the nearby homes, so they are not injured." The major paused. "The gangs want their actions perceived as anti-American, not as terrorism."

The words of the man on the loudspeaker system changed. The major translated, "They will shoot down this helicopter and any others if we don't retreat immediately." The major studied the scene below with binoculars as the tarp was pulled off the first truck. "They have the necessary equipment."

The pilot circled the helicopter away. The major ordered the state military troops to speed up their movement from a nearby location to the consul's house. He estimated it would take five minutes for them to arrive.

Sanders's phone pinged and he turned it on speaker mode. The voice of leader of the SEAL team who had flown in with Sara rang out, "Zack here. We're almost in position. We are behind two houses across the street from the consul's house. We can take out the trucks and the equipment they carry, but the gangs were smart to bring civilians out on the street."

Sanders felt acid rise from his stomach into his throat.

Zack continued, "But the federal military police were smarter. They emptied the houses of all civilians on the street over an hour ago before the gangs arrived. Everyone exiting the homes is a federal military police officer. I'm told the gangs were sloppy and didn't search them for weapons. The federal military police are prepared to act when you give the okay."

The major gulped. "I told the state military troops to be noisy as they approach to get the attention of the gang members."

Sanders through his binoculars could see the scene unfolding. The state military troops, led by two tanks, were ready to turn onto the street two blocks in front of the barricade.

The major said, "Now."

The tanks turned onto the street and advanced forward. All the so-called civilians ran in the opposite direction toward the two cars blocking the other end of the street.

Gang members turned a large grenade launcher loaded on the first truck toward the tanks.

The tanks fired. Shots rang out from multiple locations.

There was an explosion. The first truck blew up and its debris hit the second truck.

The tanks kept moving. While several gang members aimed the grenade launcher on the second truck at the tanks, other members of the mob directed smaller, but still powerful, weaponry at the consul's house. Other gang members fired weapons toward one of the houses where the SEALs had been located. Sanders guessed they had figured out the source of the grenades which had destroyed the first truck.

Another explosion. Then another. And another. All the time the rat-a-tat-tat of repeating guns came from multiple locations.

The resulting cloud of debris and dense gray smoke hid the view of the main action, but Sanders could see the far end of the street with his binoculars. The federal police disguised as civilians had already moved the two cars which previously blocked the street. They had guns pointed at several gang members who were lying on the ground. He couldn't tell if those on the ground were wounded.

Sanders squinted as he tried to peer through the smoke over the main action on the street. He thought he saw the second truck. It looked like a mechanical dinosaur lying on its side with flames bursting from its guts. The houses from which the original grenades had been launched were now heaps of rubble. Then Sanders looked across the street. The consul's house was ablaze. No one in it could have survived. He swallowed hard and continued his assessment.

One tank had pushed aside one of the cars blocking its entrance to this block of the street. The other tank had climbed over the second car and squashed it into a metal pancake. Sanders thought the action was an excessive show of force, but it certainly precluded escape in the car. The troops behind the tanks had fanned out and were shooting at anything moving in the street.

An announcement blasted from a speaker system. Sanders recognized the voice of the SEAL team leader, Zack. "You're surrounded. Lay down your arms." It was repeated in Portuguese by another voice.

The reply was gunshots toward the speaker and the tanks from gang members on the street.

One tank exploded after it was hit by a grenade.

The response was rapid. The state military police barraged those on the street with gunfire. No one was left standing.

A speaker on the second tank made an announcement in Portuguese. The order was repeated in English from another speaker. "Throw down your arms and sit down or kneel on the sidewalks."

Troopers—they looked like U.S. SEALs—walked from between the houses toward the debris which had been the consul's home. A few of the gang members lying in the street crawled or limped to the sidewalks.

                                                J. L. Greger

The military police cautiously moved forward picking up guns and throwing them into the back of a truck following them. Fire trucks entered the street from the end cleared by the federal police and began to douse flames on homes hit by stray artillery.

Sanders wondered how many had been killed. He announced on his hotline system. "It's over except for the cleanup. Camille, aren't you glad we evacuated you to a house on another side street last night?"

Camille replied, "The four agents and two contract guards are grateful you removed them from the center of the action but kept them close enough to see and hear the action. Personally, I want to be on the first flight out of here. But why did the gangs attack the consul's house?"

"I don't know. One reason might be this was a diversion to distract us from the warehouse at the pier." He didn't add another potential reason was Bridgit wanted Camille dead or captured. Somehow, he thought Camille was hiding something that made her valuable to Bridgit.

CHAPTER 25: Surprise Packages on the Pier

At ten to six, the state civil police announced they and the Manaus police were overwhelmed by their tasks at the warehouse owned by St. Bridgit Enterprises on the pier. A mob of dock workers and probably gang members was out of control.

Reinforcements from the state military police and four Navy SEALs arrived around ten minutes later. At six-thirty, a state military police captain announced his troops had forced the mob to retreat behind a barrier of sealed storage container on the pier. Thus, the local and military police were finally able to search the warehouse for Bridgit Tarantino.

Meanwhile, the four SEALs had focused their attention on one moderate-sized ship owned by Braga Industries. The ship had arrived at the pier around two a.m. from the Braga ranch with a cargo of high-end wood products—Brazilian oak, Brazilian walnut, and tigerwood paneling and flooring—ready to be loaded into containers bound for the U.S. on ocean liners. The SEALs had found no contraband or passengers on the ship or among the cargo.

When Sara and Latoya arrived a little after seven, they were glad an officer in the military police quickly escorted them away from the surly crowd and behind the barrier of sealed storage containers on the pier. Sara watched as military police checked every item—mainly hardware for wood processing tools and food—being loaded onto the Bragas' ship. The captain of the ship, with his hands waving in the air, was yelling at a woman officer. Latoya translated the gist of his rants. "If he is delayed much longer, he can't get to the ranch in time to unload this cargo and pick up another load of lumber, which is to be on an ocean liner leaving at five this afternoon."

Sara couldn't believe the heat even though the sun was low in the sky. She drained a bottle of water and wondered how hot the temperature got inside the unrefrigerated containers at midday. She doubted most produce in a container for a day in Brazil would be edible afterwards and wondered whether coca and its derivative cocaine ever degraded in the tropical heat. She'd never heard heat was a concern of drug traffickers, but they didn't seem to care about impurities in their products. Sara stopped daydreaming and forced herself to be alert to her surroundings.

***

A state police officer explained the loading of the ship bound for the Braga ranch was slower than expected because a large shipment—mainly saw blades and precision equipment—had been delivered at the last minute for delivery to the ranch.

Sara and Latoya watched one officer debating with two dock workers, who refused to open a crate marked: *MANUSEIE COM CUIDADO*. Latoya explained the marking meant "Handle Carefully."

Finally, the officer whispered into his headpiece, climbed into the cockpit of a crane, and "accidentally" dropped the crate into the water. Two dock workers immediately dove into the river and pulled the crate to the surface. The officer was smiling as he and several other officers opened the crate and pulled out a spluttering woman—not cutting blades or precision equipment—from a vented wooden case within the crate. The police immediately arrested the two dock workers and the woman. After the incident, the dock workers seemed to be more cooperative with the police.

***

A captain in the state military police guided Sara and Latoya to the area in the warehouse where the SEALs were working. The military captain's English was good, but he added a soft "e" to the end of many words. "Your *mene* have intercepted a *shipmente* of three barrels just brought to the warehouse. They noticed *odde* airholes in the lids of the kegs. You need to see the contents."

Sara saw three barrels marked *EXPLOSIVA*. All were open. Military police had handcuffed the three men who had delivered the barrels. A canvas tarp lay over objects on the ground. Military police circled the area so outsiders could not see the ground.

One of the SEALs strode forward and lifted a corner of the tarp.

Sara suppressed a scream. It was Jorge Braga. His face was red, and he was perspiring heavily. He appeared to be having difficulty breathing with a white rag stuffed in his mouth. Sara pulled the tarp back further. His hands were tied with ropes across his bare red chest.

"You know this is Jorge Braga. He's overheated and needs medical attention."

The captain replied, "He'll get it as soon as you finish the identification."

While one SEAL covered Jorge with the tarp, another SEAL turned up another corner of the tarp. A woman lay there. Her face was turned to the side with pinkish hair covering her face.

Sara leaned forward to brush the hair aside.

The captain snorted, "No! Too dangerous." The captain used a short stick to push the hair from the woman's face.

Sara gasped. The woman was fair skinned and had a small nose. In general, her features were childlike, and she seemed to be barely breathing. Her face was extremely pale and covered with fine beads of sweat.

"I don't know who she is." Sara leaned forward and pulled the rag from the woman's mouth before the captain could stop her. "Do you work in the massage parlor?"

The woman didn't respond in any way. Sara pulled the tarp back further to reveal the woman's small, thin body, clad only in a bikini swimsuit. A tremor moved through the woman's body. Sara was relieved. At least the young woman was alive.

Sara looked toward one of the SEALs. "Do you have ice? She's in heat shock."

The SEAL shook his head.

"Then throw some cold water on her and Jorge. We need to lower their body temperatures."

The SEAL looked between the captain and Sara.

Sara noticed the captain was scowling. She must have overstepped her authority. She thought for a second. "Okay cover their faces but uncover and wet their bodies so they can cool off. We gain nothing if they die."

The captain nodded. Two of his men ran from the circle.

A SEAL pulled up the third corner of the tarp. The woman lying there was panting as she lay on her back. Her skin was pale, her hair was short and dark. She too was perspiring heavily and appeared to be having trouble breathing with the rag in her mouth.

Sara focused on the woman's narrow face. The nose was thin. Her skin was covered with a heavy coat of makeup. Her eyes were unflinching and blue. Sara suddenly realized she'd never noticed the color of Bridgit's eyes. She'd probably would have remembered if they were blue or black. "I'm not sure."

The SEALs and the captain all groaned.

"I'd be sure if her makeup was washed off. Bridgit has freckles across the bridge of her nose and high on her cheeks."

The two men had returned with pails of water. One dribbled water on the woman's face and threw the rest of water in the pail over Jorge and the other woman.

The captain clicked his fingers and said something in Portuguese. It must have been a threat because Latoya gasped.

The woman didn't move as the aide pulled the rag from the woman's mouth and wiped her nose and cheeks.

There were no freckles. The woman's eyes were wide open with the whites creating a wide frame for her blue irises. Sara thought Bridgit when captured would show anger more than fear. This woman was terrified. Sara leaned forward and pulled the tarp down to show the woman's shoulders. They were muscular. Bridgit had narrower shoulders. "Do you work in the gym?"

"*Sim.*"

Sara glanced at Latoya. "Is that a yes?"

Latoya nodded.

"Do you know where Bridgit is?"

The woman whispered and then spat.

Latoya translated, "You'll never get her, bitch."

Sara laughed. "This one is less afraid than I thought." She looked at the captain. "Sorry. Neither woman is Bridgit."

The captain nodded and clicked his fingers. The military police immediately began to wrap the three prisoners in wet sheets—almost like a straight-jackets—and carried them to a waiting vehicle. The barrels were recapped and rolled toward the pier.

The captain spoke rapidly in Portuguese. Latoya translated. "The SEALs and I agreed it would be best if few knew who we found in the barrels."

"Slow down," gasped Latoya.

The captain straightened but then spoke rapidly again with Latoya trying to keep the translation in pace. "The SEALs and my men have kept the attention of the crowd on the woman found in the case by the pier. Now we will load the empty barrels on the ship and allow it to sail. With luck, the captain and crew will not check the barrels." He began to walk away.

Sara hated to delay the captain, but she needed details if she was to be useful. "Who was the woman in the case?"

He winked. "One of my officers. So were the two dock workers. The SEALs are clever. So, am I. We needed—how do you say it— a *diversione* as we waited for late arrivals to the warehouse. I'd hoped Bridgit would be one the late deliveries."

CHAPTER 26: Nothing Adds Up

Sara wanted to cry. Her workroom was smoky but looked better than she felt. She was tired and ached all over. It wasn't surprising. The trips to and from São Paulo had been stressful. Then too, she felt like she'd put in a full day's work, although it was only ten in the morning.

The last email from Sanders was the final straw. She knew he was busy, but he really should have asked how she was.

Ray knocked and entered her office. "I tried to talk Sanders out of it, but he wouldn't listen."

Sara looked up from her laptop's screen. "He's convinced he's got to complete his assignments in Brazil."

"Which are? He's never told me the details of the Undersecretary's requests." Ray pulled up a chair to Sara's desk.

"The Undersecretary is as ruthless as any drug lord and knows Sanders is more compulsive than any other of her ambassador-level staff. *But* he won't listen to me." Tears dribbled from Sara's eyes.

Ray pulled a large red bandanna from his jacket pocket and gave it to Sara.

"He really isn't up to playing James Bond anymore. Besides, he was always better as a tactician than an action hero. Look at this email." She turned her laptop so Ray could read the message:

Sara,
We stopped the gangs this morning, but they'll
be back with a vengeance if we don't apprehend
Bridgit. I've got to try to finish my assignments.

Ray stopped reading and stared at Sara. "He doesn't appreciate you... at least not emotionally."

Sara bit her lip. *What could she say?* Her relationship with Sanders had deteriorated into a close business partnership. She knew it was a possibility when she refused to move to Brazil with him several months ago. If she was honest, she had probably undermined their romance when she suggested they exchange rings but not marry a year ago. But it had been her desperate attempt to force him not to take her for granted. It hadn't worked.

What could she expect from a man who had been raised by emotionally, and often physically, detached rich parents and boarding schools? They had drilled into him the Spartan phrase—*Return with your shield or on it.* She reflected a second. Her sharecropper parents hadn't been much different, except they had phrased the maxim as: *We don't' want to look like trailer trash and will disown you if you embarrass us.* No wonder most of Sanders's behavior was logical to her.

She looked up and saw Ray was staring at her. This was not the time for regrets. "Have you noticed anything unusual about Camille?"

J. L. Greger

"Er, er... yes." He looked down and rummaged in a bag on his lap. "I found this clunky picture frame on Camille's desk." He shoved a picture frame, which looked like a cutting board made of various types of wood, toward Sara.

Sara studied the picture in the frame. It was a group shot of the staff at the consulate. "

"When I played with the frame to remove the photo, the pieces in the bottom of the frame moved. Guess what I found?" He laid a tiny bag of white powder on the table.

"Batrachotoxin?"

"More likely cocaine."

"Do you think Camille knew it was there?"

"No idea."

Sara looked at her watch. I know what Sanders thinks he wants, but I think my time would be best spent popping into the last session at the conference. I want to see if Manuel Braga and Gabriela Gómez are still there. They can flee more easily than Camille. Just in case, you'd better notify customs to not to allow Camille to leave Brazil."

Ray nodded. "For the time being, I've got to focus on cleaning up and fortifying the consulate. It's up to you to continue gathering information. I assume you'll want Latoya to go along. Why don't you take Marty Santos, too? He'll keep you from taking too many risks."

"Are you saying I take too many risks?"

"Yes." Ray didn't take a breath before he continued. "Remember Marty is a klutz, but Sanders says he's a super extraction expert. Pedro can be your driver."

"I've been thinking. Maybe I'm particularly cynical today, but the relationship Bridgit has with either Emilio or Manuel Braga could be just a close, trusted business, not a romantic, relationship."

***

Sara slipped into a chair in the back row of the closing session of the conference less than ten minutes after the session began. Carlos Moreno—as usual—was already in the back row. He seemed startled to see Sara and coughed as he texted rapidly on his phone.

Sara was surprised to see Manuel Braga at the head table. She assumed he knew about the rather ignominious capture of his brother at the warehouse. She studied him. His clothes looked fresh; his hair was in place; and he looked calm as he gazed at the audience. She doubted she looked as neat.

Suddenly Manuel's head jerked in her direction. He stared at her and then smiled.

Sara walked to the back table to get a bottle of water and have a better view of the audience. Gabriela Gómez was sitting at the end of a last row on the right side of the room. Sara remembered yesterday or was it the day before—time was badly jumbled in her mind at this point—Ray and she had reviewed Gabriela's application for study in the U.S. They had agreed Gabriela didn't need another postdoctoral position. Gabriela needed an introduction to an appropriate bigwig in a major pharmaceutical company. Of course, Sara cynically thought the main purpose of many postdoctoral positions was to get students noticed by desirable employers.

However, Ray and she had wondered if Gabriela had other motives. Her bravado had seemed too contrived. No rational person was so oblivious to danger. And her answers were too perfect.

Sara was irritated as the chairmen of the breakout groups reported their conclusions. They had made the recommendations she had predicted a day ago. She didn't feel like listening and walked over to sit by Gabriela.

Gabriela didn't seem surprised to see Sara.

Sara whispered, "How soon would you be willing to go to the U.S.?"

Gabriela yawned. "Nothing is keeping me here. I can write up my data from here at my new workplace."

"Don't you need to talk to Jorge Braga? He pays your rent."

Gabriela frowned. "I expected you would check me out thoroughly, but this seems like overkill."

Sara shrugged her shoulders.

"The Braga family..." Gabriela studied Sara. "...is rich. They felt—after a little encouragement from me—they owed me. Jorge, poor Jorge, always does what his father tells him to do."

"What about Manuel? Does he do what his father Emilio tells him to do, too?"

Gabriela shrugged.

"Maybe we should step outside so you can explain to me what you really want and what you know? I doubt Manuel will race from the podium to stop you and Jorge is in police custody."

Gabriela stood. "Let's go."

***

"Gabriela, I'm puzzled. You seem unafraid of speaking against gang leaders even though your family has been decimated by them."

Gabriela fluttered her long black eyelashes. "I only say things everyone knows."

"You maligned Jorge Braga."

"Jorge may be the son of a drug lord, but he's a minor mouthpiece for his father."

"How do you know that?"

"Everyone does."

Pedro, who was sitting in the front seat of the van with Latoya, snorted. "That's for sure."

Gabriela smiled. "See, even your driver knows I'm right. Jorge's father basically disowned Jorge after he and his wife moved out of the ranch complex." Gabriela tossed her long hair. "Why do you think the captain who worked with you this morning was so angry? He knew he'd wasted his time when he recovered Jorge from the barrel at the pier."

"You know about Jorge's capture? It was supposed to be secret."

Gabriela giggled. "The raids were hard to ignore. Someone, probably a police officer, got several shots of Jorge and put them on Facebook. One of the shots included a military police captain getting into a van with Jorge. I saw you in the distance in another shot."

Marty, who was sitting in the back row of the van, had been silent as he recorded the conversation; now he was making little squealing noises. Sara suspected he was frantically searching Facebook for the photos Gabriela mentioned.

Gabriela sneered at Marty and played with her phone. She handed him her phone with an ugly shot of Jorge on display. "Jorge's dumb enough to sue the photographer for defamation of character."

Sara couldn't understand Gabriela's brashness and thought it was an act. Then again, Sara thought it would be easy to be cynical about the police in Manaus. "Let's go back a bit. Why did Jorge and his wife move out of the ranch complex?"

"The Bragas fixed the police report of an accident about five years ago. They claimed Emilio's wife was driving the car in an accident near the ranch because she was killed and couldn't be charged. Jorge's wife was driving. She'd been drinking—as usual—and rolled the car in a minor rut."

Sara was tired of hearsay evidence. "Sounds like gossip. There's no way you'd know those details."

"Sound right to me," said Pedro.

Sara didn't feel like being polite. She was tired and cranky. "Pedro, I'm trying to interview *Gabriela*, not you." She focused on Gabriela. "Be honest. How could you possibly know those details? Your entry into the U.S. is not dependent on telling a grand story."

Gabriela made a hoarse sound. "I don't gossip. Emilio's wife was my grandmother's half-sister. One of the last things my grandmother did was to convince Emilio not to kill Jorge's wife. He did worse and imprisoned her in a gilded cage in Manaus with a husband who doesn't even like her."

Everyone in the car gasped. Sara wondered how she had missed the relationship between Gabriela and the Bragas in her earlier genealogical search of the Braga family. Sara guessed a half-sister might mean one of the women, had been illegitimate.

Throughout Sara's conversation with Gabriella, Marty typed wildly and made purring noises. Suddenly, he yelled, "I found it! She's telling the truth about being a grandniece—at least by marriage—to Emilio Braga."

Sara thought a moment. The situation still didn't make sense. "Do you really think you can move to the U.S. and get a high-profile job in the drug industry without some consequences? I'm sorry but you sound more like a candidate for the witness protection program in the U.S."

All noises in the car stopped. Pedro coughed. Latoya sighed. Marty said, "I can make it happen."

Gabriela shrugged. "I'm... as you say... reckless because I can't change the inevitable." Tears rolled down her face. "But I'd like a chance at a long—even if it's not glamorous—life."

Sara knew her mouth was agape but all she could do was stare. "I think you and Marty have a lot to talk about. I have just

                                            J. L. Greger

one question for you now—what's Manuel's' role in the family business?"

"I don't know, neither does Manuel." She sniffled. "It depends on Bridgit Tarantino."

CHAPTER 27: The Clock Is Ticking for Sara

Ray was waiting when Sara entered the back entrance to the consulate. "Let Marty and Latoya take care of Gabriela. We gotta talk." Ray pulled into a waiting room. "Everyone saw you lead Gabriela from the conference. I don't know who will come looking for her—gang members, police, or her colleagues at the university—but they will be arriving soon." He pointed at the plywood over a section of wall where a window once been. Broken glass was still on the floor. "Now look at this consulate. I've got workmen doing repairs, but we couldn't defend ourselves against another attack. Hell, we'd have trouble answering even simple diplomatic requests."

Sara knew he was right but felt she had to explain. "I know, but... when the conference ended, I figured Gabriela would disappear—either voluntarily or because someone forced her disappearance."

Ray sighed. "You did what you had to do, *but* I don't know how to get Gabriela out of Manaus. The SEALs under Sanders's direction have been studying satellite images. They know the ranch has anti-aircraft guns. They've also noted increased activity around the silos on the ranch where weapons are stored."

"You're saying gang leaders can just blast any planes from the air around Manaus?"

"Yep. And a land route out of here is not an option."

"It can't be that bad."

"It is. The shortest land route is over two thousand miles through areas controlled by the drug gangs. It takes forty-six hours on good days and involves several ferries. I'd have to send a convoy because the roads are bad and car repairs—if needed—are nearly impossible to arrange."

"I think I know the answer, but can we sit it out until Sanders and the SEALs decommission the big guns at the Braga ranch?"

"Get real. We lost the consul's house. I need to find safe housing for over thirty people for tonight. I had staff call hotels and other consulates. They don't want us because they fear retaliation from the gangs."

"I guess I now understand Sanders's comments. He always said Manaus was like an island in the South Pacific surrounded by jungle instead of ocean."

"Yes, and the ocean is easier to navigate than the jungle." Ray began to pick up pieces of debris and throw them into a waste basket. "Sanders ordered me not to try any military actions unless he was killed. He thinks the SEALs on the ground can destroy the silos at the ranch, but it will blow their cover. He believes it's essential to complete several other goals first. Besides, destruction of the silos at the Braga ranch could be considered an act of war."

"Doubtful, but it could create an ugly international incident." Sara sat hunched over a small table and massaged the temples of her head with her fingers. "It depends on the deals that Sanders's has struck with Brazilian officials. I bet the major from the military police is involved." She looked up. "Did Sanders give any practical advice?"

"Use the Amazon."

"Okay. Can we rent a ship?"

Ray stopped his cleanup activities. "Most of the tour boats and ferries in Manaus only go a few hundred miles on the river. Many aren't outfitted for overnight trips."

"How about ocean-going cargo vessels? Most cargo ships can transport a few passengers beside crew. Surely, there are ocean-going vessels docked here with registration, or at least owners based in the U.S., Canada, or one of our European allies?" Sara could see Ray was skeptical by the vague stare he gave her.

"Getting the ships doesn't solve the problem. We'd have to create a diversion so the gangs—and even local police—didn't realize many of us were leaving Manaus. You know we all should evacuate."

Sara stood and began to also pick up pieces of debris and throw them in the garbage can. "If we used different types of ships and put only a few of us on each ship, our exit wouldn't be obvious."

Ray pulled his hands through his hair. "Travel on the river is slow. It takes a little over three days to get from here to the closest ports on the Atlantic coast of Brazil. The facilities on the cargo ships are primitive. Passengers and crews often sleep in hammocks on open decks. While on most ships, you don't have internet access."

"But satellite phones make communication possible. Does anyone in this office know executives in the shipping industry?"

"This office didn't have experts on anything but party planning and security under Hinkley." Ray hammered at his laptop. "Jake might be helpful, but we'd only tell him we were shipping out his guards. I don't think he'd set them up to be killed."

Sara frowned. "He might try harder if he was also on the ship." She paused for only a second. "We'd have to do something in parallel and even more secretly for Gabriela." Sara thought for a minute. "I'd really like to get Gabriela out first and not involve Jake."

"Agreed."

Sara picked up the last large piece of glass. "Don't cargo ships often stop at a Brazilian port on the Atlantic before they sail to a foreign country. We could fly Gabriela in disguise out of a port city on the Atlantic coast as soon as the ship arrives."

Ray sighed.

"Any chance we could get help from the SEALs."

"I think Sanders and the SEALSs are committed to their current assignment."

***

The rush was on. It was already almost three in the afternoon. The tasks seemed impossible as Sara conferred with Marty and then called the Undersecretary.

Sara had choked when Marty originally explained the cover story he had dreamed up for Gabriela. One FBI agent would pose as a nephew of a sheik in the United Arab Emirates, and Gabriela would pose as his bride. Two other FBI agents would be in the entourage.

Marty had also identified a private yacht moored at a pier near Manaus. The yacht was set to sail at five. As Ray would say—

J. L. Greger

Sara and Marty were lucky, not smart. The owner had sailed this yacht once to Florida to meet with Sanders and the Undersecretary. He agreed to let the newlyweds join him on his yacht because the Undersecretary personally called him.

The agent selected to be the bridegroom had been posted in the Emirates and spoke Arabic; the other two agents did not. It was a problem that Marty couldn't solve. Luckily, the yacht owner didn't know Arabic either. Latoya managed to find a hijab for Gabriela and flowing robes and head gear for the agents, but Latoya found only a single change of clothes for everyone in the entourage.

Sara was relieved Gabriela had lost much of her fiery spunk. Gabriela accepted that none of her possessions could be retrieved from her apartment because it might signal her escape. However, Sara had to make two promises to Gabriela. She didn't have to wear the hijab in her cabin on the yacht, and Gabriela's supposed "bridegroom" would sleep on the floor.

Sara gave a sigh of relief when the agents notified her that the yacht had left the pier on time. Ray had four fewer people to house tonight. All the important documents and forensic items in the consulate, including Camille's picture frame with the mysterious powder, were in the sheik's luggage. Ray had decided not to have forensics analyses done locally because it might alert the drug gangs.

Although the SEALs were too busy to be distracted by problems at the consulate, they identified two cargo ships that they were considering for their own evacuation. One—an ocean-going container ship with a twenty-man German crew—was leaving at six. The problem was the ship had room for only twelve adult passengers. Ten could sleep in an open area on hammocks and two more in a small alcove. The SEALs had thought they might have to evacuate Sanders and Sara and would need the extra bunks.

Ray picked those to be evacuated on the cargo ship carefully. It would include: the two arrested contract guards, three FBI agents to escort the arrested contract guards, four of the five U.S. citizens who worked in the consular offices, and the children of the staff members.

Those to be evacuated on the first ship did not include Camille, Jake, or Pedro. Both Sara and Ray thought Camille was too unpredictable and would endanger others. Jake did not want to be shipped out ahead of the women who worked in the consulate. Sara suspected Jake considered himself a dead man anyway and wanted to see Bridgit get her comeuppance. At least she hoped those were his thoughts. Pedro was convinced as a Brazilian he could easily get to the embassy in Brasília by a land route without attracting the notice of gang members.

The disguises for the fourteen to be evacuated were problematic until Sara suggested an honest—well, a *semi-truthful*—policy might be the best. The two contract guards would be handcuffed and labeled as U.S. citizens being extradited from Brazilian jails. The two women and their three young children were families of the prisoners. The three FBI agents and two male staff members in the consular offices were contractors hired by the Department of Justice. The nine adults and three children had been booked on a ship leaving this morning but in the chaos at the piers, they had missed their connections.

The German captain insisted the passengers could have only limited luggage and must be at the pier by five-thirty or he would sail without them. When the fourteen passengers left for the consulate a little after five, Sara was exhausted.

***

Sara, Latoya, and Marty walked slowly to Hinkley's old—now Ray's—office to report their two assignments were completed. Sara hoped they would not need to utilize Mary's plan for evacuating themselves, Camille, Ray, and the rest of the agents. Three days in hammocks on the open deck of a cargo ship didn't appeal to her.

Ray finished his phone conversation phone before he spoke to Sara. "The lead agent in our last group just notified me they were on the cargo ship. The two women wanted to thank you for allowing them most of the baggage space so they could salvage bits and pieces from their apartments."

"It was easy. There was nothing left at the consul's house to salvage. Latoya and Pedro bought underwear and shirts en masse. Each of the adults on the ship have one change of underwear and an extra shirt. Latoya also bought enough for us to have a change of clothes."

Latoya smirked. "I bought laundry detergent and shampoo, too. Did you know the washer and dryer in the pantry and our shower work?" She sniffed. "You three should use them." She stood. "I'll bring you clothes while you three plot who gets out next."

Ray did a mock bow to Latoya. "All hail our queen of clean."

Latoya snorted and rushed out.

Marty waited until the door closed after her. "I don't think we made too many false promises today to those who left." He pulled out a white handkerchief and cleaned his glasses. "Except for one. Do you think Gabriela guessed it was likely her apartment would be ransacked?"

"Probably, but I thought it best to take an upbeat approach with her." Sara studied her hands. "I was under the care of U.S. Marshals about a year ago before a series of trials of gang leaders. It was a horrendous to realize my past might be wiped out completely if I entered the witness protection program. My life lost most of its value. I doubt in the blitz today, Gabriela realized how gutsy her decision was. I couldn't tell her the truth."

Marty blew his nose. "It's what I hate most about working with the U.S. Marshals Service. "Witnesses get a raw deal. Getting a new identity is like a... lobotomy."

Sara looked around the office. Ray was a real neatnik. The office looked tidy. Then she searched the refrigerator under the desk. "There are only two diet colas, a lemon soda, and water left." She placed the choices on the desk for the two men after she took one of the diet colas for herself.

The men each grabbed a bottle.

Sara took a gulp of soda. "Ray, you've had staff so busy I bet you forgot to send anyone for groceries. Do you think the hotel could lay out a big buffet tonight for the remaining staff?"

He finished his can of cola and crushed it in his hand. "The Ramada Hotel had the gall to call an hour ago and ask if they could cancel our six room reservations for tonight. What's crazy is I wanted to reserve more rooms. Six rooms are not enough space to house the three of us, Latoya and the seven other agents, Jake, and Camille. I'm sure I can't bribe the hotel enough to get our dirty group inside their restaurant."

"You know an army moves on its stomach." Sara took another swig.

Ray laughed, "I'm ahead of you. I had to keep Camille busy. So, I had her arrange for deliveries from several local delis, bakeries, and grocery stores."

Sara' phone pinged. After Sara smiled, Rays said, "What's the word from Sanders?"

"He and the SEALS are exploring the ranch. The major, whom Sanders appears to trust, hasn't spotted any vehicles, other than log trucks, entering the ranch. They have no idea on Bridgit's location."

"Okay." Ray studied Sara. "Are you still planning on interviewing Jorge's wife, Francesca, in an hour?"

"I wish I could postpone the interview, but Gabriela spent a lot of time arranging the meeting. And I think Francesca will talk more if Jorge hasn't had time to silence her. I doubt the police can hold him for more than a day. It's not illegal to be shipped in a barrel."

"You're wrong." Ray appeared to wait for Sara to respond. She didn't.

"Jorge was fleeing arrest. They can keep him in jail until he's arraigned. I pulled strings. He will not be arraigned until late tomorrow."

"So, I guess I could postpone the interview, but I don't think I should." Sara looked around the consul's office with most of its windows boarded over with plywood. "I'm glad Gabriela arranged for me to visit with Francesca at her home. This consulate doesn't inspire confidence in the U.S. Can you spare Pedro, Latoya, and another agent to go with me? It may be the last useful thing I do here before we leave Manaus."

***

The drive to the outskirts of Manaus was scary. Latoya and Sara constantly studied the cars around them looking for potential attackers, even though Ray had sent two additional agents in a second car to follow them.

The house looked like a fortress. It was a three-story building surrounded by a gray concrete wall topped with a chain-link fence. It was the sole house at the end of a long side street. The iron gate swung open slowly after Pedro negotiated their entry using the intercom.

J. L. Greger

A maid in an old fashioned black and white uniform escorted Sara and Latoya into an ornately decorated green room.

A thin—emaciated was a better descriptor—woman with blonde hair sat on a chair upholstered in green brocade at the far end of the room. She didn't stand but merely nodded to two nearby chairs before she began to speak slowly in English. "My dear Gabriela said you would bring me news of Jorge. I have not seen him in weeks." She sniffed. Her voice was suddenly lower and softer as she said, "Which is how it should be."

Sara thought Francesca had established that she and Jorge were not on good terms. Francesca had been less clear about her relationship with Gabriela. "Senhora, may I call you Francesca?"

The woman smiled slightly.

Sara noticed the woman had applied her makeup carefully. Her skin looked flawless. Her earrings and necklace looked like black pearls and accented her tailored, expensive-looking black silk dress. Francesca had worked hard to look her best for this interview. "We're honored to be in your home and to meet you. Gabriela told me you were known as a great beauty."

Sara saw no reason to add Gabriela had actually said, "Francesca *was* a great beauty thirty years ago. The Bragas considered her the perfect match for Jorge because she had completed two years at Vassar and spoke fluent English."

The woman gave another slight smile. Sara suspected Francesca didn't want to mar her perfect makeup job with smile lines.

"We at the consulate would like to understand how the Bragas—at least the men—became so attached to a U.S. citizen called Bridgit Tarantino. How did they meet her?"

The woman lips puckered. "What a disgusting woman. She came to Brazil almost ten years ago with her husband. She immediately started looking for artifacts and shipping them everywhere. Of course, my husband found her interesting." She rolled her eyes. "He outsmarted himself." She smiled so much her face showed laugh lines. "He even introduced Bridgit to Emilio."

"What happened?"

Francesca snickered. "Emilio was pleased when Bridgit dumped Jorge."

"How did Emilio show his pleasure?"

"He set her up in her own beauty salon about nine years ago after she pointed out it would be a great place to recruit society women as sources of artifacts and as mules to transport those items to international markets." Francesca coughed repeatedly.

Sara suspected the woman was as frail as she looked but wanted to gather as much information as possible. "Did Emilio make any demands of Bridgit?"

Francesca looked surprised. "Oh, no. He was always loyal to his wife." She paused. "But he did suggest Bridgit hire Lolita as a manicurist." She sighed. "I guess, it was a favor to me. Lolita had been one of Jorge's many dalliances, and she hated Jorge."

"Do you know of any other connections between Emilio and Bridgit?"

"There's St. Bridgit Enterprises."

"Oh?" Sara didn't want to act too enthusiastic. "Doesn't St. Bridgit Enterprises own several properties in downtown Manaus? I can't find its charter."

"Its ownership has changed over time, and I was never told the details. You see I stopped being one of Emilio favorites twenty years ago." She waved one hand. "It was when I suggested my children be sent to boarding schools in the U.S. because the schools in Manaus were bad."

"What happened?" Sara wondered if that was around the time Francesca started drinking heavily.

"My children were instead enrolled in a Catholic boarding school in São Paulo. I've only seen them on holidays since then."

Sara didn't want to be impolite, but she wanted to learn more about St. Bridgit Enterprises. "Let's get back to St. Bridgit Enterprises. Is it a family-owned holding company?"

Francesca raised her eyebrows, and her voice trilled. "I said I don't know much about the company."

"I'm sorry. We're trying to learn how money from illegal sales of drugs and artifacts is laundered."

"I only know what happened at my last meeting with Emilio. It was about five years ago—after my accident. Emilio had just learned he would never walk normally again." Francesca's hands trembled as she rang a small silver bell.

A maid carrying a silver tray with iced tea and finger sandwiches appeared. Francesca was silent as the maid offered food and tea to Sara and Latoya. Francesca ignored the food and only took a glass of tea.

When the maid departed, Francesca said, "She reports on me to Emilio weekly. It's only a small annoyance because I give her little to report. You see at the meeting five years ago Emilio handed to Jorge the deeds to two houses—this one and the one Jorge now lives in. He also told me if I ever tried to leave Brazil, I'd have an accident like the one I caused. Jorge's punishment was worse, I suppose. He couldn't divorce me because he'd turned me into a drunk—you don't need to hear the exact words Emilio used—with his constant philandering."

Sara felt sorry for the woman and put her arms around Francesca's shoulders. "Now I understand why Gabriela said you were an injured bird in a gilded cage."

Francesca patted her eyes with an embroidered handkerchief. She shrugged. "I might as well tell you what I know. All Emilio can do is finish killing me." She sniffed. "I guess Jorge and I were... given special considerations because.... we were family. You see, Emilio normally has close employees... those he is around regularly... executed... if he discovers they're addicted to drugs of any sort. Alcohol is a type of drug, I guess."

Sara nodded to Latoya who went to the door to see if the maid was listening. No one was there. Latoya continued to walk around the room checking for devices but found none.

Francesca continued to whisper. "Emilio is afraid of all drugs. He always refused to take any pain medications. Manuel says Emilio retreated to the ranch five years ago because he didn't want outsiders to see he was crippled. Emilio's pain is intense, but he won't take any medications."

Sara thought the insight into Emilio's character was interesting, but her goal was to find Bridgit and understand her relationship to the Braga family. "So, tell me about Emilio's legitimate—and illegitimate—businesses."

"Most of Emilio's legitimate businesses are officially owned by St. Bridgit Enterprises. Emilio gives shares in the St. Bridgit Enterprises to family members and Bridgit based on the income they bring into Emilio's businesses. The last I heard Jorge owned nothing. My son owns ten percent of St. Bridgit

Enterprises because he manages the warehouse properties for Emilio. My daughter manages the gym and massage parlor and has shares for five percent of the Enterprises."

"What about Manuel?"

"He and his wife own five percent because she stays at the ranch with Emilio and cares for him." She peered at Sara. "You've been too polite to ask the big question. How much does Bridgit own?"

"Well?"

"At least thirty percent. She also partially owns Emilio's lumber business."

Sara did the math in her head. She had estimated earlier the properties owned by the holding company were worth at least fifty million. She had no idea of the value of the lumber industries. Emilio had rewarded Bridgit well. "Will Bridgit or Manuel inherit control of Emilio's ranch and other businesses when he dies?"

"I don't know." Francesca stood with difficulty. "I suggest you leave Brazil immediately. You know too much."

"What about you?"

"It doesn't matter. I've been a dead for five years."

Sara smiled at her sympathetically.

Francesca shrugged. "I've accepted my fate. Gabriela called me around five today. All she said was: 'This is our final goodbye.'"

Sara wondered who else Gabriela had phoned after she left the consulate. *Talk about bad news.* Sara recognized she had to warn the agents on the yacht immediately.

Francesca gave a broad smile for the first time. "You should know Jorge's pathetic behavior at the opera house occurred because you look a lot like one of his past mistresses. Poor man... his brains are in the wrong place."

Sara felt Francesca push something into the left pocket of her slacks.

CHAPTER 28: Sanders Waits at the Ranch

A slash of lightening and a clap of thunder on the right were followed by even a bigger flash and roar on the left. It had rained almost continuously since Sanders and the SEALs had arrived at an outpost less than a mile from the Braga ranch three hours ago. He knew rainstorms occurred daily in the jungle, but this storm seemed especially long and violent. Storm clouds and the vegetation filtered the sunlight so much that the jungle floor was an eerie twilight zone. Sanders squinted at the messages from Sara and Ray on his satellite phone.

The leader of the SEALs had divided his ten men into three groups as soon as they created their base camp. The three exploratory units had just reported their findings.

***

The three SEALs in Team A had gone to a complex of four buildings about a mile from the homes at the Braga ranch. They reported trucks had delivered logs to the largest of these building three times since the SEALs arrived. The whines of saws emanating from this building were overpowering and almost continuous. The cut lumber was processed in a nearby large building. The mechanical buzz emitted from the second building was softer, but a mix of noxious odors wafted from all its windows. Trucks departing from the second building were heavy with lumber. Team A thought the trucks were hauling high-end wood flooring but weren't sure because tarps covered the loads.

Team A thought the two smaller buildings about a quarter mile from the lumber-processing area were more interesting. One small building with its windows and doors open emitted the sounds and odors typical of a woodworking shop. Two women sat under the veranda at the front of the shop polishing small wood sculptures—like those sold in tourists' shops in Manaus.

The other small building had elaborate air conditioning units on its roof. All the doors and windows were closed. A variety of tanks were stored under the veranda surrounding the building. The SEALs' microwave and ultrasonic devices suggested two rooms inside the building were filled with high benches with stone-like surfaces—probably lab benches—covered with metal equipment. Two people were in those rooms. A third room with a few high benches seemed to be maintained at a high humidity. No one was in the room. A fourth room with windows appeared to be an office and had two occupants. When one left or returned to the room, the other always followed.

There was no evidence to suggest coca was processed to cocaine in the building. Sanders noted this was consistent with Sara's last text. It was doubtful Emilio would allow the processing of cocaine near his home. Sanders guessed the lab with the high humidity was probably used for growing the beetles. Caputo must have lived up to his reputation and found a way to extract compounds from the beetles which his lab group converted into batrachotoxins.

Team A concluded Caputo could be extracted quickly from the building with minimal resistance once the guard with him in the office was eliminated.

***

The members of Team B had gone to a separate clearing about two miles from the housing complex at the ranch. Satellite transmissions had ascertained the two missile silos at this location were large enough to launch missiles capable of demolishing the airport at Manaus. It was assumed the small building at the site was the entrance to the controls for the missiles and the larger building was a storage area for additional armaments.

Satellite transmissions over the last week had indicated only one vehicle was usually parked at the site. When Team B arrived, three vehicles were there. As the SEALs explored the area, three more vehicles arrived. Their ultrasonic and microwave surveillance devices suggested five individuals were in the larger building, but only one was in the small building. The SEALs assumed the rest of the men must be in a nearby underground bunker. At first, the SEALs couldn't locate an entrance to the bunker except through the two buildings. Then they spotted two men in the nearby jungle suddenly disappeared.

The SEALs focused on the area where the men disappeared. Their patience was rewarded, and the team not only identified the bunker's entrance but also filmed the use of the access system by other men arriving at the site. While satellite LIDAR (so-called light detection and ranging) surveillance technology had already identified the size of the underground bunker, tunnels in the moist jungle soil were less clear.

***

The members of SEAL team C had investigated the area around the houses on the Braga ranch. Three two-story buildings of about equal size were positioned around a plaza with a pool, garden, and shaded patio. A long parking garage formed the fourth side of the plaza.

The center house appeared to be the hub of the ranch. Two guards were positioned at the front door. They patted down visitors who were driven from the wharf on the Amazon a mile away and workmen who walked or drove up from the lumber-processing area but waved through women who worked in the complex.

Most of the visitors shortly after their arrival in the house were escorted into a walled backyard garden where a gray-haired man sat in a wheelchair. He appeared to be the boss because all visitors bowed slightly when they entered the area. There were no guards in the backyard, but two large German Shepherd dogs roamed the area freely. There were sensors around the property's wall.

The SEALs recognized the man in the wheelchair was Emilio Braga but could identify only one of the guests entering the house. He was the major whom Sanders had worked with earlier in the day. The dogs prevented the SEALs from getting close enough to assess thoroughly how many people were in the house. The SEALs guessed six.

Team C twice saw a woman with a small dog walk from the second house across the plaza to the main house. She remained in the main house for only a few minutes each time. Team C identified her as Manuel's wife. The team noted no activity in the house on the far side of the plaza and assumed it had once been occupied by Jorge and his wife.

About a quarter mile from the plaza were two one-story buildings. They looked like mid-century motels in the U.S. with eight entrances on both their front and back sides. Several acres of gardens were behind the buildings. Only three cars were parked in the asphalt parking lot in front of the buildings.

Children streamed in and out of two doors of one building into a fenced playground. Otherwise, few noises came from the buildings. The SEALs assumed these two buildings, besides serving as a school or day care center, were housing for employees in the compound.

Analyses of satellite images suggested a narrow passageway ran underneath the cleared area and led from the garage near the main houses to the missile silos. Team C located entrances to the tunnel in the garage and in a gully at the side of the road. The tunnel appeared to be heavily lined with concrete.

Team C advised further effort should focus on exploring the tunnels. They thought if explosives were planted strategically that it would be possible to trap individuals in sections of the tunnel.

***

Zack, the leader of the SEALs, had made few comments as each team reported in. After the last report, he said, "You've got to prioritize your goals. We can make the air space around Manaus safer at least for a few days by wiping out the missile silos and ammo dump here."

Sanders shrugged. "The gangs could still shoot down planes with modern grenade launchers and drones."

"Okay, that goal just became a third priority."

"My highest priority is to make a long-term difference. I want to curtail—or at least cut the legs off—the drug gangs in Brazil."

"We can kill Emilio, capture Caputo, destroy the silos, potentially reduce the number of gang members, and get out of here safely."

"Those actions would make great PR in the U.S. and would please honest Brazilians, *but* they would only be a bandage—granted a large one—on our Brazilian problems. Your

                                    J. L. Greger

goal should remain as it was in Manaus—to capture, but not kill, Bridgit Tarantino.”

Zack scratched his head. “Don’t forget our mission was also to protect the U.S. personnel in the consulate and consul’s house in Manaus. We did.”

“But you didn’t save the consul’s house. Do you know why?” Sanders waited only a few seconds. “Because of Bridgit.”

“Why do you think that?”

“When Camille saw the destruction of the consul’s house, she said, “Bridgit will be pleased. She always hated the house because Consul Hinkley had abused her there.” Sanders paused. “Emilio would not have cared enough about the consul’s house to give the order to raze it. Bridgit did.”

“Okay. That’s a reasonable assumption.”

‘There is one problem. Camille is... mentally unstable. I’ve asked Sara to assess Camille.”

“Damn.” Zack looked skyward and shook his head. “Shouldn’t such an assessment be done by a psychiatrist?”

“Yes, eventually but for now Sara is our best chance of learning Camille’s... and Bridgit’s secrets.”

“Okay. Let’s assume capturing Bridgit, not Emilio, is our primary goal. She could have been one of the individuals who already entered the underground bunker by the jungle entrance we found... or by another entrance we haven’t found yet.”

“True, but I doubt she got to the ranch so quickly after she escaped the raid on the warehouse, especially if she had to walk part of the way. Satellite images have spotted several vehicles on the roads between Manaus and the ranch. Ray and Sara talked to Jake and have suggestions.”

“Who’s Jake?”

“Bridgit’s ex-husband. So far, all his predictions have come true.”

Zack growled, “Why wasn’t I told about Jake sooner? We could have questioned him before we left Manaus.”

“Probably no more effectively than Ray and Sara.”

Zack grimaced.

“It’s too late to critique past decisions. They just learned an interesting point. Jake claimed that Bridgit often bragged “the surest way to avoid police searches was to hide drugs or men in the loads on the logging trucks.”

"She's right. Those trucks when moving are hard to stop—if the driver doesn't want to be stopped—without injuries. Team A found those trucks were entering the compound hourly. Bridgit could have already ridden one of them in."

"I doubt it. Team C didn't report seeing her in the back yard with Emilio. I think he would be eager to see her. However, Sara thinks Bridgit who usually has long pink hair might be disguised as a man. Have Team C look for small, thin man entering the main house or talking to Emilio in the back garden."

"Done. I'll also have Team A move their focus from the lab to the large building where the logs are processed."

"I've already talked to the commander of the Amazona State Military Police. They're going to create a log jam. It should help us control entry to this compound."

***

Zack and Sanders peered at live images on their computers. Helicopters operated by the Amazonas State Military Police were buzzing noisily over the roads from Manaus to the ranch. Seven of the vehicles on the roads had turned around when the helicopter pilots announced a logging truck had jackknifed and logs were now blocking the main road into the Braga ranch. The drivers of the vehicles, which turned around, were not told they would be stopped at barricades before they re-entered Manaus.

Five of the trucks and cars on the roads had stopped apparently awaiting instructions from the helicopters. Passengers wandered from four of these vehicles into the jungle. All the passengers had reappeared after several minutes to find military police officers monitoring their cars. After the passengers and vehicles were searched and photographed, three of these vehicles returned to Manaus. Two appeared to have logical destinations in the jungle between Manaus and the ranch and were allowed to continue. The officers guessed those who had wandered into the jungle for a few minutes had hidden drugs or other contraband they were carrying, but the police thought it was a waste of time to search for the items now.

Three vehicles within five miles of the ranch had turned off their headlights as the helicopters approached and continued to move toward the ranch. The military police were prepared for this contingency and had drones ready to follow the three vehicles.

Two of the vehicles were logging trucks. Neither truck appeared to have a full load. Zack and Sanders decided to keep monitoring the trucks but to make no effort to stop them.

The other vehicle—a dilapidated truck—pulled off the road not far from the location of the identified entrance to the secret tunnel. Team B captured the four individuals in the truck as they tried to hide their parked vehicle with branches in the jungle. The four men captured by the SEALs laughed when the SEALs tried to question them. The captives stopped laughing when they were gagged, bound, and marched through the jungle to a spot near the wharf. There each captive was suspended in a cage. Sanders hoped those at the missile site wouldn't find the truck or the cages and would blame the road closure for the absence of the captured men.

***

Sanders peered out of the blind in the jungle where he and the best sharpshooter among the SEALs were hidden. It was fifty feet from Emilio's enclosed back yard. If they were any closer, they would be visible in the lights surrounding the cleared area of the ranch.

The sharpshooter watched the backyard of the main house and monitored cameras he had managed to position with views into several rooms of the main house and the front door of the house across the plaza. Occasionally, the sharpshooter spat on the ground and complained because he'd been unable to place any monitors giving him a view of the third house.

Sanders monitored feedback from the devices the SEALSs had planted around the compound while Zack personally checked out the scene at the lumber-processing area.

The aroma of meat grilling wafted from the front verandas of the staff quarters to Sanders's and the sharpshooter's hiding spot. It smelled tempting, especially as Sanders chewed his dry military ration. The loudest noises from the staff housing were the screams of children playing soccer on the paved parking lot in front of the apartments. Occasionally, Sanders saw on a monitor that the ball rolled into the gravel drive connecting the main plaza to the staff housing. If staff had been warned of potential raids by Brazilian police or U.S. SEALs, Sanders doubted they would allow their children to be outside and unprotected.

The sharpshooter saw lights turned on and off in the rooms of two of the three houses around the plaza. He even spotted through a second-floor window of the main house an old man—probably Emilio—watching a movie.

In general, neither Emilio nor anyone else appeared to be tensely peering out a window awaiting the return of Bridgit. Yet, Sanders was nervous.

Sanders called the major in the federal military police who had been seen with Emilio Braga. The major had calmly lied that he had searched jungle roads for Bridgit all afternoon. Sanders had been equally devious and praised Ray for the facilities he'd found to house himself and the SEALs in Manaus.

Around nine, Zack joined Sanders and the sharpshooter in their blind. He reported the drivers of the two log trucks, which escaped the blockade, had arrived around eight in the lumber-processing area. The drivers had walked to the staff housing without stopping by the main house. The workmen in the large log-processing facility had only exchanged quick greeting with the drivers and continued to sweep up the facility. They didn't seem to notice the SEALs searching the two trucks for passengers or drugs.

After Zack adjusted his monitors, he lay on the ground. In less than two minutes, he was snoring.

Sanders tried to sleep, but he couldn't. Instead, he kept enumerating problems in his mind. The major one was the SEALs team had not anticipated a prolonged mission in the jungle because Bridgit had escaped their net in Manaus. Thus, they had less than their usually detailed profile on their current site and had wasted daylight hours scoping out the ranch and planting monitors. Their extended mission also meant they didn't have all the equipment they needed and were shorthanded.

As Sanders looked at the multitude of monitors, he recognized another concern. The Bragas and their staff seemed too confident and too calm. This was just another day for them. Two guards remained posted at the front door of the main house and four men remained stationed at the wharf. Otherwise, no guards were visible. Team A reported the cleanup crew had even left the lumber-processing area.

Sanders kept wondering. Was it possible Bridgit and the crew at the ranch didn't know of the SEALs presence? Or was she biding her time until she was ready to respond? So, Sanders waited in the dark.

CHAPTER 29: Sara Learns Secrets

Sara was struck by the view when she stepped out of Francesca's house. The lights of Manaus shone below on one side of the house, but only a couple of lights pierced the darkness on the other side of the house. Overhead the stars seemed brighter than usual. She guessed the absence of light pollution made the stars over the river and jungle seem brighter.

Latoya wasn't enchanted by the sky and pushed Sara toward the waiting car. Within seconds Pedro had the car moving rapidly. The second car from the consular offices was right behind them.

"The *agente* in the other *care* spotted *mene* climbing the hill to the back of the house."

Latoya looked back at the house. "They notified the police."

"They will come too late." Pedro sighed. "*Birde* finally free *frome* cage."

Sara gasped when she finished *translating* Pedro's English. "Can't we save Francesca?"

"Too risky." Latoya nervously peered into the blackness for movements to the side and back of the car and didn't utter another word during the tense drive. Pedro muttered prayers as he drove.

***

Sara was amazed by the changes in the consulate. All the broken glass and debris had been swept away. New lights and cameras had been installed by the doors. Wooden beams were now strategically placed to support the walls. The consulate was no longer crowded with off-duty agents and staff trying to sleep on broken chairs. There was only one agent monitoring various devices, while two other agents moved about the consulate.

An FBI agent gave her a schedule for use of the hotel rooms. He'd already sent the drivers of the second car sent to Francesca's house to the hotel. "Your bed at the hotel won't be available for another two hours. Ray would like to talk to you ASAP."

***

She found Ray lying on the recliner in the consul's office. He looked better than she felt. It was amazing how good a young man could look with a six o'clock shadow and wearing a sloppy tee shirt. *The wonders of youth and adrenaline highs.*

He sat up as Sara sat on a nearby chair. "I was trying to rest while I could."

"You've performed a miracle here."

"It was easy with fewer people and no leads to follow."

"You know you could use your organizational skills to advance in the State Department without doing information gathering."

"It'd be less exciting,"

"But it might lead to a more normal family life. Think about it."

Ray pulled out a stick of gum and popped it into his mouth. "I already have."

Sara suddenly remembered the wad Francesca had slid into the pocket of Sara's slacks. She pulled it out and unfolded the wad until it was a half sheet of paper. "I think your rest is over. Francesca handed me a message as we left but I couldn't read it in the car."

The script message written with a fountain pen was difficult to read. Sara began to cry as she read aloud the first line of the note:

> *By the time you read this, I'll be dead. I hope they will not bomb my beautiful house.*
>
> *Manuel will be helpful if you get his wife out of Brazil. She's a hostage at the ranch. Don't trust Gabriela.*
>
> *Bridgit left Manaus by boat this morning before the gangs were unleashed. I believe she*

*went to the ranch. She usually stays in my old
house.*

*Light a candle for me at the Cathedral of Our
Lady of Conception. I went to confession there
every day at seven a.m. It was the only travel I
was permitted. Manuel confesses there daily at
6 a.m.*

Ray sprang to his feet and began fiddling with a satellite phone. "Sanders needs to know these details."

"Let's think a moment before we bother Sanders. How did Francesca know about Bridgit? I doubt Gabriela told her."

Ray nodded. "The priest could have told her. But how did he know?"

I think Manuel is the key to a successful resolution of this mess. Do we know where Manuel is now?"

"Or to put it more honestly, he's the only one left of the Braga family who might help us. The Manaus police posted officers outside Manuel's condo ever since he returned from the conference this afternoon. They claim he hasn't complained about the surveillance, and no one has visited him."

"Let's assume we can trust Manuel."

Ray smacked him gum. "Okay."

"We know Manuel will leave his condo around five-thirty in the morning to go to the cathedral. We can assume Bridgit knows it, too. She also knows which priest is usually on duty then."

"You're guessing the priest knows a lot and hasn't felt constrained by sanctity of the confessional because he kept Francesca informed."

"We need to find that priest."

"Two problems. Neither of us have close contacts with the Catholic Church. And we're short on staff."

Sara looked around the room. "I didn't see Camille when I came in. Where is she? She had strong ties with the nuns at the orphanage. She might know the priests at the cathedral, too."

"She's in the press office. I put her to work identifying the two women in the barrels. She was acting squirrelly, and I wanted her out of my hair."

J. L. Greger

"Define squirrelly."

He moved one hand in a circle by his ear. "She seemed fine when she returned here after the destruction of the consul's house. But from four on, she sent me notes every half hour asking when she would be evacuated." Ray ran his hands through his blond hair. "I didn't think she fit into the two groups we got out. I also didn't have the time or guts to question her about the interesting picture frame on her desk. Every time I started to talk to her, she recited the rosary or asked to see the teenage girl who had been injured trying to protect Sister Rose. I...."

"It's okay. It wouldn't surprise me if Camille had a nervous breakdown of some sort. She's been under stress for months. The shootout in the garden at the orphanage was... way past scary. Watching the destruction of the consul's house from close by would be terrifying. Sanders even was amazed at the destruction. I ignored her questions this afternoon, too." Sara stood. "Here's the deal. You update Sanders. I'll talk to Camille."

Ray raised a finger. "Be careful."

"I know. We can't be sure of Camille's allegiances."

***

Camille was on the phone with her back to the door when Sara arrived in the doorless press office. "Bishop, please excuse my English but your English is better than my Portuguese. Please let me take Elena, the girl who was injured trying to protect Sister Rose, back to the United States with me."

There was a long pause. Sara decided not to interrupt.

"I know there are rules. I've been told that by a mother superior and two priests. Each of them also said you could waive the rules."

There was a short pause.

"Please reconsider." Camille's shoulders heaved up and down as she almost howled, "I can't wait another day for your decision! I'll be shipped out tomorrow on...."

Sara couldn't believe her ears. She grabbed the phone and disconnected it. "Camille are you crazy? You just signed a death warrant for yourself and those to be evacuated with you tomorrow if the gangs have tapped this line."

Camille looked at Sara defiantly. "Mr. Sanders deceived me. He... he promised. He said he'd get me out of here before he left. Today Ray got eighteen people out but left me here to die."

She swiped her hand along her desk scattering papers. "Then I found Ray had stolen from my desk the only memento of Brazil I wanted to keep. He had no right."

Sara tried to not panic. The first thing she needed to do was calm Camille enough for a logical discussion. No, the first thing she needed to do was summon help. She pushed Ray's number on her phone. She hoped Ray could hear her. "Camille, calm down."

Before Sara could say more, Camille yelled, "Ray wouldn't even let me out of here to see my daughter in the hospital."

Sara felt like she'd been punched. "The teen age girl..." She didn't add the descriptor sulky. "...in the office at the orphanage is your *daughter*, Elena?"

"I officially adopted Elena a month ago. Sister Rose didn't think it was a good idea, but she processed the papers on condition that Elena remain in the orphanage until I was ready to leave Brazil."

Sara thought Sister Rose knew Camille was unstable and couldn't provide a good home for the girl in Brazil or probably anywhere. Sara pushed the unproductive thought out of her mind. She decided asking Camille about the girl might calm Camille. She pushed Ray's phone number again on her phone. "Tell me about Elena."

Camille smiled. "She's smart. A real whiz at games. That's how we became friends. I gave her a smart phone so she could game more. But...." Camille looked startled as Ray entered the office. "What are you doing here?"

Ray's voice seemed to be at a higher pitch than usual. "I... I wanted to visit my two favorite ladies."

Sara noticed Ray was staring at something on the credenza behind Camille. He must have spotted something she had not. Sara scanned the credenza and saw a handgun but tried not to show fear on her face and in her voice. "Did you know Camille adopted the injured teenage girl from the orphanage?"

Camille's smile turned to a frown when Ray said, "No."

Sara tried to improve Camille's mood and give Ray time to think. "Camille, you met a lot of children at the orphanage. Why did you pick Elena?" *That didn't sound right.* Sara added, "What made Elena so special?"

                                    J. L. Greger

"I told Bridgit about my visits to the orphanage whenever I went to the salon. About three months ago, Bridgit suggested I adopt an orphan. It got me thinking."

"But why Elena?"

"Bridgit knew of a girl in the orphanage who might be just right for me."

"Oh, how did Bridgit know this girl?"

Camille's voice became softer. "Elena was left on the streets when Lolita was jailed for trumped up charges a few years ago."

"Lolita?"

"Yes, the woman who manages the beauty shop where Bridgit works."

Sara was having trouble processing the new data. Camille knew Jake worked for the gangs of Manaus. Why didn't she realize that Bridgit did, too? She heard Ray smack his gum and decided she should try to keep Camille talking. "So, are you friends with Lolita, too?"

"No, Bridgit says Lolita's too angry to talk."

"But didn't Lolita want to know about her daughter?"

"Not really. Bridgit said she was pleased I planned to take Elena to the States with me. It..."

Sara could see Ray was circling the room gradually moving toward the credenza. Sara thought she needed to keep Camille focused elsewhere. "What else did you and Bridgit talk about?"

Camille pulled at her top. "It's hot in here." She pointed at Ray who was had almost reached the credenza. "Mr. Big Shot can't seem to make the air conditioning work. You know I should have gotten your job. I'm the one who first told Mr. Sanders about the problems in this office."

Sara could understand Camille's annoyance. Sanders had used Camille to get information but hadn't rewarded her. Sara couldn't worry about it now. She needed to keep Camille distracted long enough for Ray to get the gun. "Ray doesn't understand how unfairly you were treated because he's a man. Did Bridgit understand?"

"Yes. She often talked about how hard she had to work to survive in a man's world." Camille frowned. "Did you know eighty percent of the business owners in Manaus are men. Bridgit told me."

"Interesting. Who owned the shop Bridgit worked in?"

Camille frowned. "She didn't say exactly. She said it was a company headed by a man, but it wouldn't stay that way for long."

"Oh, really?"

The last time I saw her, Bridgit was happy. She said, 'We women have finally gotten control of the shop.'"

Sara figured Francesca's information about the distribution of shares in St. Bridgit Enterprises was outdated. Together Bridgit and probably Lolita must now own at least fifty-one percent of the shares.

Ray had grabbed the gun and was circling back around the room to the door.

Sara decided she could risk Camille becoming more emotional now that Camille couldn't use the gun. *But* Sara didn't have the guts to admit Elena, too, had been evacuated and was in a hospital in São Paulo, "Enough about Bridgit. We need to talk about your problems. Let's start with the item missing from your desk. What was it? Why was it important?"

"It was a picture of Elena and me."

Sara was caught off guard and gasped. "I don't remember seeing a picture of you with Elena on your desk."

Camille giggled. "Of course not. I put my picture under the picture already in the frame. I didn't want anyone to know I'd adopted Elena."

"I understand, but how did you get the frame?"

"Oh, Jake was cleaning up his office about a month ago and pitching stuff. He asked me if I'd like the picture of my co-workers. I took it because Sister Rose had photographed me and Elena a week before. I needed a picture frame."

The answer was fast, and Camille's voice had sounded natural. Sara concluded Camille had told the truth—at least as she understood it. Jake could have forgotten the secret compartment in the frame *or* could have been setting Camille up. She guessed the latter was true. Jake must have known Camille was ratting on him to Sanders.

"Camille, it will take a while, but I'll try to get the picture back for you. Now, I need your help. We need to find a priest who listens to confessions at the cathedral early every morning."

Ray gave her a high sign after he handed the gun to an agent who had appeared at the door.

"Do you think the bishop will know who is assigned that responsibility?"

Camille looked surprised. "Why ask him? It's Father Alfonso. I talk to him a lot. He's...."

Ray interrupted, "Camille, I'm leaving now to talk to Mr. Sanders. He will be relieved to hear you are okay." He winked at Sara. "Then I'm going to see how helpful Father Alfonso can be."

Sara noticed Camille's shoulders sank. "Don't forget to arrange a seat for Camille on the next plane out of here."

***

Camille's comments were those of a hysterical, aggrieved employee, but Sara recorded them because she figured it might calm Camille if she had a chance to vent her frustrations. Besides, Sara found Camille's drone easy to shut out as she made a list of things to be done.

First, Sara did a background check on Father Alfonso and texted the info to Ray. Father Alfonso Braga had been ordained as a Redemptorist priest forty years ago. He was Emilio's brother.

As she crossed out the first point of her list, Sara interrupted Camille monologue and asked, "Did you learn who the two women in the barrels at the warehouse were?"

Camille stared at her.

"You know—the two found when Jorge was arrested?"

"Jorge's daughter and granddaughter. The hospital is keeping the granddaughter overnight for observation, and her mother is staying with her."

Sara crossed the second point off her list and gulped repeatedly as she thought how to approach the next. She sent a text to Latoya and then smiled. "Camille, did you ever see Elena's birth certificate? Exactly what did Sister Rose tell you about... your daughter?"

"Sister Rose said Elena had appeared at the orphanage about six months ago without any identification. It didn't matter because Bridgit had told me Elena's sad story of being left on the streets when Lolita was jailed several years ago."

Sara wondered whether Bridgit had planted Elena in the orphanage to monitor Camille. Was it possible the gang members attacked Elena, not because she was protecting Sister Rose, but because she hadn't reported Camille's location to Bridgit? It would be nice to think the girl had bonded to Camille. No time to think about that possibility now.

Sara went to the fourth point on her list. "Camille, Sanders told me why you forwarded Will and Juan Anderson's file to him, but he never told me what made you notice Gabriela González Gómez."

Camille's eyelids fluttered. "I... I guess... I saw her here visiting Jake several times. I remember because he seldom had visitors and he always closed the door to his office as soon as she arrived." Camille sighed, "When I learned she was a scientist, I thought Mr. Sanders might like to meet her. Mr. Sanders was interested in scientists, and I wanted Mr. Sanders to listen to me." She gulped. "Is there a problem?"

"No... I'm just cleaning up the office's files." Sara decided she couldn't sort facts from fiction in Camille' statements. "I want you to write a statement outlining how you gathered the data on Gabriela you sent to Mr. Sanders." Sara figured the writing exercise would keep Camille busy and might yield insights into Camille's thought processes for others to assess.

***

Sara was asleep in the recliner in Hinkley's old office when Ray returned to the office around midnight. "We've made several mistakes."

Sara sat up. "I agree. Gabriela played us. I already sent a coded message using a satellite phone to agents on the yacht to search Gabriela thoroughly and not allow her access to any communications device or to others on the yacht. I have arranged for a forensic psychiatrist to meet with Camille as soon as she returns to the U.S. By the way, rapid DNA tests proved Elena was not Lolita's daughter."

Ray pulled a stick of gum out of his pocket and began to chew. "Forget the small stuff, like Elena. We may have facilitated the annihilation of the entire Braga family—the good, the bad, and the ugly." He snorted at his own joke.

"Oh God, no. What did Father Alfonso say?'

"Little but he allowed me to hear Manuel's confession."

"How?"

Ray smacked his gum. "It was crowded on our side of the confessional, but both Alfonso and I are thin."

Sara didn't want to dignify the comment with a laugh. "That's not what I meant. I thought Manuel went to confession at six a.m. What was he doing at the cathedral tonight?"

"The police called Father Alfonso to give Francesca last rites. He called Manuel to come to the cathedral afterward. I arrived at the cathedral just before Manuel."

"You must have been seen."

"It doesn't matter. I was dressed as priest and wore a wig. It gave me a bald spot like a shaved tonsure." He pulled his hand through his hair. "Most uncomfortable disguise I've ever done. Francesca was right. Manuel has been careful because his wife was a hostage at the ranch. But here's the kicker—so was Emilio."

"How long has Bridgit been in control?"

"Two years, ever since Bridgit arranged for Gabriela to move here and be her second-in-command. Evidently, Jorge and his family hadn't wanted to go to the ranch this morning. When the granddaughter resisted getting into the barrel, Bridgit's men showed Jorge and his daughter how easy it was to suffocate someone like the granddaughter without leaving any evidence."

Sara turned pale. "Did Manuel give you any reason to think the yacht owner was in league with Bridgit or Gabriela?"

"We can ask Manuel when he arrives in a few minutes. Father Alfonso insisted Manuel must not return to his home. They exchanged clothes and Alfonso returned to Manuel's home. Manuel had to complete evening confessions as Father Alfonso and then take a walk. Pedro and an agent will pick him up and bring him here by a circuitous route allowing Manuel time to change his clothes."

"Will the priest be safe?"

"Probably not, but he insisted."

Ray's phone pinged. The text from Sanders was brief:

Get a ship to the wharf at the Braga ranch by four-fifteen—not more than ten minutes earlier or later. Have on it 3 backhoes, 3 EMTs and 4 agents.

If no white flag is flying at the wharf, the crew should NOT land but should call in the military police.

Then Sara's phone pinged. This text was even briefer: *Sara, thank you for your love.*

CHAPTER 30: Sanders Is Still in the Jungle on Day 5

Living with the SEALs—even for just one night—was not easy. They slept on the hard ground oblivious to the dampness and a variety of musty odors emanating from the rotting flora and fauna on the jungle floor. Their military rations were edible but not desirable. The SEALs' ability to function after only four hours of sleep was amazing.

Sanders knew he had facilitated their efforts by doing all the negotiations with Brazilian authorities, but he also recognized he'd slowed the speed of their movements. Now he waited not far from the ranch's wharf gathering data from the dozens of monitors the SEALs had planted. He knew they had placed him in the safest spot.

When the SEALs planned this mission, they had determined an alternate way out of Manaus—if the Manaus airport was closed for any reason—was to have seaplanes flown the seven hundred miles from Paramaribo, Suriname to Manaus. This was an unusual solution and would be totally unexpected by anyone familiar with their standard operating procedures. The U.S. military had ceased using seaplanes after World War II because land runways were available in most locations. Unfortunately, most of runways in the Amazon basin were controlled by drug gangs or those engaged in other illegal activities.

The SEALs had identified an "entrepreneur" in Suriname willing to rent his seaplanes before their mission. They had secretly retained his services.

After Sanders had clarified the goals of the mission yesterday, he and Zack made several calls. The net result was another team of ten SEALs had arrived on a military jet from Miami to Paramaribo, Suriname around midnight.

***

It was now almost four in the morning. The new batch of SEALs was due to arrive at the ranch's wharf in less than a half hour. Sanders thought he had set the stage.

The residents of the ranch were isolated as much as possible. The Amazonas State Military Police had kept the major roads to the ranch blockaded. Sanders had occasionally monitored their live feeds but noted only two vehicles had been stopped and forced to return to Manaus after nine yesterday evening. He hoped that meant no one wanted to drive in the jungle at night but accepted drivers could have found alternate routes.

Sanders thought the SEALs on the ground were as ready as possible. They had not seen lights in the third house on the plaza. However, based on Ray's last message, he feared Bridgit was there. The SEALs were monitoring the exits from the house and a tunnel entrance in the parking garage. However, the house, like most building built by Emilio, probably had at least one secret exit.

Several SEALs were near the pier were ready to decommission the guards at the pier before the new batch of SEALs arrived.

The area around the silo was problematic. The SEALs estimated the twenty men at the silos could launch missiles to destroy the Manaus airport and kill anyone nearby—who was seen as a threat—with only a minute's notice. Thus, the attack on the missile site had to be well-coordinated, massive, and deadly. In preparation, the SEALs had explored the ranch's tunnel system and planted explosives to collapse it at several key locations. They also had aimed rocket launchers at the two silos.

Sanders recognized two unfortunate aspects of the attack occurring before sunrise. The capture of Caputo and Manuel's wife would be difficult. The SEALs had watched Caputo leave the somewhat isolated lab after sunset and go to a hard-to-reach apartment in the middle of the staff housing complex. The SEALs had no idea where Manuel's wife slept in the second house on the plaza.

Sanders was prepared, but he had to assume Bridgit was, too. He had told Ray to send a ship with at least three backhoes and several EMTs and agents to the ranch for arrival by four-fifteen. He hadn't mentioned the ship might have to pick up his body and those of several of the SEALs.

***

The action exploded when two incoming seaplanes signaled their arrival. The four SEALs near him at the wharf crept forward and quickly garroted or stabbed one guard after another. None of the guards appeared to have hit any alarms. Sanders alerted the pilots of the seaplanes to land while the four SEALs readied rowboats, not noisy powerboats, to pick up the incoming crew.

Sanders was worried when the seaplanes were nosier than he expected. He studied the monitors before him, but he could see no movements in the lumber-processing area or around the silos. He hoped Zack, who had placed his command center near the plaza, was observing no movement in the plaza and the staff housing units on his monitors. He readied the grenade launcher that he'd been trained to use last night.

Sanders was relieved when four rested SEALs led by a SEAL who had been posted at the ranch all night trotted past him. They were on their way to the silos. The seconds dragged on. A second group of four fresh SEALs led by another SEAL who had spent the night at the ranch rushed past him. They were going to join Zack near the residents' housing. He studied the wharf. Four men were refueling the planes and searching the sky for any drones.

He studied the monitors. The seconds dragged by as he noted no action around the silos or in the lumber-processing area.

Sanders looked at the time on the monitors and held his breath. One missile site exploded. The ground shook. As the flames shot up from the first one, the second site exploded. A ball of fire shot into the air. The ground continued to tremble as low roars came from a distant site—probably the entrance to the tunnel in the jungle—and a closer location—the tunnel entrance by the road leading to the missile site.

He could see clearly now because the sky was lit by the fires. It was terrifying to see how rapidly the fires spread from the missile sites. He doubted the SEALs had adequately calculated the fire's speed. He now realized why the cleared area around the ranch was so large. It was to prevent the spread of fires from the jungle into the ranch.

***

The ship from Manaus had arrived on time. Sanders assumed the SEALS at the wharf would instruct the agents and EMTs on board.

The scenes captured by monitors from the lumber-processing area were troubling. Two individuals had jumped inside the cabs of two lumber trucks and were gunning their engines as they prepared to rush forward. Sanders feared one of these individuals might be Bridgit. He yelled into his mouthpiece, "Stop the trucks! Bridgit might be on board."

Sanders couldn't see on his screens all of what happened next, but he heard the results. One logging truck crashed near the staff housing complex. The second logging truck—seen on the monitors at the lumber-processing area—braked to a stop. The driver of the second truck jumped from this cab and raised his hands. Two SEALs moved cautiously forward.

Sanders spoke more softly this time into his mouthpiece. "Check the trucks for passengers. Better check both big warehouses, too." He figured Bridgit must have found a weak spot in the SEALs surveillance system of the plaza and its three houses. If she'd been spotted, Zack would have detonated the explosives at the tunnel entrance in the parking garage.

Zack's voice roared from a speaker. "Come out with your hands up. You will not be hurt." A second voice repeated the announcement in Portuguese and continued to repeat it again and again.

Sanders heard gunshots coming from the plaza and the housing complex. He wished he had time to look at all the views transmitted by the monitors placed around the housing units and from the body cams wore by the SEALs but recognized he couldn't and keep up with his assigned responsibilities.

There was another explosion. One of the cameras focused on the lab stopped transmitting. The other showed a ball of flames where the lab had been before it, too, stopped transmitting. The SEALs must have found no one inside the lab and—had as planned—eliminated it.

                                                    J. L. Greger

The views captured by monitors from around the missile site were horrendous. Two individuals afire and screaming ran from the larger building within seconds of the attack on the silos. The individuals rolled on the ground and their screams continued for at least another minute. Blasting noises accompanied by intense sparks of fire came from the buildings by the silos as they were engulfed in flames. Sanders assumed the sparks and sound were generated as various munitions exploded.

***

Sanders found it impossible to watch closely all his assigned monitors at the missile site. He focused on the monitor at the entrance to the jungle tunnel first because the monitors focused on the missile silos only showed flames and clouds of smoke.

Three SEALs shot open the exit. They found as expected the tunnel was smoky. Rocks, pieces of concrete, and dirt blocked the tunnel where they'd placed the explosives. They thought they heard men coughing and dug through the debris enough to allow more air to enter the tunnel. However, they could do little to enlarge the air passage without a backhoe. Sanders directed the first backhoe off the ship to proceed to the jungle site.

Flames and smoke were still all he could see at the site of the erstwhile silos. So, he focused on the exit to the tunnel in the gulley by the road leading to the silos. The area was now a much bigger ravine. He could see the parts of two bodies in the debris. A man caught under collapsed support beams was screaming that several men were trapped behind him in the tunnel. The second backhoe carefully removed debris, but the two SEALs at the site were only able to pull two live men from the debris.

Sanders focused on the silo site when the flames had subsided. The SEALs at the silo site were cautious because they feared the damaged floor of the once larger building would give way under the weight of a backhoe. They scraped away the debris by hand and found a trap door in the floor. Several SEALs used iron crowbars to wedge open the trap door while others focused their guns on the potential opening. The SEALs tugged and tugged. Finally, they lifted the evidently heavy door. Smoke, not men, poured out.

Sanders didn't closely watch the ensuing rescue operations. They were too grim. He notified Ray that the Manaus airport was now safe from missile attacks but not from attacks by smaller weapons. He also suggested Ray start apologizing to Brazilian officials. Ray already had photos of the missile sites taken yesterday to prove the attack on the ranch was necessary. Sanders forwarded to Ray the most sanitized recent photos—those without any bodies—to prove the sites had been destroyed.

***

An EMT reported it was doubtful the driver of the first logging truck, which had jackknifed, would survive. The driver and two passengers in the second logging truck were uninjured. Sanders was told the prisoners would be brought to him as soon as the situations at the plaza and the staff housing compound were controlled.

Sanders figured he had time to check the monitors focused on the plaza. The views were disappointing. Six women in nightgowns and a small dog stood there. *Where was Emilio? Where were the two guards who usually stood at the door?* Two SEALs stood in the plaza with their guns focused on the houses.

He heard one SEAL—presumably in the main house—report, "One old man is dead in his bed. Throat slit."

The report confirmed one of Sanders's assumptions. Bridgit was in control.

Sanders checked the monitors showing the lumber-processing area, the lab area, and the silos. There was nothing new. WAIT.

The door of the small workshop by the lab was open. It had been closed when he checked earlier. He signaled his findings to the nearest SEALs—those in the lumber-processing area.

He took a quick look at the views from the monitors focused on the staff housing area. SEALs were still entering and leaving individual apartments evidently looking for hidden workers About fifty men, women, and children were seated on the paved parking lot with temporary metal fencing surrounding them.

One gray-haired man was handcuffed to a post away from the others. Sanders enlarged the view of the man. It was Caputo.

A male voice on Sanders's earphone diverted his attention. "Found a woman in the workshop. EMT needed."

He was surprised to hear a woman's voice seconds later. "We're bringing the driver and passenger from the second truck to the wharf in a Jeep. Will pick up the EMT and injured woman at the workshop."

Sanders knew all the SEALs were men and thought the EMTs were all men. *Could the voice be Bridgit's?* If so, Bridgit had gained access to their communications system. She'd hear anything he transmitted. He had to warn the men at the wharf directly. He ran from his blind at the edge of the jungle to the wharf.

***

The Jeep raced toward the pier until the driver apparently saw logs had been placed across the road. The Jeep sent up a cloud of dust as the driver braked hard.

Two SEALs fired shots at the Jeep's tires and then advanced with their guns aimed at the driver. "Hands up or we'll shoot."

The driver—a woman in an EMT uniform—got out. Her clothes hung loosely from her shoulders. She raised her hands.

Sanders nodded. While the two SEALs kept their guns focused on the woman, two other SEALs frisked the three male and one female passengers. The men were armed with knives and handguns. Sanders recognized the woman passenger as Manuel's wife. She was unarmed and had red puffy areas and cuts on her face. She looked like she'd been beaten.

Sanders pulled the cap from the woman EMT's head. Long pink hair fell to her shoulders. He stared at Bridgit's thin face and narrow nose. He nodded.

The SEALs handcuffed her.

CHAPTER 31: More Surprises

"It's over." Sanders's whisper sounded tired but triumphant.

Sara couldn't express the relief she felt when she heard Sanders's voice. She sobbed, "Good."

Sanders continued, "The Undersecretary knows ten SEALs departed with Bridgit two hours ago after I negotiated with the Mayor of Manaus, the Governor of the State of Amazonas, and heads of the various police units."

Ray interrupted, "Why didn't you call us for help? At least in setting up the calls?"

"I didn't want you blamed if the Brazilians disagreed with me."

Sara thought Sanders was enjoying the hero role too much but didn't want to ruin his announcement—just to speed it up. "What did you promise them?"

"I convinced them the only place for Bridgit was in isolation at the maximum-security prison in Colorado. It was easy after I told them she personally had slit Emilio Braga's throat and carried plans on her phone for the assassination of several Brazilian officials."

"What else?"

Sanders snorted. "Sara, you know me too well." He paused. "A military plane will be landing at Manaus airport in a few minutes. Two other jets will circle the airport to provide protection."

Ray interrupted. "That explains the call we got from a Navy commander five minutes ago. He told us to have Jake and Camille ready to be transported by an armed convoy in an hour."

"Yes, ten more SEALs, Caputo, Manuel's wife, and I should be arriving at Braga's warehouse pier in thirty minutes on the ship you sent last night to the ranch. Twenty-eight prisoners and the three EMTs will also be on the ship."

Sara was confused. "Wait! Where did you get all the SEALs. I thought Brazilian officials only approved the use of one U.S. military unit of ten men on their sovereign territory."

"I didn't tell you about the second group of SEALs because I wanted you two to be able say honestly you didn't know the U.S. government used more than the agreed number of troops in Brazil." He paused. "We can discuss those details later. Brazilian federal and state military police want to take custody of the prisoners—all believed to be gang members—as soon as the ship arrives at the warehouse. However, one EMT and several of the prisoners are severely injured and need immediate hospitalization."

Sara thought Sanders must be so tired he was being naïve. "Are you sure this isn't a set-up for an ambush?"

"I doubt it. A major in the Amazonas State Military Police will supervise the transfer of prisoners."

"The major you saw on Emilio's patio?"

"The same. We've been working together for months. His visit to the ranch yesterday was designed to lull Emilio into a false sense of security and to assess whether our plan was compromised. My call to him last night was routed through a phone line out of the consulate and cemented the gang members' belief that Ray had all the SEALs housed at the consulate."

"So, what else did you promises?"

"I promised I would leave Brazil with the SEALs and the three U.S. citizens being extradited."

Ray interrupted, "But there's five—Bridgit, Jake, Paul, Caputo, and Camille."

"Bridgit doesn't count. She just seems to have escaped Brazil and will be caught illegally entering the U.S. later today. Remember, I promised we wouldn't extradite Paul. We'll let him rot in a Brazilian jail."

"Do you...?"

"Please let me finish. Sara, do you want to come with me? It will be a typical military transport plane."

Sara wanted to punish Sanders for his callousness towards her, but she wanted to escape Brazil even more. "Those planes are ghastly."

"Low on passenger comfort but safe with two other jets flying interference."

"I'll round up all the blankets in the office." I want to be warm and comfortable."

"Good. One of the armored vehicles in the U.S. military convoy will pick you and the three U.S. citizens to be extradited in the next hour."

"What about me?" said Ray.

Sanders laughed. "I guess I forgot to tell you. You officially became the U.S. Chargé d' Affaires to Brazil an hour ago when I resigned."

Ray laughed hysterically. "Mom will never believe it. Even if the appointment lasts only for a day or two."

"Don't laugh too loud. You have four agents stranded at the ranch. They're guarding over a hundred Brazilians who need to be screened for their loyalty to what's left of the drug gang."

"Sounds easier than handling the unhappy agents and staff now at the hotel and in this dilapidated consulate."

"First off, realize you must worry about all the U.S, citizens in Brazil now, not just this consulate. The Undersecretary will approve your appointment of Latoya as the temporary consul for Manaus and rescind Gabriela's application for asylum in the U.S. Marty Santos can handle the latter once you give the order. Warn him the Brazilian officials are keen to question Gabriela. They don't think they will allow the Colombians to extradite her because they want her out of the drugs business for a long time."

Ray smacked his gum. "What a waste. I wonder if she'll look like Lolita when she's eventually released from jail in ten years or so?"

***

"I thought we were flying in the military transport plane." Sara let out a low whistle as she looked around the burnished metal surfaces and navy, suede-like upholstered reclining seats on the executive jet.

"So did I until the Undersecretary notified me as my ship arrived at the warehouse in Manaus. The Secretary thought we deserved better. The Undersecretary arranged for one of the State Department's executive jets to fly from Miami to Manaus last night. It arrived at the airport minutes after the military planes.”

***

Sara waved the steward to the galley after he handed Sanders a laptop and told him to read his emails immediately. “We must talk. You were reckless to rush off with the SEALs.” She knew her voice was getting louder but she couldn’t stop herself. “Much of what you’ve done since you arrived in Brazil has been rash.” She pointed at Sanders. “I realize you’ve been heroic and... smart in a calculated way as you did what needed to be done. But I should have been warned.” Tears rolled down her cheeks as she slammed her fist on the chair rest. “I was so worried. I tried... I tried so hard to help. But this was just too much.” She sobbed.

Sanders sat staring at her. “We succeeded. I couldn’t have done it without you.”

“What does ‘succeeded’ mean?” She glared at him. “Don’t say the Undersecretary was pleased. All we did was cause a drug gang to hiccup.”

“No, we cemented Brazil and the U.S. together in major efforts to reduce drug trafficking and save the Amazon.”

“I doubt it. And you’re missing the point. You made too many assumptions... about me.” She started to pace about the cabin.

Sanders read his emails. “The Governor of the Amazonas State and Mayor of Manaus sent thank you emails to the Secretary of State. They specifically thanked ‘Special Envoy Sara Almquist.’”

She walked over to a burnished tissue holder, pulled out a tissue, and wiped her eyes. “I’m not a dog panting for a pat on the head. I know we did a good job—with a lot of help from impressive FBI agents and SEALs—of cleaning up a real mess. *But* you should have been more honest... more forthcoming at the start with me... before I even left New Mexico.”

“Oh, here’s the email from the President of Brazil to our President.”

Sara stamped her foot. “You’re not listening! I’m not a star-struck kid... like you apparently are.”

Sanders gulped. “I guess I deserved the last comment. You’re right. I apologize.” He paused. “The main reason I resigned was I knew we couldn't survive emotionally, if not physically, another episode like the last five days. I'm ready to move to New Mexico and be with you."

Sara put her hand on his shoulder. "I don't expect you to be a martyr. You belong in Washington. I've got to cool off now." She walked to the bathroom door. "I noticed this plane has a shower and a change of clothes for both of us. After lunch, I'll be capable of a reasonable discussion."

***

Sara's stomach was upset, and she only picked at the sandwiches and salad the steward served. Sanders was ravenous. Sara suspected he wouldn't go on another mission with SEALs because he commented several times about how bad their field rations tasted.

She picked up an oatmeal cookie and started munching. "I'm too wound up to sleep. We might as well attend to a few details."

Sanders smiled and reached across the table to rub Sara's hand. "I'm not the only workaholic." He studied his laptop. "I thanked Carlos Moreno by having a selection of cheeses sent to his office in Havana. He admitted to me the one thing the Cubans can't do well is make good cheese."

"Good. I sent copies of the two pages of Will Anderson's diary which mentioned a Cuban drug dealer to Carlos. I hope he finds them useful." Sara studied her laptop. "While you showered, I read documents we recovered from the orphanage but didn't have time to evaluate earlier. Sister Rose was a wise woman. She didn't process any adoption papers for Elena and called Camille a "tortured" soul in her files. I hope the FBI gets psychiatric help for Camille before they charge her with anything. I'm still not sure how much she played us."

"Agreed."

She looked down at an email for a few seconds. "The Tupi translator at the Library of Congress thinks Maria will be admitted to the linguistics program at Yale." A tear ran down her cheek. "I was worried we couldn't help her. By the way, Juan has his choice of two medical schools."

"See? We had a positive effect on the lives of the Andersons. And probably on the lives of Jake Tarantino and Al Caputo. Those two will probably end up in the witness protection

                                J. L. Greger

program after they spend a few years testifying in RICO trials against Bridgit and her many contacts in the U.S."

Sara smiled only slightly. "Then there's the Bragas."

"I know you think Jorge should be left to rot." Sanders tried to stop snickering and instead began to cough.

"Jorge Braga is not funny. The only reason he's not a gang leader is his father recognized Jorge was a philandering fool with a hot temper." She studied her laptop. "I asked Ray to debrief Manuel Braga and his wife. I'm surprised. They decided to stay in Manaus because it's the only home they've known. Together they think they can run Emilio's lumber business and turn it into an operation noted for preserving the unique ecology of the Amazon. They said Jorge and his kids can have the rest of Emilio's holdings or whatever is left after the Brazilian government confiscates illegal enterprises. Father Alfonso has applied to the bishop to be allowed to retire from his duties at the cathedral and to work mainly with the nuns at the orphanage."

Sanders rose and put his hand on Sara's shoulder. "Ray is a good man, but he's not up to the job of being the chargé d'affaires for long, especially if he keeps smacking his gum. You know you could do it. The Secretary of State would like to know if you'd like to be vetted for the appointment. You have no stains on your record, like I do."

"As I told you earlier—I'm not begging for attention. I want to go back to my dog Bug, in New Mexico, do occasional consults, and... strengthen our relationship."

"I promise I've learned my lesson. I'm too old for another assignment like I had in Brazil."

Sara brushed a kiss on his cheek.

"Did I tell you that the major, whom I worked with, wants to run for political office?"

Sara suddenly recognized Sanders's second secret assignment had been to identify potential future Brazilian leaders with positive sympathies toward the U.S. She sighed. "Some things never change."

THE END

THE SCIENCE AND HISTORY BEHIND THE STORY

This novel is packed with details from international headlines, scientific journals, and historical records. The points below may help you learn more about the issues discussed in the book.

The Amazon River and the surrounding jungle are vast. Consider these relevant statistics (https://en.wikipedia.org/wiki/Amazon_rainforest) and (https://education.nationalgeographic.org/resource/amazon-deforestation-and-climate-change):

• The Amazon biome (predominantly rainforest) is twice the size of India. About 60% of the Amazon rainforest is in Brazil where it occupies about 40% of the country. Note: Brazil has a larger land area than the contiguous United States but is 87% the size of the total U.S.

• The Amazon River originates in Peru and meanders almost 4,000 miles through nine countries in South America. Moderate-sized ocean-going ships can reach Manaus—almost a thousand miles from the Atlantic Ocean—at the point where the Rio Negro flows into the Amazon. The Amazon River provides 20% of the ocean's freshwater supply.

• The Amazon rainforest is a worldwide resource for slowing climate change. It absorbs one-fourth of the carbon dioxide absorbed by all the land on earth. The amount absorbed today is 30% less than in the 1990s because of deforestation.

- The Amazon jungles harbor 10% of the world´s known species and are the home to 350 ethnic groups.

The conference on Vector Control of Tropical Diseases in this novel was fictional but the problems discussed at this fictional conference are real and complex:

- Over 600 million people died of **malaria** in 2020. (https://www.who.int/data/gho/data/themes/malaria). Malaria is caused by single-celled parasites (called *Plasmodium*) which are transmitted to humans through the bites of female *Anopheles* mosquitos. These parasites have complicated life cycles and the ability to constantly change their surface proteins. So far, scientists have been unable to develop an effective vaccine against malaria (Science [2021] vol 372, issue 6541:448).

- **Dengue, zika, and chikungunya fevers** are severe viral diseases spread by *Aedes* mosquitos in the tropics (https://www.who.int/news-room/fact-sheets/detail/dengue-and-severe-dengue). All produce fever and flu-like symptoms. Zika virus is believed to cause severe birth defects in infants (Science [2016] vol 351, issue 6278:1123-4). Approximately 100 million people are sickened with dengue fever, and 40 thousand die of it each year.

- The lack of effective vaccines for these tropical diseases have caused a lot of public health efforts to be focused on controlling the **vectors—mosquitos**—spreading these diseases. Traditional approaches include insecticides and mosquito netting. Mosquito control through the use of genetic modification, irradiation, or infection with *Wolbachia* bacteria have been shown to be effective in reducing the incidence of Dengue fever and other viral diseases spread by *Aedes* mosquitos (https://www.cdc.gov/mosquitoes/mosquito-control/community/emerging-methods/index.html) However, these modern techniques are not effective in preventing the spread of malaria (https://doi.org/10.1590/S0074-02762011000900026).

• The number of cases of tropical diseases seen in the U.S., especially in Florida, have increased in the last few years (https://www.cdc.gov/dengue/areaswithrisk/in-the-us.html). This is troubling because both *Aedes* and *Anopheles* mosquitos are common in many areas of the U.S.

Citizens of the U.S. generally know little about Brazil beyond its beaches, soccer teams, and the Carnival in Rio. These following items are important for understanding Brazil's history and culture:

• The **colonial history of** Brazil began in 1500 when Pedro Álvares Cabral landed in South America and officially claimed the area to become known as Brazil for the Portuguese. The Portuguese colonization of Brazil differed from the contemporaneous Spanish colonialization of its territories for several reasons. No exploitable mineral wealth was found in Brazil until the 1700s. The indigenous people of Brazil had no complex civilizations like the Incas. New research suggests this assumption by the Portuguese explorers is questionable (Nature [2022] vol 606:325-8).

• The Jesuits were important in the colonization of Brazil. One of their achievements was to create a written "national" language in Brazil. The Jesuits were expelled in 1759, and the popularity of Tupi declined rapidly.

• In general, few scholarly experts on the Portuguese colonization of Brazil (as opposed to experts on Spanish colonization of the Americas) can be found in the U.S.

• In 2019, only 5% of Brazilians could communicate in English.

• Transportation systems in Brazil differ from those in most developed countries. Road and railroads are limited and do not traverse much of the Amazon region. There are no bridges across the Amazon River. Air and river transportation systems are highly developed.

• Like many countries, Brazil experienced political turmoil recently. Jair Bolsonaro, as president of Brazil from 2010 to 2022, aroused the ire of scientists, public health workers, and environmentalist (<u>Science</u> [2021] vol 373, issue 639:225).

The golden poison dart frog (*Phyllobates terribilis*) is mentioned frequently in the novel. Here are a few facts about this amphibian species:

• The frogs live in the jungles of the Pacific coast of Colombia (not the Amazon jungle) and can be yellow, green, or orange. They are arguably the most poisonous animals on earth. Each wild frog in its skin contains enough poison to kill ten humans.

• **Batrachotoxins** (a type of neurotoxin) in the frogs' skins are derived from compounds in insects, probably beetles, consumed by the frogs (<u>National Academy of Sciences</u> [2204] vol. 101, issue. 45: 15857-15860). DOI:10.1073/pnas.0407197101). Generally these frogs do not have toxins in their skin when raised in zoos and not fed special beetles.

ABOUT THE AUTHOR

J. L. Greger is a biology professor and research administrator from the University of Wisconsin-Madison turned novelist. The pet therapy dog, Bug, in her mysteries and thrillers is based on her own Japanese Chin. She includes tidbits about science, the American Southwest, and her international travel experiences in her Science Traveler Series.

The Flu Is Coming. In the first book in the series, a woman scientist traces the spread of a deadly new flu virus among the frantic residents of a quarantined New Mexico community. (New Mexico/ Arizona Book Award Finalist)

Murder...A Way to Lose Weight. A dean in a medical school helps police discover whether an ambitious young "diet doctor," disgruntled patients, or old-timers with buried secrets are killers. (Winner of the 2016 Public Safety Writers Association contest and New Mexico/Arizona Book Award Finalist)

Ignore the Pain. A woman scientist learns too much about the coca trade and too little about a sexy new colleague while on a public health assignment in Bolivia.

Malignancy. A woman tries to escape the clutches of a drug lord and accepts a risky assignment as a science consultant in Cuba. (Winner of the 2015 Public Safety Writers Association contest)

I Saw You in Beirut. A woman's past provides clues for the extraction of a nuclear scientist from Iran. The author's experiences as a science and education consultant in the United Arab Emirates and Lebanon are featured.

Riddled with Clues. A homeless man and a woman scientist are targeted by drug gangs after she listens to the strange tale of an undercover drug agent about his war experiences. The memories of an actual CIA agent in Laos during the Vietnam War are featured. (New Mexico/Arizona Book Award Finalist)

A Pound of Flesh, Sorta. The police and a woman scientist can't decide whether a package contaminated with the bacteria that causes the bubonic plague is a plea for help by a whistleblower or a threat from gang leaders awaiting trial. (New Mexico/Arizona Book Award Finalist)

Dirty Holy Water. A woman who usually serves as a science consultant for the FBI learns there is a thin line between being a victim and being a villain when she becomes the chief suspect in a bizarre murder case. (New Mexico/Arizona Book Award Finalist)

Games for Couples. Did lethal compounds in a cultured meat product—meat made in a test tube—kill a man in a clinical trial? Or did the toxic competition between biotechnology companies and spite of battling couples cause his death? (New Mexico/Arizona Book Award Finalist)

Fair Compromises. Sara Almquist and her FBI colleagues rush to find the culprits who endangered the lives of a hundred attendees at a political rally by poisoning the food with botulism toxin. Their target was a woman candidate for the U.S. Senate. (New Mexico/Arizona Book Award Finalist)

Bungle in the Jungle. The U.S. consular office in Manaus, Brazil, is a "Bungle in the Jungle." Can Sara Almquist and the new Acting Ambassador to Brazil figure out how the staff became enmeshed in the illegal international trade of drugs and cultural artifacts?

See more at: http://www.jlgreger.com